Love is a State of Mind

Sarah Catherine Knights

Published by Sarah Catherine Knights, 2015.

LOVE IS A STATE OF MIND

First edition. October 28, 2015.

Written by Sarah Catherine Knights.

ٺ

Chapter One

I have a desire to dive into the water and never come up again, but instead, I lower myself quietly into the medium lane and stand there, at the shallow end, surveying the scene.

I catch the eye of the young boy on the top of the lifesaver's chair; he looks away, embarrassed, and I realise he's probably thinking exactly what I'm thinking. I look ridiculous. Why do I tog myself up like an Olympic athlete, with my cap and goggles and Speedo costume, when I'm blatantly not?

Although I haven't been here for ages, I can see the normal crowd are in: the three, who are always in the fast lane doing flashy tumble turns and timing themselves, are showing off, as usual. In my lane, there is the annoying guy who thinks he's a good swimmer and will insist on overtaking but who won't go in the fast lane; the older woman who was obviously a really good swimmer in her time, but who is now past her sell-by date (which is rich, coming from me) and a youngish guy, who has the most extraordinary style. He looks as if he might die at any minute, as he flails his arms around, making huge splashes. When he comes towards me, I can't help thinking he looks comical: mouth wide open and a look of surprise on his face, as if he can't believe he's survived yet another stroke. In the slow lane, there is the little group of ladies who spend most of their time chatting in the shallow end and then struggle up to the other end, to continue

1

their discussion, hanging onto the rails and getting in everybody's way.

Nothing changes.

And yet it does, doesn't it? Things change a lot.

Like when your husband of twenty-nine years, leaves you for someone else.

I push off, leaving a good gap between me and the person in front. The water feels warm and comforting, holding me in its embrace. I swim breaststroke, not putting my face in at first, just allowing my body to get used to the motion and letting the water sooth my limbs and clear my head. The end of the pool seems too far away.

Wishing I could do a tumble turn, I touch the end and change stroke; this time it's crawl. Face down, I breathe in rhythmically, under my left arm. In, out, in, out ... well, that's the theory. Half-way down the lane, I'm kicked hard on the ankle, which completely disrupts my style and I end up having to stop, spluttering, while someone piles into the back of me. "Sorry!" I mouth, as he angrily ploughs past me, kicking his legs with ferocity.

I continue to the end and stand there, lifting my goggles to let out the inevitable water and shaking my head, to clear my ears. Two lengths done and I already feel exhausted and water-logged.

Why am I doing this? To get fit, lose weight, feel younger and drown my sorrows, I tell myself.

I begin to get into my rhythm, without further interruptions. There's something about the action of swimming that allows me to forget everything and just focus on breathing. My thoughts float off into the artificial blueness and I become simply a physical being, without the mind-shattering inner life that haunts me on dry land.

I constantly have to count my lengths – is that the tenth or the twelfth? Eventually, convinced I've done twenty, I stand at the shallow end, probably getting in other people's way, but I don't care. I want to savour the moment.

This is the start of the new me, post David.

I'm pretty sure I've actually lost weight already as I walk towards the shower area, resting my hand gently on my stomach. I hold my tummy in and catch a brief look of my outline, reflected in some glass. I see an 'mature' woman with a swimming cap on, goggles and a fat stomach staring back at me – and instinctively turn round to see who it is. There's no one else there.

It's me.

Kids stare back at me through the glass, while they queue for the vending machines, causing mayhem in the reception area. I hurry away, glad to be in the shelter of the changing area, hidden from young, prying eyes.

Having got dressed, I go to the hairdryers which are placed by a large mirror – my face is blotchy and there are deep red lines around my eyes. My skin looks like one of those 'before' adverts, only there isn't an 'after' in my case and in the fluorescent lighting, my eyes look hollow. I stand under a fixed machine that's more like a hand dryer and blow my hair about, to get it dry. The end result is, quite frankly, a mess, but I don't care.

I'm invisible at my age, aren't I?

I DRIVE THE FEW MINUTES it takes to get to my house, park the car and open the front door.

The silence and absence of another human being, hits me in the guts, as it does every time; I close the door behind me and stand in the small area I think of as 'the hall'. I hang my jacket up on the hooks that used to house his coat and the kids' anoraks and beneath which was a selection of wellies and old trainers. Now, I notice once again, as I do every time I come into the house, there are just my things: my jacket, my dog-walking coat and a pair of old, green wellies.

This is what my life has come to.

"Gaz, I'm home," I shout to the emptiness. My only companion, my labrador, asleep in the kitchen. I can hear his tail thumping against the side of his plastic bed, as I walk down the corridor. At least he's pleased to see me, I think, although he can't even be bothered to get out of bed.

"How are you, Gorgeous?" I say, going over to him, bending down and giving him a kiss on his dear, black head. "Busy day?"

He looks up at me, smiling. "It must be knackering, lying there all day," I say and he gets up slowly, to follow me over to the kettle. He's such a presence in the house and I'm grateful for him. Just imagine if I came home to nothing ... no one? I shudder to think of it.

I make my instant coffee and sit down with Gaz by my side. We have an old sofa in the kitchen – rather a nice idea we thought at the time – David used to sit and read the paper and chat, while I cooked the supper. Now, just Gaz and I appreciate its cosiness – we snuggle up together in the evening and watch the small portable telly on the dresser: him, gently farting by my side and me, trying to get absorbed in other people's miseries on 'Eastenders'. There's always so much angst on that programme – it makes you feel your life is a bed of roses compared to the goings-on in Albert Square. Maybe the script writers are doing the public a service, by making us feel that our lives aren't so bad, after all.

We've lived in this house for nineteen years, David and I; it's full of 'us' still, except the other member of 'us' has left the building, a bit like Elvis, except that my husband isn't dead. He's taken some clothes, some books, his toothbrush of course, and some of his tools from the shed, and gone ... but most of what we bought together, is here. He's been gone a month now and despite what he's done, I miss him with every ounce of my being.

I can see the years of our marriage spread out before me, wherever I go in the house: the dresser in the kitchen we saved up for; the dining table and six chairs, we bought ten years ago from a neighbour who was getting rid of them. The three-piece suite in the sitting room we said Gaz would never be allowed to sit on (and within three days, he'd reminded us that dogs have rights too and he'd commandeered the armchair). We were thinking of re-covering it, just weeks before David told me his news. When I showed some material to him, was he secretly thinking, well, that'll never happen ... I'll be well gone by then?

There was no indication that he had other plans.

There are still photos of 'us' everywhere – I can't bring myself to take them down. 'Us' alone at the beginning of our marriage, looking lovingly at each other in some forgotten restaurant; a faded wedding photo (I remember Holly saying when she was tiny, Why aren't I there? How we laughed.) A group shot of all the family, as it was before the children: his parents, my parents (now all dead) his sister, Clare, and my sister, Jane. God, we look so young. Like children. Why were we all together? Was it Mum's seventieth birthday, celebrated in a hotel, in Surrey? Yes, that's it. David's got his arm around me and he's laughing, as if he hasn't got a care in the world.

And then the children – photos of them all over the kitchen walls, growing up before my eyes. Babies to toddlers, kids with toothless grins, to sulky teenagers; graduation photos of Holly ... and Adam in his beloved wetsuit.

It's as if they are designed to sit there and taunt me, with all the life that's now gone.

One picture, in particular, catches my attention: David, now affectionately called 'The Bastard' in my mind, running towards the camera on a beach down in Cornwall, the children each holding one of his hands. He looks young, handsome (he was – not quite George Clooney, more Ewan McGregor; wholesome, sandy-haired, golden tanned – without the Scottish accent).

I remember that holiday so well; we were staying in a small cottage, right by the sea. The children built endless sand castles, and we lolled on towels, on the sand beside them. The weather was hot and once the children had gone to bed, we sat and watched the sunset, drinking chilled white wine ... and made love all night. Those are my rose-coloured memories of it; maybe it wasn't so wonderful at all, but the truth is, that's how I think of those days. We were happy ... we had two beautiful children, we adored each other and we had our future in front of us.

I realise I've been staring at the picture, for at least three minutes. My mind wanders these days. The picture has been in this position for so long, it's almost part of the wall now. I get up to lift it up and yes, the wall paper is a different colour underneath and when I look closely, there are little black bugs under the surface of the glass, stuck like specks of black rain.

I feel a longing for the children, now so grown-up. I reach for my mobile to check that I haven't missed a text ... but no, nothing.

I read their last messages.

Adam's: *Just arrived Sydney. Shit, its a long way. Will email tomorrow.*

I haven't heard another thing from him – oh well, no news is good news, with Adam.

Holly's: *Hope you're ok? Spoke to Dad last night. I might come home Sunday, will text. Love you, Holly xxx*

Always kisses from Holly but again, nothing since, so I have no idea if she's coming tomorrow or not. I'm tempted to text her but ... I've told myself on lots of occasions, I must let them go. If she wants to come, she'll come. I don't want her to feel she's *got* to.

Gaz gets up and stands right in front of me, staring me out.

Are you going to take me for a walk, or what? he says.

Well, he doesn't say that, obviously, but that's what I do ... I imagine great long conversations with him. He's my best friend now – he listens to everything I have to say and never criticises me.

If he was a human he would, however, no doubt, be having counselling. He has a lot of 'issues', does Gaz. He's frightened of loud noises, including fireworks and thunder (which is understandable) but also includes very distant gunfire, hairdryers and hoovers. He also has a complex about anything that goes wrong in the house; if I drop a mug on the floor, he thinks it's his fault and rushes to his bed. He can't go through doors, if they're not wide open and doesn't like being in the garden on his own. He's not really a 'dog person', either – he has a great capacity to blank other dogs, but will rush up to complete dog-walking strangers, as if he knows them.

These are but a few of his little foibles. He doesn't seem to be particularly worried about David's absence – I was always his main carer.

"Well, go and find your lead and ball, then," I say, and he runs off. I, meanwhile, continue to sit on the sofa, too tired and fed up, to move.

Here I am, I found the ball and I'm now going to drop it on your lap to remind you that you said ... and with that he lets the ball roll down my legs into my lap, again staring at me, willing me to get up.

"Where's your lead?" I say, not really expecting him to know, but deliberately winding him up. He does a quick circle, as if chasing his tail and barks.

"Okay, okay," I say and I drag myself up. I pull on my dog-walking coat and we go into the outside world together, like an old married couple.

WE LIVE ON A SMALL estate (that word 'we' – I must start saying 'I'). Nothing very exciting ... but it's home and everything around me is familiar. I feel safe here ... it's my little universe, but since David left, I'm just existing in a bubble, floating about ... alone.

I turn left and walk down the enthusiastically named, Primrose Avenue. I don't think I've ever seen a primrose and it's certainly not avenue-like – I would expect an avenue to have towering trees, on either side. On the contrary, there are just rather average-looking houses and bungalows, circa 1970 on either side, with well-kept, small front gardens.

I pass John, washing his Escort – which always looks as if he's just polished it – and we exchange a few pleasantries about the weather, along the lines of, "Not very summery today, is it?" from John and "No, but at least it's not raining," from me. Our conversations usually go like that, with a few variations about the sun, the sky or the frost. We've never got past this level and neither of us show any desire to do otherwise. I know his name purely because I heard his invisible wife call to him through an open window once. I'm not sure he knows mine. He's more likely to know Gaz' name, as I sometimes bring him into the conversation with something like, "Gaz doesn't mind the rain." John's seen me with David, of course, in the past. I wonder if he's registered that he's gone? Probably not.

I pass June, a few doors down, who's hanging out her washing – and the old man at number seventy-five, who seems to be permanently pruning his roses. June says, "Hello, dear" and number seventy-five, grunts. I don't really mind that no one wants to talk to me. I'm not in the mood, to be honest.

We walk across Tulip Close and into Daisy Lane (yes, a pattern is emerging) and reach the main road. I cross over and go down towards the 'rec' as we locals call it – an open space where people play football and cricket and where dog-walkers allow their dogs to foul the grass, much to the indignation of sports lovers. I try to be community spirited and always take my plastic bag to collect the evidence. It makes me gag every time, but I do it and then place it in the disgusting bin that is certainly not 'fit for purpose' as it's over-flowing and hanging off its post. Gaz always looks embarrassed by it all, as if he knows he shouldn't relieve himself there, poor thing.

There's a bench at the rec where I often sit, while Gaz wanders around, sniffing aimlessly. Today, is no exception; I sit down and watch him as he walks the periphery of the grass, lifting his leg on various blades of grass.

This is the bench – I mean … *the* bench. The bench where David told me his 'news'. I still go all funny when I think about that afternoon.

Chapter Two

You'd been quiet all morning – not unusual for you, really, but looking back, you were less smiley – more intense. It was a Saturday and we were both tired, for different reasons.

You'd had a particularly difficult week at school; we'd discussed various problems you were facing as Headmaster at supper every night that week – funding, inspections, discipline – the list was long – and I'd tried to be as sympathetic as possible, but I sometimes felt as if I was on the opposing 'side', as a mere teacher at the coalface, so to speak. You were now so cut off from the reality of actual teaching, you'd forgotten what it was like to be confronted day in, day out with rows of teenagers, concealing their mobile phones, talking, plotting and throwing things. I felt you'd forgotten why you'd gone into teaching in the first place, but I didn't say that ... anyway, the reason I was tired was unrelated. My hormones have been all over the place for months and the consequence is chronic sleeplessness. At the time, it was getting ridiculous ... each morning, I was feeling as if I'd had no sleep at all. I was lying awake most of the night and then falling asleep at around 4.30 am and being dragged out of semi-unconsciousness at 7 am, by Jim Naughtie on Radio Four.

So, all things considered, I wasn't surprised that we didn't talk to each other that Saturday morning. We'd got up late; we sat together at the breakfast table, you looking at your iPad and me, reading the Times. Married couples do that though – you don't have to talk to each other all the time, do you? Sometimes, it's nice to sit companionably silent.

Our routine at the weekend was usually: me going to the supermarket to do the weekly shop, while you took Gaz for a walk. We'd go to the pub for a drink at lunchtime and in the summer, we'd go down to the club and play tennis in the afternoon, either as a mixed doubles pair, or as singles. We had friends and acquaintances down there and we could usually find someone to play with. We made good doubles partners – you were good at the net and I was good at lobs, at the back. If it was winter, you might still go to tennis, but I was strictly a fair weather player, so I'd stay at home and catch up on housework or marking. If you didn't play tennis, you'd watch rugby and shout at the television or, do the Telegraph crossword.

That Saturday morning, you'd suggested we went for a walk together, which, although it wasn't unprecedented, was unusual enough for me to take note.

What's that about, I remember thinking? Little did I know what was coming.

We did our usual walk – Gaz was pottering happily and you suggested we sat down on the bench. I didn't particularly want to, it wasn't that warm and I wanted to get on, but you insisted – so we sat and I remember watching, as Gaz triumphantly found a ball in the undergrowth and ran over to us, with it gripped between his teeth.

That image is burnt into my brain now – the happy dog running towards me, the yellow of the tennis ball – it's as if he's running in hyper slow-motion towards a truck that is going to come out from nowhere and run him over ...splat. That's how it felt – it was as if you'd run me down, and then reversed over my prone body again and again, to make sure I was dead.

"Anna, I need to tell you something," you said. I can remember hearing those words and not thinking anything much. I can remember not even turning to look at you; I was watching Gaz, wasn't I?

"Anna, did you hear me?"

"Yes, well ... get on with it, then," I said, sort of jokily ironic, in the way we were prone to speak to each other.

There was a long pause and this made me turn towards you. You looked pale, your eyes had black rings under them, and for the first time, I wondered what was wrong. Maybe he's ill, I thought. Maybe he's going to say he hates his new job and wants to quit?

"Anna, there's no easy way to say this ... I'm sorry ..."

"What?" I said, finally realising it was something important.

"Anna ... I've fallen in love with someone else ..."

Those words still have the same effect on me now, when I think about them. I hear your voice, I see your face ... and I feel the pain that *literally* hit me in the stomach that day. I can remember momentarily wondering if this was your idea of a sick joke ... maybe it's an ill-thought out jape and you're suddenly going to burst out laughing? But it was fleeting – I only had to look at your face to see that it was true. The pain I felt, flashed through my entire body, leaving me breathless; at that moment, the life drained out of me. I felt I was going to faint.

"Anna ... Anna ... did you hear what I said?"

"Yes, I heard."

I remember leaning forward, putting my head in my hands, my elbows resting on my knees and almost blacking out. It was such a shock. I had no idea you were going to say that to me, no idea at all. No inkling.

"I'm so sorry," you said. "I *had* to tell you. It's been killing me. I couldn't live like this, any more."

You put your hand on my back but I couldn't bear your touch. I stood up and almost fell over, as my legs gave way. Gaz, ever hopeful, thought I was going to throw the ball and spat it out at my feet, looking up expectantly.

"Anna, say something... anything... shout at me, if you want," you said. I turned towards you and for a split second, I can remember feeling sorry for you – your face looked haggard, ravaged even, but then I remembered what you'd said.

"Who is it?"

Your face took on a guilty look and I understood, instantly, that it was someone I knew.

"WHO?" I SHOUTED TO the air, not caring that an old couple walking nearby were staring at us. They were quite blatant – they didn't try to hide their interest at all.

"Sit down," you said. "Sit down and I'll explain."

I didn't want to hear your explanation; I thought it might, quite literally, kill me. But I sat down, like one of your pupils about to be told off. I couldn't look at you, so I set my eyes on Gaz who was standing in front of me, still holding the ball, with a look of disappointment on his face.

"I'm so sorry, Anna, I really am. I never meant this to happen. I never set out to hurt you. It crept up on us."

The 'us' pained me like no other word could. 'Us' now referred to you and someone else, not you and me. It was as if you'd stabbed me with a knife, right through the ribs. I drew my eyes away from Gaz and turned to face you.

"It just happened," you said.

"That's what they all say," I said. "But it doesn't *just happen*, does it? "

There was a long silence. The old couple had moved on now, so had Gaz. There was no one else on the rec. I noticed a small flock of black birds swooping overhead; the only sound I could hear was the distant rumble of traffic from the dual-carriageway.

"So ... who is she, then?"

You looked directly at me, opened your mouth, closed it again and then whispered, "Suzie Barton."

Why didn't I see that coming? Suzie Barton. The woman all the men drool over when she bounces through the staffroom door in her tracksuit, whistle round her neck, blond ponytail swinging. She can't be more than thirty-six, for God's sake. I've never really got to know her – the PE staff are a group apart, with all their energy and outdoor activities.

These thoughts were rushing through my head as I stared at you, your face now white, your eyes, haunted. If you're so in love, why don't you look happier?

"Well, say something ..." you said. "I'm so sorry ... but ... you needed to know."

"She's married, isn't she?"

"She was ... she left him. She and her daughter ..."

"How old?"

"Her daughter? Gemma's three – they moved out ..."

"So ... was this before or after you 'fell in love'?" I said, in the most damning, hurtful tone I could muster. I wanted you to see how ridiculous you were being, to make you see how clichéd it was to 'fall in love' at your age. I wanted to hurt you, as much as you'd hurt me.

"Before ... they'd split up months before – I wasn't the cause of their breakup ..."

"How convenient," I spat, "for her, I mean, to fall in love with someone on a good salary ..."

"It wasn't like that."

"How long ... how long have you been screwing her?"

"Anna ... please ... it's not like that ... if it was just sex, it'd be easier."

"Easier?" I shouted.

"Yes ... because it ..."

"Because you could just screw her and not tell me – is *that* what you're saying?"

There was a pause. "Yes, I suppose it is." You looked down and probably without realising it, you began twisting your wedding ring around your finger.

"You didn't answer my question ... how long has it been going on, whatever 'it' is?"

"About six months. It crept up on us both. We didn't deliberately try to hurt you ... you must believe me. I tried to fight it ..."

"Oh please – don't make out you are the *victim*. It's quite simple, David ... you've been having an affair ... and now you're trying to justify it, by saying you're 'in lurve.'"

You said, very quietly and without any sense of triumph, "As I said, I've fallen in love. I thought you deserved to know the truth."

"Well, I don't want to hear any more. I want to get as far away from you as I can, right now. Come on, Gaz, we're going home." And with that, I walked away from you, my whole body shaking and feeling as if I was going to be sick. In some ways, I wanted to hear all the gory details ... in others, I wanted to pretend you'd never said it. I wanted to shout and scream at you, to hit you, to cry ... but I walked away.

I hoped my back seared into your eyes with its sadness.

When I was out of sight, I stopped and leant against a tree, my breath coming in gasps, my heart racing, as if I'd just run the whole way. Gaz looked up at me with a worried gaze.

I stumbled home, my body using its own sat nav system. I could have been walking on Mars for all the awareness of my surroundings I felt. Gaz knew where he was going and kindly led me home, like a generous, old uncle.

I opened the front door, hung up my coat and leant back against the closed door. It looked a very different hall from the one I'd left an hour before.

I didn't recognise anything.

Chapter Three

So, that's how he told me. I suppose, looking back, there was no easy way to say it, was there? It was something that had to be said and he said it. He *really* said it.

At least he didn't leave me a note one morning – *Hey Anna, Sorry – but I'm moving in with Suzie Barton. Thanks for everything.*

That would have been awful. Or, more awful than this.

At least I didn't catch them 'at it' in our bed. Imagine the shock of that – wandering home early, unexpectedly and hearing muffled noises coming from upstairs ... thinking it's burglars ... and finding them doing something unspeakable to each other ... it doesn't bear thinking about.

At least I didn't learn about it from a colleague coming up to me in the staffroom and taking me to one side and saying, *I'm sorry to be the one to tell you, but I really feel you should know ... your husband and Suzie Barton are having an affair. Everyone knows, except you.*

Imagine the humiliation, the embarrassment.

No, when all's said and done, he told me straight. But then again, saying 'I've fallen in love with someone else' ... that's really telling you how it is, isn't it? He didn't exactly sugarcoat it, did he? Would it have been better if he'd said, I'm having an affair ... I fancy someone at school ... I don't love you any more ... there are three people in our marriage ... I'm having a fling ... or as the Australians put it, I'm giving you the flick.

All those expressions could have led to some kind of response from me – but what can you say to someone who says, *I've fallen in love with someone else*? It's so honest, so straightforward ... so truthful ... so final. That's why I walked away. What could I say?

He came back, six hours later. God knows where he'd gone in the interval. He didn't smell of alcohol, so he hadn't gone to the pub to drown his sorrows. Maybe he went straight round to Suzie's and said, '*Well, I've done it. I've told her. Can I come round tonight? I don't think I'll be very welcome at home, any more.*'

Anyway, he came quietly back through the door. I was in the kitchen, staring unseeingly at the television. Some hilarious programme was on, where they show clips of people falling over on dance-floors or hurtling down hills on bikes and crashing into trees, or water-skiers, out of control – it can really make me laugh sometimes.

When I heard the front door open, my heart began to race. I didn't know what I was going to say to him, but I knew I had to say *something*.

I couldn't just let him walk away from our marriage, could I?

I didn't move. He wandered into the kitchen without saying anything and stood by the sink, looking out into the garden. The silence between us was like a presence in the room; it prowled around like a black cat, twisting itself around the table legs.

I'm not going to be the one to break the silence, I thought to myself.

"What do you want me to do?" he said, slowly turning to face me.

Well, I thought, that's a strange question ... what could I say?

"Do you still love me?" I said, not knowing why I said it; it came from nowhere.

"Of course I do – you're the mother of my children – I'll always love you. But ... this is different ... this is ..." He ran his fingers through his still abundant hair. "This is ... completely different."

"How? Tell me ..."

"It's like ... we're soul mates. She understands me. She 'gets' me."

With wonderful comic timing, there was a burst of canned laughter from the television set.

"What ... I don't 'get' you? After all these years?"

"I don't know, it's like I've met the other half of *me*. When I'm with her, I feel completely happy." He was now facing me and came towards me and stood to the side of the TV, trying to make me see him.

This was getting worse. He was explaining, but with every sentence he was making me feel more ... worthless.

"Well, it sounds wonderful," I said, "for YOU. It sounds like love's young dream, like Brief Fucking Encounter, like Brad and Fucking Angelina. But for ME, it's truly, fucking shit ... TRULY, FUCKING SHIT," I found myself shouting. I was also, without realising it, now standing and poking him in the chest, with every foul word that was coming out of my mouth.

His face had a sort of shocked expression, as if he'd just been told he'd got terminal cancer. He was trying to step backward and I was following him now, pushing him hard in the stomach, with the heel of my hand.

"How do you think it feels? How do you think it feels ... to have YOU telling ME how FUCKING wonderful you feel with HER?" I yelled, now leaning in on him, my face right in his, spitting in his face, my veins standing out, unattractively, in my neck. Not the most endearing picture of me to take away with him. Not the best way to hold onto him, for sure.

But what did it matter? He'd made up his mind, anyway, and I'd lost all control. I'd been pretty restrained at the rec and now in the privacy of my own home, I had the right to shout at him, didn't I? I wasn't going to give in gracefully and say, *Well, go and have a wonderful life with Suzie fucking Barton,* was I? He was going to find out just how much he'd hurt me.

It left me wrung out, like an old J cloth. I was totally raving mad for thirty minutes but ... I've never been like that before and hopefully will never be like it, again. I think I had every right, every f***ing right, though. (I don't normally approve of swearing – I tell my pupils it just shows that they don't have a very good vocabulary, but sometimes, just sometimes, that word really hits the spot.)

When I'd stopped shouting, prodding and pushing, I collapsed onto the sofa. Gaz, by this stage, was showing signs of acute paranoia and had retreated to his bed, in shock. He wasn't used to us shouting – we hadn't been a couple who went in for loud arguments and yelling. We were quietly happy, until that day.

Simon Cowell was now smirking at me from the television screen in his smarmy, superior way. Do I have the X Factor for shouting abuse at my spouse, I wondered? *A thousand percent yes,* says Simon. *See you in boot camp, Anna.*

David, meanwhile, had accepted defeat and left the kitchen. I could hear him walking around our bedroom, above me; I assumed he was packing a case, putting a few clothes in one of our large cases. He wasn't a vain man, David; to him, clothes were of no interest and he tended to wear a collection of shirts and trousers, which all looked pretty much the same. As my final sentence had been, "Well, if you think you're spending one more night here, you've got another think coming" – he didn't really have much choice; or maybe he'd planned this all along – to leave that Saturday.

Whatever the case, he appeared at the kitchen door, about twenty minutes later. I'd heard him coming down the stairs, bumping the case down, so I was mentally prepared. What I wasn't prepared for though, was the feeling of love I still had for him. It's true what they say, love and hate are so intertwined.

"Well, I'll be off then," he muttered.

I stared at him. I couldn't bear the thought of me wailing, or repeating the performance from earlier, so I didn't say anything at all, except, " ... have a nice life."

We stared at each other for a few more seconds and I'm pretty sure I could detect a sheen of tears across his eyes. He honestly looked as if he'd just received the worst news you could imagine – not like someone who was going off to live with his 'soulmate'. He said, "Bye, then, see you at school," and closed the kitchen door quietly.

The front door closed and I stared at Cheryl Cole's face, wondering whether her life was as good as it looked. She's got the face, the body, the hair, the voice and now the French husband too – surely, it's a darn sight better than mine, anyway?

His parting 'see you at school' echoed round my head. The thought of going back there was horrendous. How many people knew already and how was I going to go about my day, seeing Suzie – seeing him? I had visions of them walking hand in hand down corridors; of my colleagues whispering in corners – outright laughter by the kids in classrooms.

Have you heard? Mrs McCarthy's husband's been shagging Mrs Barton? She had no idea ...

My mind froze at the thought of all the looks and the ridicule – perhaps I could pull a sickie – surely he wouldn't question it?

On the TV, the panel of judges whittled down the hopefuls to the lucky few going on to bootcamp. You knew which ones were going to be in the final twelve – we got all their sob stories. *I'm doing it for me Gran. I've wanted this ever since I was in my mother's womb. I want to make me dead grandfather proud.*

Wouldn't it be good if life was like reality TV? If you cry enough, have a good back story, you get chosen.

Well, real life isn't like that, is it, Simon?

Chapter Four

So here I am, a month after the big revelation. It's no easier – in fact, it's getting more difficult by the day. Marriage is a state of mind more than anything. It's been 'we' for so long ... now it's 'I'.

Being single when you're twenty is fun – all those hopes and dreams, all those future relationships and adventures to look forward to. Being single at fifty-five is just ... sad. All you've got to look forward to is drawing your pension, varicose veins and incontinence pads. Not the same at all.

I *did* pull a sickie on that Monday – I just couldn't face school.

I couldn't face Life, either. I lay in bed all day, just occasionally getting up to go to the fridge. Unfortunately, I still seemed to have an appetite – I obviously wasn't going to be one of those women who lose loads of weight, in a crisis. In fact, I found myself comfort eating: toast with loads of butter; chocolate digestives that were hiding at the back of the cupboard and a whole tub of chocolate chip ice cream.

By the evening, not only was I feeling sick from over-eating, but I was also feeling guilty about my classes – I have, despite everything, a deep-seated desire to do a good job. I went in on Tuesday, avoided the staffroom, kept my head down and left on the dot.

WHEN HE WALKED OUT that night, all I kept thinking about was Holly and Adam – although they're 'adults' now and have their own lives, this was going to be devastating news for them. Particularly for Holly – she worships her Dad. Adam and David, on the other hand, fight like male lions, tearing each other apart, at every available opportunity. David just doesn't understand Adam and Adam thinks his father is a 'dickhead' (his words, not mine – but come to think of it, a pretty apt description.)

Adam had been staying with a friend, the night before that Saturday, leaving the coast clear for David to do his evil deed. Holly lives in London, so was out of the picture, anyway.

They're so different, Adam and Holly. She's so focussed and hard-working; Adam's more of a free-spirit and hasn't got a clue what he wants to do – he thinks that surfing is a great career choice and that his 'A' levels are irrelevant. None of us are sure he'll pass any of them – he's a bright boy, but doesn't apply himself to anything that involves sitting down.

Adam texted late Saturday night; I was still staring at the television, unable to drag myself to my solitary bed. It read: *Staying over again. See ya tomoz.*

When the phone vibrated, I thought for a mad moment it was David – *Soz, bad joke, I know. Convincing though!*

But no, of course, it wasn't him.

Adam was always good at letting me know what he was doing and I was grateful that he'd done so this time. I had no energy left to worry about him that night.

When he eventually wandered in at two o'clock on the Sunday afternoon, he didn't even comment on the fact that David's car wasn't there – he probably didn't even notice.

I was still in my pyjamas and Gaz was looking extremely hard done-by.

"You look rough, Mum ... heavy night?" he said, as he dumped his bag in the middle of the floor.

"Thanks. You could say that, yes." I opened my mouth to tell him the news, but nothing came out. I was sitting on the sofa, surrounded by empty crisp packets. I stood up.

"What are your plans for the rest of the day, Adam?"

"Not a lot. I thought I'd have a kip now – didn't get a lot of sleep last night or the night before, for that matter. Got a cracking head."

"Can I have a word ..." I said, as he was making his way to the stairs.

"What?"

"I thought you should know ... your Dad's left." I wasn't sure how to tell him. Blunt, seemed the best way.

"What d'ya mean? Where's the old git gone?" Adam was always one for showing respect for his elders.

"He's left us. He's gone to live with Mrs Barton, the PE teacher." As I said it, it was like I was part of some awful sit-com.

Adam's face was a picture of incredulity. A smirk came over his face and he said, "You're joking, right?"

"No, Adam, I'm not. He told me, in great detail, which I could have done without, to be honest, how she and he have 'fallen in love' and that he's left ... for good, it seems."

The smile slipped from his face. He sat down on the sofa with a thump and looked at me with a face that reminded me of him when he was a little boy.

"I don't believe it. What a stupid, fucking twat he really is. How could he?" He jumped up suddenly and in a display of kindness that was pretty well unheard of from Adam, he came over to me and put his arms around me and hugged me hard. Having him show such raw emotion, set me off and tears now coursed down my face.

"Oh Mum. How could he? He'll be a laughing stock ... everyone knows what she's like. All the sixth form fancy her – there's rumours she had sex with one of the guys in last year's Sports 'A' Level classes."

"I'm sure that's not true," I said, wondering if it was. "Shall I make you a cup of tea?"

We were standing together, still with arms around each other. Suddenly, he broke away and went and kicked the fridge door so hard, he actually dented it and then hopped around on one leg holding his foot.

"Look, Adam – that won't help. Your father's made his decision ... he may live to regret it but ... he loves you both ... very much."

"Yea, right ... so much that he doesn't even bother to tell me he's leaving home. When is he planning to talk to me, then?"

"I don't know. You've got his mobile number – give him a ring, if you want."

"I'm not going to ring that pillock. Thank God I'm going to Australia – sorry Mum, I didn't mean ... but I really feel I might do something I'll regret if I see him. God, when I think about all his lectures to me – about 'knowing what you want in life' and 'focussing on your future' and all that shit, it makes me sick. Some role model he's turned out to be."

I couldn't really disagree with him. There was part of me that thought I should be sticking up for David in front of this onslaught – no son should talk about his father in that way – but there was another part of me that thought, yes, what a bloody hypocrite you are, David McCarthy. How do you expect Adam to now 'knuckle down' as you kept saying? You've given him the incentive to go completely off the rails. Thanks for nothing.

Adam did go upstairs to have a nap and the rest of the evening was spent in companionable silence, in front of the box. I was so pleased to have him there and realised it would only be a couple of weeks before he left. If this hadn't happened, I would have been excited for Adam, loving the fact that he was going off with his best friend, Jake ... having an adventure. Now, everything seemed ruined. I selfishly wanted him to stay, to be permanently 'my little boy' – but he'd stopped being that long ago.

He told me later that he'd stormed into David's office on Monday and had an almighty row with him. I bet the secretaries in the adjoining office enjoyed that. Serves him right. When Adam came home that evening, he told me that the whole school seemed to know – quite how, no one knew. Maybe they'd driven to school together, in the morning – gossip travels fast in that place. Adam said everyone was on 'my side', not David's – quite how true that was, I don't know, but it helped me decide to brave everyone the next day.

As for Holly, I rang her late on Sunday night after Adam had kissed me goodnight, more lovingly that he'd done for years. I always spoke to her late in the evenings – Holly's a great socialite and is out most nights, in clubs and bars. She's one of those people who can be both conscientious and great fun, at the same time. She's gregarious, loud, outspoken even, in social situations, but give her a job to do and she gets on with it, quickly and efficiently.

She's very close to her Dad, so I knew her reaction would be quite different to her brother's. I was, in fact, worried about telling her. I didn't want this to come between them; after all, it had nothing to do with their relationship – it was between him and me. So I picked up the phone, with my hands already sweating. I was lying on what was now *my* bed, not ours, with just the bedside light on. I was in my pyjamas and was snuggled under the duvet.

"Hey, Holly, it's Mum," I said, trying not to let my voice give myself away. "How was your day?"

"Yea, great thanks. Three of us went off on Boris bikes and had Sunday lunch in a pub down by the canal. We've only just got back. Turned into a bit of a 'sesh'. Met some great guys too. Got my eye on one – Greg. Gorgeous. I deliberately, but casually, managed to mention where I work, so maybe he'll get in touch. There was definitely a bit of a 'frisson' between us. Sorry to witter on. How was your day?"

I really didn't want to break this bubble of excitement and happiness. I always loved hearing about Holly's life; she was so enthusiastic about everything and she managed to convey it to me. She always cheered me up with her tales of London life and boyfriends. Greg was just another, in a long line of potentials. It was great the way she felt she could talk about it to me – I felt honoured that she trusted me enough.

I paused before I said anything. How could I tell her, without making her Dad out to be the bad guy? "Holly, I've got some news ..."

"That sounds ominous – your voice tells me it's not good news ..." She was always very perceptive, my daughter.

"No, it isn't, I'm afraid. I ... I mean your Dad and I ..."

"WHAT? You're worrying me now ..."

"Your Dad and I are ... separating."

I could hear a loud intake of breath at the other end of the phone. "You what?"

"I said, we're separating, Holly. I can't say it any other way."

"But Mum ... you and Dad are rock solid ... all my friends always look at you two and say you're the archetypal happy oldies. What's going on? This is just a blip, isn't it?"

"No ... Holly ... I'm so sorry, but it isn't 'just a blip' ... it's permanent – Dad's already gone."

"WHAT? WHEN? Why didn't you tell me, for God's sake. Does Adam know?"

"Yes, he knows ..."

"Why am I the *last* person to know?"

"You're not, not really – it's just that Adam was here and ... life's been a bit difficult ..."

I could now hear sniffing at the other end of the line. Oh God, I wish I could have told her in person, but then she really would have had to wait to hear. "Look, Holly, he only went on Saturday evening ... it was yesterday. I've been in a bit of a state, since then. I'm sorry I didn't ring you."

"Sorry, Mum – I'm being selfish. I'm meant to be all grown up now, but I suddenly feel like a four year old, never mind a twenty-four year old. You've always both been there for us ...

you're both *everything* to me," she said. "You're my role models ...
I thought you'd be there, together, *forever*."

"So did I, Holly. I thought I'd grow old with your Dad, but
it seems he's got other ideas."

"What do you mean? Tell me everything ... tell me what's
happened."

So I had to tell her everything. I tried not to harp on about
Suzie Barton; I glossed over her age – Holly didn't know her
from school; she'd left before Suzie flounced into the staffroom,
for the first time. She'll no doubt hear soon enough from Adam.

"I can't believe it, Mum. Why hasn't Dad been in touch with
me? When was he ever going to tell me?"

"Look, Holly, don't cry ... it'll all work out in the end. Dad's
feeling guilty ... he probably doesn't know how to tell you. Why
don't you ring him tomorrow and have a talk to him?"

"Of COURSE I'm going to ring him. How could he? Are
you okay, Mum? Do you want me to come home?"

"Well, I won't lie, I've been better, Holly, but no, you mustn't
come home. You've got work tomorrow and there's nothing you
can do, honestly. Adam's here for a couple more weeks, so I've
got company."

"He's about as useless as a ..."

"Actually, Holly, he was really sweet to me, tonight. Don't do
your brother down. He's very angry at your Dad, though."

"Yea, sorry ... Adam can be quite caring, when he puts his
mind to it. I wouldn't like to be in Dad's shoes when Adam
confronts him."

"No ... anyway, it's late now, Holly. You go to bed and get
some sleep. I'm so sorry to give you the news."

"Okay, I'll go now, Mum, but I'll ring tomorrow. Night night ... try to get some sleep."

I put the phone down and lay back against the pillows, going over the conversation in my head. I hoped I'd broken it to her as well as I could. Suddenly, there was a loud buzzing sound, which nearly made me jump out of bed. It was only the mobile vibrating, but it was on a wooden surface and the house was so quiet – it scared the life out of me. I picked up the phone.

Message from Holly: *I love you, Mum. Try to stay positive. xxx*

She was such a sweet, kind girl ... so thoughtful. Her message made me feel momentarily better, somehow.

She's right, I must stay positive – but then all the negatives of being fifty-five and alone, came piling into my head and I tossed and turned for most of the night.

That's why I pulled a sickie on that Monday. I really did feel dreadful.

Chapter Five

So, thank God the school holidays have started now and I can stay away from David and 'Love's Young Dream'. The previous weeks, since he told me, have probably been the worst of my life. I had to force myself to go to school every day. People were actually very kind to me – too kind sometimes, to be honest – giving me those sympathetic glances and offering me cups of tea. John Blair, Head of History, even took me to one side and asked me if there was anything he could do, in rather a creepy way – quite what he was offering, I'm not sure.

Suzie kept well clear of me – we were almost forced to sit at the same table one day in the cafeteria, but I gave her a filthy look and she backed off and forced herself in, somewhere else. I did consider deliberately chucking my lunch at her, but thought that wasn't such a good idea. We have, as yet, not spoken. This may be surprising, but I don't trust myself to go anywhere near her. I've had a few encounters with my husband – but that's another story.

I've worked at the school for ten years now; David joined the year before me. It was only three years ago that he got the Headship – we were so excited for him, at the time. He's one of those teachers that I've always admired – totally dedicated, a natural ... and he loves the kids. I, on the other hand, went into teaching because I couldn't think of anything else to do.

Seriously, I wracked my brains and couldn't think of anything to do with an English degree, apart from teach English.

It wasn't like it is now – today, there are so many choices for women. Then, when I left university, most of us went into teaching or nursing. Nowadays, I could do marketing, events, branding, recruitment, underwater basket weaving ... mind you, if I had my time again, I don't think I'd do English at uni at all. Why study books for three years, when you can just read the damn things in your spare time?

So ... getting back to my career choice, when I started, I was terrified of the children, useless at discipline and felt completely out of my comfort zone. The only way I survived was to work twice as hard as David and prepare every minute, of every lesson. This was exhausting and after a time, I did relax a little, but it was always stressful for me. Teaching was not what I should have been doing all these years. Unless you're in total control of your classes, it's a hell-hole.

Why couldn't I swan into school, like him? He was universally liked by pupils and staff alike, seemed to do his marking in his free periods and was hardly ever seen preparing lessons, but he got brilliant results. How did he do it? I've no idea ... but hence, the fast track to Head. I, however, floundered around, barely coping, with a reputation for being a push-over. When the kids told me their dog had eaten their homework, I'd believe them. If they arrived late to class, I'd believe some half-baked story about another teacher keeping them late, in a previous lesson. If someone in my class wasn't wearing the correct uniform, I didn't demand that they left the class, I'd say lamely, 'make sure you're wearing it tomorrow', and of course, they never were.

I was too trusting to be a teacher – you have to question everything a kid tells you and believe nothing. You have to pretend you're angry, when you're not. You have to start the way you mean to go on, not go into a class like a right old softie. You also have to like kids – and for the vast majority of my career, I've disliked them intensely.

Don't get me wrong, I love my own children, but other people's children, en masse, are another thing altogether – like marauding pack animals, who'll eat the weakest one alive – and I was the weak one. You try teaching 'Black Beauty' to a classroom full of fourteen year old boys, half of whom can't really speak English. To be fair, that didn't happen at this school, but it happened on my teaching practice, all those years ago. I was told to read a book about a girl and her lovely black pony, to a load of kids who lived in the roughest area in Birmingham and whose relations were often living at her Majesty's pleasure in the prison, opposite the school. Not a good start – and I don't think I've ever recovered from it. I was set on a path towards a career where I was permanently ... bewildered, for want of a better word.

So, all things considered, I wasn't cut out to be a teacher, but I'd done it for years ... and survived. My results were average, my attendance was good and I was conscientious – David had helped me through ... bolstering me up when I'd had a particularly bad day, telling me I was a good teacher, even though I wasn't.

Without his backup and with the situation now so impossible, I began to wonder why I was doing it.

The end of term was always such a relief – I'd walk out of school on the last day with my heart lighter and my head, stress-headache free. David, on the other hand, would always miss school and find the holidays 'too long'. This seemed unbelievable to me – surely most people go into teaching for the long holidays, don't they?

This particular end of term was a two-edged sword, however. It was going to be so good to get away from David and Suzie; so good not to have to mark endless essays ... but so odd to be on my own for six weeks. What would I do with myself?

That swim was the start of my new regime. To get out, to get fit ... to get a life. The other part of my plan was to face the fact that I didn't want to do it any more – teaching, I mean. Surely, I'd tried long enough? Surely ... enough was enough?

My only real friend at school, Lisa Parsons, a colleague in the English department, put the idea into my head. Lisa is also single – she got divorced five years ago and lives with her two sons of twelve and fourteen. She's a good person to talk to about my current situation; she's younger than me, but her husband left her for someone else too, so she knows what I'm going through. I think we became friends originally as we could see in each other a fellow soul – neither of us found 'Macbeth' particularly riveting and we both regarded trips to the theatre with thirty teenagers, pretty much like torture.

We were talking in the staffroom one Tuesday afternoon, when we both had a free and should have been marking; she said, "Well, if you hate it as much as you say, why don't you leave? What are you waiting for? Death in the classroom? Life's too short to do this, if you really hate it. It's a big world out there – think of all the things you could do? Why don't you take early retirement? I've heard you can get a lump sum, if you want. And if you didn't find something else to do, it wouldn't be a disaster – they're always crying out for supply teachers or you could find a part-time position somewhere else. You need to get away from here, Anna, you really do. You can't stay here with David and Suzie ..."

Well, it was like a light switching on in my brain. I'd never really considered it before – I thought I'd go on till I dropped; David and I would retire at the same time and go off into the sunset together, as two old pensioners.

But what's to stop me? I've worked long enough to have an okay pension and it would mean that whatever I did, I could do it part-time. I could get some perspective on my life – I'd have time to think ...

I SAID I WASN'T SURE if Holly was coming home on Sunday or not – well, I was feeling really pathetic that Saturday after the swim and I was really praying she'd come. All this bravado about leaving work ... starting a new life ... boiled down to me feeling lonely, vulnerable and in desperate need of seeing my daughter. I kept checking my phone – had I got it on silent? Had I missed the sound of a message arriving?

It wasn't until 7 o'clock that night that my phone made a sound. Grabbing it, I read:

Hi Mum. Will be on the 11am train. Can you pick me up? Should be in at 12.15. Will text if a prob. xxx

I felt ridiculously pleased that I wouldn't have to spend a Sunday on my own. What was it about Sundays? How can a day of the week have an atmosphere? To me, it did, and this would have been the second one on my own. Sundays felt as if everyone else, in the entire world, were happily ensconced with their family: having walks together; sitting round the table eating roast pork and playing games round a roaring fire. Probably an over-exaggerated view, but that's how it felt. Not to mention the thought of him and her snuggled up together ...

My first Sunday on my own (after Adam had left on the Saturday) had been awful. Staying in bed till midday and then feeling guilty for being so lazy; walking Gaz in a solitary fashion – even he chased his ball in a rather desultory way; reading the Sunday newspapers for a couple of hours and then watching 'Countryfile' and 'Antiques Roadshow' on the telly – designed to be comforting Sunday night viewing, an end to a cosy family day, which just served to show me how sad I really was.

I texted back immediately. I wanted to sound pleased, but not desperate.

That's brill. Will be there. Can't wait to catch up. Are you going to see Dad while you're back? x

Another one from her:

No way. Can't face him. Will talk tomorrow. Love you. xxx

Me:

Love you too. xxx

SINCE DAVID LEFT, THE gap on the left-hand side of the bed seems huge. His body was always so warm – we'd cuddle up together, legs entwined, every night. In the winter particularly, I'd regard him as my human hot water bottle; my feet were permanently freezing and he was so good about letting me put my two blocks of ice, on his legs. We'd always read before turning off the light, we'd talk about the day, we'd discuss problems. All that's gone – now, there is just me with my thoughts and a sea of space, that no one will fill again.

The night before Holly came, I slept particularly badly. I went to sleep okay and then woke about an hour later. I couldn't believe it when I saw the time on the clock – 1.30 am. The night spread before me like a long, dark tunnel of nothing, swallowing me up in its choking darkness.

I got up several times and gazed out of the window; the amber street lights made the road look eery. A fox barked, a sound that gave me the creeps whenever I heard it and then there he was, walking down the centre of the road, like a sly old ghost. He peeled off into my neighbours' front garden, no doubt on a mission to kill something. The scene made me shiver.

The sky was clear – the stars pulsed and glittered, even through the light pollution. Looking up made me feel totally insignificant ... and I longed for David to be there in my bed when I turned. But, of course, he wasn't.

I eventually fell asleep around four, but it was one of those sleeps full of disturbing dreams where you feel you'll never wake up again. I was lost in a huge city. Like all dreams, it made no sense; I was trying to get somewhere and everything was stopping me: I couldn't get out of the car; the train I was suddenly travelling on, never got to the station; when I did get to a street, my legs wouldn't work – I was trying to walk, but my feet were stuck in some sort of mud. Holly was shouting at me, from a window high up on one of those buildings like the Gherkin – all glass and metal – and when I looked up and saw her, I tried to shout back, but nothing came out of my mouth. I woke myself up, trying to shout; my heart was beating fast, I was sweating and exhausted.

I lay back, trying to recover, feeling wrung out. The digital numbers on my alarm clock read 7.15. I got up and made myself a cup of tea, now a solitary and rather sad event that used to be David's treat for me. Every day, he'd say, "Would you like a cup of tea?" and every day I'd say, "Oo, yes please," as if it was the first time he'd ever asked me. He brought me one, even on school days. He was like that.

I took my tea back to bed and lay there listening to the World Service on my mobile. I've learned so much about the world over the years, listening to the radio in the dead of night – I'd plug in my ear phones, so as not to wake David and drift off to other countries and hear about lives that made mine seem okay.

I CATCH SIGHT OF HOLLY in amongst other people getting off the train. It's like my eyes are drawn to her – I've always been able to pick my kids out of a crowd so easily, as if their DNA drifts through the air to me. She looks as gorgeous as ever, her hair catching the light as its blond waves flow around her shoulders. I enjoy watching her as, oblivious of me, she strides purposely along the platform. She's wearing a floaty floral top over washed out blue jeans and, despite the warm weather, she has on a pair of clumpy boots. How does she manage to look so stylish in jeans, I think to myself?

She disappears up the steps that take her up and over the line towards the car park where I'm waiting in my car. Gaz is sitting on the floor of the front seat and when I say to him, "Can you see Holly? Where is she?" he starts to look interested. He stands up with his front paws on the seat and sticks his head through the window that I've opened for him. His whole body begins to wag, as he catches sight of her, emerging from the steps.

"Hey Gazza!" she calls as she walks towards the car, finally running the last few steps. She leans in the window and kisses his head, his whole body now trembling with excitement. Who says dogs don't have a sense of time? If they don't, why is he so excited to see her, after a gap?

She opens the door, saying, "Get down, old boy, let me squeeze in next to you. Hi Mum," and she sits down, leaning over to kiss me. "Okay, Gaz, calm down ... no more slobbery kisses, please." She pushes him down so he's now in the well of the seat, crammed in, next to her legs. He manages to get his head wedged between her right thigh and the gear stick, looking up lovingly at her.

"He's so pleased to see you, Holly. I swear he knew you were coming – I told him where we were going and he definitely understood."

"How are you, Mum? Are you okay?" Her voice sounded more serious now. "I'm so sorry I haven't been down before, but it's ..."

"Don't worry ... it's fine. You've been great to speak to on the phone, anyway. I *can* remember what it was like to have a social life, you know."

"Yea, it's been manic at work too and with Fiona's hen do last weekend, there just hasn't been a moment. Still, I'm here now," she says with her warm smile lighting up her face. She gently squeezes my arm.

We drive back home and decide to take Gaz for a walk, before lunch. Holly misses him in London. She insists on taking his ball thrower and we set off together, Holly holding Gaz' lead. The sun is out, there's a light breeze – and for the first time for what feels like weeks, I begin to feel a lifting of my spirits.

We're walking, as we often do, arm in arm, and talk about trivial things for a while – the latest developments in Albert Square, the owners of the shop down the road that's changed hands and Fiona's hen night. It feels like old times ... as if Adam is just out with his friends and David is playing tennis at the Club and we're going to go back to have Sunday lunch, all together. We both avoid the subject ... it's not as if anything's changed since we last talked on the phone.

Down at the rec, we pass the bench and I can't resist saying, "That's where he told me, you know."

"Oh, Mum ... really?" She looks at it, as if she can visualise the scene. "How horrible. I just can't imagine what you must have gone through. I'm so sorry ..."

I look away. Her words manage to bring tears to my eyes, but I don't want her to see.

"Mum, you don't have to be brave on my account," she says. She's not dim, my daughter.

"It was awful, Holly, I have to admit. But I've got to somehow move on. I can't ..."

"It's such early days, Mum ... you can't expect to move on yet. You were married for a lifetime."

"I know ... but he's not coming back ... I've got to accept that."

"How do you know? Maybe he'll realise what an idiot he's been ... she's so much younger than him, for a start ... it must be a real shock for him, her having a young child ... do you really think it'll work?"

"I don't know ... maybe I don't want him back."

"Really? Wouldn't you forgive him if ..."

"No, Holly, I'm not sure I can. He's broken my heart. I know that sounds dramatic but ... that's how it feels. I feel as if I'm being punished for something I didn't do."

"Oh Mum," she says, putting her arm around my back and squeezing me hard. "I wish I could say something to make it better, but I can't ... when I speak to Dad, he always asks about you, you know. *Have you spoken to Mum? Is Mum okay?* I think he's worried about you."

"And so he should be ..." I say, bitterly. I really don't want Holly to feel trapped in the middle of us, though.

I say, "Do you know what his plans are, at all? Has he said anything to you about anything?"

I know ... I'm fishing for information and yes, I'm using Holly like a go-between. I must stop it, but ...

"Well, I don't think he likes living in a small flat, that's for sure. He mentioned in passing once, that Gemma's room is tiny and she won't be able to be in there much longer."

"Oh God ... he'll want us to sell the house and split the money ... why should I move? I've done nothing wrong."

"He didn't say that to me, Mum ... but I suppose ... realistically ... that may have to happen, one day."

I know she's right, but I can't even bear to think about it, at the moment. I say, "Does he sound happy, when you speak to him?"

"If I'm honest, no, not really. He sounds wracked with guilt, apart from anything else. It can't be a good way to start a relationship. Dad's a good person really, Mum; he must really love her to put you through this. And he's decent enough to know he's done a bad thing. He wants me to go round there sometime soon and meet her ... but you know what? I don't want to meet her ... not yet, anyhow. She's come between you and Dad ... and I hate her for it."

"You'll have to meet her sometime ..."

"Maybe ... but at the moment, I'd prefer to meet Dad on his own, on neutral territory."

We walk back home, leave Gaz to his own devices and then I take her to our local pub for lunch.

I always notice men's admiring glances, whenever I'm with Holly. She's totally unaware of them, of course, but I see their eyes follow her across a room. It's no different this day – there's a group of guys at the bar, all about thirty, and when we walk in, they all look towards us. Some of them try to hide their interest and go back to their pints, but two of them blatantly stare at Holly, who strides across the room, with confidence. She goes up to the bar and says loudly, "What would you like, Mum? A G and T?"

I watch as the two lads try to look away and continue their conversation but, one of them in particular, looks at Holly again. He is, I have to admit, extremely good-looking. Tall, about 6'2", dark-haired and dressed in jeans and a smart, expensive-looking leather jacket. I'm convinced he's going to talk to her.

I don't want to cramp Holly's style, so I grab my G and T and wander over to a table by the window, leaving her at the bar, while she waits for her drink and the menu card.

Once seated, I look over and they are, indeed, chatting. I can't hear what's being said as the pub's busy and Nat King Cole is singing loudly through some speakers, but I can see them both laughing. I can see the chemistry fizzing.

I like this pub – there's a good atmosphere, friendly staff and good value food. In the winter, there's usually a roaring log fire and Gaz is welcomed with dog biscuits and a water bowl. I rather wish we'd bought him now, but he was muddy and I couldn't be bothered to clean him.

I get my phone out – like everyone else these days, I use the mobile phone more as a distraction, than for making actual phone calls. I've previously logged on to the pub's wi-fi, so I check my emails to see if Adam has written. Nothing. No surprise there, then.

I go onto Facebook to while away some time, while Holly flirts at the bar. I use an alias so my pupils don't know who I am. Being a teacher, I really don't want my private life splattered all over social media. All my friends and family know my 'other' name and it's a way of keeping up to date with people – it always adds to my conviction, though, that everyone else is having a better life than me. Status updates, ranging from *Wonderful evening with friends in fab restaurant!* to *Off to Bali for a month!* to *Wow! Look at the view from my mountaintop hotel!* with all the compulsory accompanying pictures of smiling, happy faces and brown bodies, adding to my conviction that I'll never go anywhere exciting, ever again.

When I sent Adam a friend request, he came home that night and said, "Mum, what on earth's possessed you? Why would I want you as a 'friend'? How uncool would I look with my mother on my friend's list? No, the answer is definitely no – you can't be my friend. Is there nowhere I can be, without parental supervision?"

I let it go for a while, but when he was nearly off on his adventures to Oz, I asked again and after much soul-searching, he allowed it. I expect he thought he wouldn't be able to post drunken pictures of himself, but I persuaded him to accept me

– I put a positive spin on it, by saying he wouldn't have to send me any emails when he was in Oz, if I could just see what he was doing on Facebook.

I scroll down and – there he is – a selfie of him and Jake on a beach with the comment *Oz is Awesome!* He looks healthy and happy and the two of them seem remarkably sober. Well, that's a mother's optimistic take on a perfectly innocent photo; we clutch at straws when our children are so far away. The location information says Bondi Beach. I stare at the picture, trying to glean any information I can from it. I feel like a combination of a spy and a detective and kind of understand where he was coming from, when he objected. When we were young, there were just long distance phone calls and letters; parents had to accept long silences. Now, with the constant updates on Facebook, we expect to keep up to date, daily.

Should I comment on the post or not?

I write *Looks Amazing!* and hope it's completely neutral and non-judgemental.

Another comment pops up from someone I've never heard of.

Cool Dude. Didn't know you were out here. PM me and we'll meet up.

I click on them – it's some sexy-looking girl, who has very little on. So, the stalking commences. I now go from feeling happy he's having fun, to worrying about predatory females, in the space of about five seconds. The joys of smartphone technology.

At that moment, Holly wanders back and sits down. "You look engrossed Mum. What is it?"

I hand her my phone with the picture of Adam displayed. "Hey, that's cool. Jakey looks as gorgeous as ever! God, I wish he was a bit older ... why do you look worried, Mum?"

"Because ... some girl in a bikini has just asked to meet up with them ..."

"Oh Mum – you are funny. For a start, she probably doesn't wear a bikini full-time, and secondly, what's wrong with that? It's good that they're making friends out there. You're going to have to get used to this, Mum. As you've insisted on being his Facebook friend, you'll see all sorts of things."

"Yes, you're right. It's awful being a Mum sometimes, though. You have absolutely no control and all the angst. Anyway, who was *he* at the bar? You seemed to be getting on rather well?"

Holly looks surreptitiously over towards the bar and catches his eye – a sizzling smile burns back across the space. She smiles and then deliberately turns towards me. She lowers her voice and says, "Well, it turns out we went to school together – primary – but he was a few years ahead of me. He claimed to recognise me, but I think that was just a line. His name's Jed and he's just down for the weekend, like me. Lives in London too." She looks bright and her eyes have a certain happiness about them.

"Are you going to meet up, in London?" I ask.

"Maybe," she says, cagily. "We found out that we work pretty near each other."

"You seem to have found out an awful lot of information in a short space of time," I say, leaning over and nudging her knowingly. How lovely to be so young – life's so easy – you see someone you like the look of, you flirt, you meet up for a drink and these days, the next step is probably, bed.

How am I ever going to meet someone now, at my age? The thought of taking my clothes off in front of someone, other than David, makes me feel sick.

"So, enough of me," says Holly. "Let's order lunch and I want you to tell me what you're going to do with the rest of your life. There's a big world out there, Mum, and now's the time to go and find it."

So, over roast pork and all the trimmings, I tell her what Lisa suggested, about retiring early and we go on to talk about what I'd do if I took that option. She has me travelling the world – studying yoga in India, going to Peru to see Machu Picchu, flying by helicopter across the Grand Canyon. "You could do *anything*, Mum ... it would be amazing ... like a grown-up gap year. You could just spend the lump sum ... life's too short to be sensible."

"It does sound fantastic, Holly, but the the reality is, I'd be on my own. I haven't travelled without your Dad for ... ever. Imagine me, wandering around the world ... I don't think I've got the confidence and anyway, I wouldn't want to spend the whole lump sum on ..."

"But Mum, you might meet some gorgeous Indian guru or some Peruvian horseman ..."

"I don't think so, somehow ... you read about the stupid older women going out to the Caribbean and meeting young Jamaicans who are just after their money ... I wouldn't want that ..."

"You're not *that* stupid, Mum ..."

"Oh, thanks ... maybe I *could* do some travelling, though – I've wanted to go and see Jane in Adelaide ever since she went out there, but there's never been the money ... or the time. At least then, I wouldn't be completely on my own."

"Hey, well, there you are ... that's a really good idea. If you gave up teaching, you could go out there for weeks, months even ... you could escape the winter here and go out in the new year. I think that's a brill plan, Mum. Resign now and take a long break away and come back with a renewed outlook."

"It does sound good. Jane's always going on at us to come out and I haven't seen her for years."

"Well, then, what's stopping you?"

I look at her and we both laugh. She has such an infectious enthusiasm for life and it's rubbing off on me. In my head, I can see a much younger version of me, floating across an Australian beach in a bikini, the waves catching the sun with glittering stars and some young bronzed life-saver dude, running towards me. He's got a surfboard tucked under his arm and one of those ridiculous life-saver hats on his head.

"What's stopping you?" Holly repeats, louder. Reading my mind she says, "You might meet some old Aussie guy wearing one of those hats with corks dangling from it!"

She brings me back to reality – my Aussie dude was like something out of 'Endless Summer', not some raddled sixty year old.

"Why don't you email Jane and ask her if it's possible first and then go on from there. I think you need something like this, Mum. God, I'd be so jealous ..."

"Adam would have a fit – he'd accuse me of following him out there ..."

"Well, Australia's big enough to miss him, Mum ... but if he wanted to meet up, you could. He won't mind. Don't let that put you off."

We finish our main course and then share a sticky toffee pudding and ice cream. There's something really nice about one pudding and two spoons; David and I used to share puddings all the time.

When it's time to go, I give Holly the cash and she goes up to the bar to pay. I notice a lot of chat again, with Jed, and I see them both get out their phones. The modern way of swopping numbers – no paper required any more – just a quick call. He bends down and kisses Holly's cheek; I stand up and walk towards them. She introduces me and I'm slightly mesmerised by his stunning, piercing blue eyes which twinkle at me. I can see that Holly's cheeks have a pink blush and I'm pretty sure it's not the alcohol having that effect.

"I'll be in touch," he says, as we walk towards the exit.

"Okay," she says, holding the door open for me, her eyes looking back to him.

When the door closes and we're walking home, I take her arm and say, "Jed's rather nice. What's he do for a living?" A typical mother comment, but it does tend to show you a little bit about the person.

"He's a barrister."

"Wow. Impressive."

"He's certainly got the gift of the gab ... funny to think last time I saw him he was probably a scruffy little boy, with dirty knees. I certainly didn't recognise him."

"Do you want him to get in touch?"

"Yea, I do ..." she says, laughing, " ... lovely eyes."

"Yes, I noticed," I say. "Rather a catch ... is he single? He seems too eligible to be ..."

"Well, he said he's just split up from his girlfriend. She's gone to work in America and they thought they'd be able to maintain the long-distance thing, but she's already found someone else. He seemed pretty cut up about it."

"I'm sure you could cheer him up," I laugh.

When we get home, Gaz is pleased to see us, but somehow manages to come over put out, at not being taken to the pub. "Sorry, Gaz. I know it was mean, but you were filthy," I say to him, and he waddles off to get on his chair, with a resigned look. We settle down to cups of tea and the Sunday papers and talk about the latest news.

Soon, it's time for Holly to catch her train. I'm always sad when she goes, but this time it seems particularly bad. I know the house will feel devoid of life when I get home; the smell of her lovely perfume will linger around the sitting room.

When we arrive at the station, we sit in the car for a few minutes, as we're a little early. "So, we've sorted you out, Mum. You're going to hand in your letter announcing early retirement, you're going to email Jane and ... you're going to come up and stay with me for a few days and we're going to go to a show – right?"

"Okay, I promise I'll think about it ..."

"No, Mum. Don't think about it – just do it. Promise?"

"I promise. Now off you go, it's five minutes till it comes and it says it's on time."

As she gets out of the car, a look of depression comes over Gaz and I know exactly how he's feeling. I get out too and come round to her side. We throw our arms around each other and hug hard. We both have tears in our eyes when we separate, but both of us try to ignore them.

"You'll be all right, Mum. I'll text you when I get home," she says and she begins to walk away. Just before she enters the little bridge, she turns and waves and I blow her a kiss.

She emerges on the platform and we wave again. The train approaches the station and she disappears from view.

I get back into the car and sit, feeling sick with sadness. I stay and watch the train leave the station – I put my hand on Gaz's head and say, "Well, it's just you and me again, old chap. What would I do without you?"

Chapter Six

The Saturday before, when Adam left, was a day I'd like to forget. David leaving me, had left me feeling old, useless, unattractive and ... need I go on? The only thing I had left that I was proud of, was being a mother. I felt I'd done a pretty good job – the kids had turned out okay and we had a great relationship. They talked to me, confided in me even, and I loved every day I spent with them.

It was inevitable, of course it was, that Adam would leave, but somehow it happened so quickly. One minute he was studying for his 'A' levels and the next, he'd taken them, booked his flight and was gone.

The plan to go to Australia in his gap year had slowly evolved during the sixth form and I blame my best friend, Laura. She and I went to school together and had been friends all through university, marriage, children and jobs. She's got two boys, Rocco and Jake and they're similar in age to my two. We spent a lot of holidays together and inevitably, Jake and Adam became great friends. Rocco's a bit older than Holly and they got on well but had, in recent years, gone on different paths and didn't see each other that much – but Jake and Adam were inseparable – when they weren't together physically, they were chatting on FaceTime, playing computer games in cyber space and texting each other. They were so similar that Laura and I used to laugh that we'd both used the same sperm donor for IVF, which of course wasn't true, but it was as if they were cut from the same cloth.

Laura and John live in Cornwall – they'd met at uni, like us, and had spent summers down on the beaches of North Cornwall, working and surfing. They never really came back up – they loved it too much down there. John got a teaching job, which suited him down to the ground – he'd surf before school – and Laura worked in shops and painted, in her spare time. Over the years, her seascapes became popular and in the end, she was able to paint full-time and they took over a little gallery where she sold hers and other people's paintings.

David and I had wonderful holidays down there, with them. At first, they didn't have room for us to stay and we'd hire a cottage or a caravan just up the road, so we'd be near them. They eventually bought an old, rundown farmhouse just outside Newquay, which they did up slowly, even converting some of the outbuildings to holiday homes. The cottages were posh, compared to the somewhat ramshackle state of their own home; they bought in some much needed revenue. So, we would hire one of their cottages and it meant that we could all be together. David and John got on well – they had their love of teaching in common and although David wasn't a surfing fanatic like John, he'd go out with him every day and the two of them would chat on their boards, while waiting for the 'big one'. It was lucky that the two men liked each other – just because Laura and I were best friends, it wouldn't automatically follow that the men would be.

Jake followed in his father's footsteps. He was in the sea at every conceivable opportunity and he often got into trouble at school for bunking off to go surfing. He entered competitions and got a reputation – he was good. All he wanted to do was surf and it was with great difficulty that Laura and John managed to persuade him to stay on and do his 'A' levels. He worked in cafés to fund his passion and the moment he was seventeen, he took and passed his driving test and used all his savings on an ancient VW camper van. This gave him the freedom to pursue the best surf – if it wasn't 'up' at Watergate, he and his mates would tour the coastline looking for alternatives – Constantine, Boobies, you name it, they went there.

Adam worshipped Jake – he was everything he wanted to be and over the course of several long summer holidays, Adam acquired Jake's expertise in surfing. The summer Jake got his camper van, I didn't see Adam at all. They lived in it together, refusing to join us in the cottage.

Laura was the one who suggested they took a year off in Australia. "It'll give them a year of freedom and, hopefully, they'll get surfing out of their system. It'll be an adventure for them – my brother's out there and we've got other relatives they could stay with. It'll do them good."

"Don't you think they ought to fund it themselves, though? You're not just going to give Jake the money for it, are you?" I wanted Adam to learn the value of money and so did David. We didn't believe in handing our children things on a plate.

"No, of course not. I'm going to say that he's got to save half the air fare and when he's out there, he's got to work for at least half the time. Do you approve?"

"Yes, that's okay – but do your relatives really want two teenage boys turning up? I can't imagine them being particularly tidy guests ..."

"Yea, they'll love it – Aussies are very hospitable. They've got huge houses. My brother's got a caravan park in Byron Bay – the boys could probably work for him and have their own van. I'll find out if it's possible and then discuss it with Jake."

So that's how it came about. The boys, to give them their due, raised the money for more than half the fare and Laura said they'd have no trouble finding temporary work out there – one of John's cousins owned a string of cafés around Sydney and would be able to sort them out as waiters there. The thought of Adam waiting made me laugh; at home, he left everything on the table, never dreamed of taking it over to the sink or putting it in the dishwasher. He didn't know what a drying up cloth was for, and hoovers were just noisy things used by parents. It was probably my fault for not making him do domestic things ... this gap year would certainly make him grow up.

The day they left, Laura and I had arranged to meet at Heathrow. Their flight was at 3.30 pm – we met in departures at 11.30 am, so we had plenty of time to have coffee all together, before the boys went through.

I had tried to get David and Adam together before he left, but Adam refused outright saying he 'no way wanted to be anywhere near that wanker' and when I rang David's phone, suggesting he came over unannounced to say goodbye, he just said, 'I think it's best if I leave him to it. Tell him I'm pleased he's going and to have a brilliant time. Give him my love.'

What can you do? You can't force people to be sensible. Didn't David realise he wouldn't see his son for a whole year? Didn't he care? I told Adam what his father said and I was sure I saw a hint of sadness pass over his eyes, at the realisation that his father wasn't interested enough to come and say goodbye, but he just said, "What does he care? He's got another family now."

So, it fell to me to take him to the airport. I'm sure in the past, we would have gone together and made a day of it, but it was just me and him and although Adam was beyond excited to be going, I could sense his nervousness. It was a big deal – this was the first time he'd been properly away from home and he was flying to the other side of the world.

I caught sight of Laura – she was waiting where we'd arranged, by the check-in desk. She waved madly through the crowds and I could see Jake with a huge rucksack on his back, beside her. They were so alike those two – they both had distinctive light auburn hair, green eyes and were now about the same height. Laura was dressed in her usual, slightly hippy, way: long floral skirt with a lacy white shirt over the top; dangly earrings and beaded bracelets. Jake, in his faded jeans, with his ear studs and lip ring, his hair long and sun streaked, his face brown – looked every inch the surf dude, down to his flip flops (or 'thongs' as he must now call them in Oz).

We all hugged – I love the way kids nowadays are so much better at this than we used to be. All Adam's friends hug each other – boys, girls – it doesn't matter who. The boys threw their arms round each other, with a lot of back slapping and *Hey Dude* and compared the size of their backpacks. Adam had had quite a lot of difficulty even getting his on his back – we were hoping it wasn't going to be too heavy for the flight.

"So ... the big day's arrived," smiled Laura. "How are you feeling, Adam?"

"Yea ... awesome," he said, sliding the rucksack off his shoulders. "Man ... that's heavy." It fell in a heap on the floor, next to Jake's. Both of them were dressed identically and looked so young. They were mere boys ... surely they were far too young to be setting out on their own? My stomach lurched at the thought that soon they'd walk away and I wouldn't see Adam for a year. Tears sprung to my eyes and I had to look away and surreptitiously wipe them away. Maybe it was a mother's intuition – Laura put her arm round me and whispered in my ear, "It's hard, isn't it?" The boys were thankfully laughing at something on Jake's phone. She linked arms with me and said, "Come on, let's go and get rid of their bags and then go to Costa and get a bucket of coffee."

Any nerves that Adam had felt in the car, seemed to disappear in the company of his friend – they were writing status updates on their phones, as they joined the queue and discussing which films they were going to watch on the plane. We shuffled along with them; when they reached the head of the queue and their rucksacks disappeared behind the flaps, the reality really began to hit me.

Laura and I sent them over to a free table in the café and for the last time, I bought my son a coffee and a huge piece of chocolate cake. I bought myself a skinny latte, which was rather pointless, as I couldn't resist a large flapjack. "Still half-heartedly dieting, I see," said Laura, grinning. "Why don't you just give in to middle-aged spread, like me?"

"You never seem to change shape at all. I've only got to look at a piece of chocolate, to put on weight."

"Who cares?" said Adam. "Just be happy with who you are, Mum. Eat what you like, life's too short."

"Says he, who's always trying to become an Adonis with a six-pack, in the gym," I said. "You wait till you're my age – you'll see the problem. You're right, though, life's too short," I repeated, stuffing the flapjack into my mouth. "Anyway ... tell me about life down in Cornwall – how's the gallery going?"

"Fine ... yea, fine. The summer's been really busy, so far. Thank God for tourists. It's dead in the winter. John's job's going well. We've just heard that he's been given deputy head, so we're really pleased."

"His tendencies towards world domination can be given free reign," said Jake, sarcastically. "Thank Christ I'm not there any more. How horrendous would that have been."

"Now you can see how I've suffered, can't you?" said Adam. "Being at the same school as your teaching parents is bad enough, without one of them being Head. Especially when he makes a complete dick of himself by going off with a woman half his age. God ..."

"Adam, don't talk about your father like that."

"Well, what does he expect? He's an idiot. I guarantee when I get back from Oz, she'll have got bored with him and he'll be out on his ear ... serve him right."

Laura and I exchanged glances. We'd discussed the situation endlessly on the phone, so she knew everything there was to know. She said, "You two will find out that life isn't as straightforward as you think. It's not all surfing and parties. We parents make mistakes and do stupid things too, you know."

"Too bloody right," said Jake grinning at her. "I know you're on Adam's friend list, Anna, but there's no way I'd let my mother anywhere near mine."

"Oh well, I'll pass on any info to your mum, anyway so ..."

"I'll make sure that nothing of any note gets on my wall, anyway," said Adam. "All you'll see is innocent pictures of us – you won't be able to glean anything. Trust me."

"You *will* promise to ring if you have any problems, won't you?" I said.

"Yes, Mum ... don't fuss. It's going to be fine. Jake's family will help if there's anything – if I have my leg bitten off by a shark, I'll drop you a line."

"Oh, for God's sake, Adam, don't even think about it ... and make sure you wear factor thirty at least ... "

"Mum ... STOP it ... we'll be fine. I'm a big boy now – cut the cord."

"Well, that's nice ..." said Laura. "Your mum's just looking out for you, Adam. You're lucky to have parents who care ..."

"Mum, don't *you* start," said Jake, "don't start the whole *there are kids out there whose parents don't care what happens to them* bit. We know we're lucky, but there comes a time when a man has to leave the tent and go out and kill food for himself, you know. If we were in some African tribe, we'd have gone off with our spears, years ago. It's time for us to go and find a nice Aussie girl to ..."

"Yea, that's enough," said Laura. "Just look out for each other. That's the main thing. Make sure the other one is safe ..."

"Yes Mum," said Jake, raising his eyebrows and sighing at Adam. "Of course we will. Come on, Ad, I think I've had about as much as I can take of 'mothers united' here. Let's get the hell outta here." He pushed his chair back with a loud scrape, picked up his hand luggage rucksack and put it on his back. Adam stood up too. He glanced across at me and said, "Mum, we'll be fine.

Don't worry ... but we've really got to go. Waves to catch ... beers to drink ... girls to ..."

"Yea, thanks, Adam," I said, smiling at him. "And don't get anyone pregnant!"

"Oh, for God's sake, Mum, I'm not stupid."

He too put his small rucksack on and they started walking towards passport control. Laura and I linked arms and walked behind them. We could hear them laughing together ahead and when they got there, they turned round and Adam said, "So ... this is it. See you in a year," and he flung his arms around me. He whispered, "Find yourself another man, Mum. Dad's not good enough for you. Love ya." He kissed my cheek and I hung on to him for perhaps a bit longer than I should. I breathed in that unique Adam smell and tried to fix him in my head. He extricated himself from me and the two of them walked away. We stood and watched as they showed their passports and as they turned towards an unseen corridor, they both waved back at us ... and were gone.

"WELL, THAT WAS RELATIVELY painless, wasn't it?" said Laura. We were still standing watching where they'd gone. I was almost hoping Adam would pop round the corner again.

"Yes, it was, I suppose. God, I'm going to miss him dreadfully ... are you?"

"Yes, of course, but I wouldn't want him to live with us forever – they've got to go out there and make their own lives, haven't they? Just like we did. We'll get used to it ... I'm sure we will. But I know it couldn't have come at a worse time for you, Anna ... shall we go and have another coffee?"

"Okay ... you've got a much longer journey home than me ... are you sure?"

"Yes, let's ... you can tell me what your plans are."

We went back to Costa and sat down at the same table. The boys' absence permeated the atmosphere. Drinking tea this time, I told her about potentially leaving teaching; she made a good point – was now the right time to make such a dramatic change? I had to agree with her that maybe too many changes were not a good idea, but ...

She told me about Rocco – he'd had to go to Manchester with the BBC – he'd started off with them as an intern in London, but had done well and been offered a contract. He was now working in Sport and was often going to all the big sporting events. There was even talk of commentating. "Who would have thought Rocco would've done so well?" she said proudly. "They've all turned out all right, haven't they?"

"I know. Manchester's a long way from Cornwall, though, isn't it? Have you been up there yet?"

"No ... he only went a couple of weeks ago. He's got some holiday coming up – he's coming down to us for two weeks. So we'll catch up with him then. Is Holly coming to visit soon?"

"Next weekend, hopefully," I said. I knew she would have discussed my situation with John. I said, "What does John think about David?"

"Well, you know what men are like, he didn't say much, but ... he did seem quite shocked, actually. His words were, *Poor Anna. She doesn't deserve that.* I still just don't get it, myself. What's he playing at, for God's sake?"

"I don't know, I really don't. It was so out of the blue. If we'd been unhappy or just drifting apart ... anything ... but there was no indication. I keep wracking my brains to see if I missed something ..."

"Looking back, were there any strange occurrences – did he stay late at work or were there any unexplained phone calls?"

"No, seriously ... either I'm naive, or stupid ... that's why it's been so awful, I think. And if Adam's right and she gets bored with him and chucks him out ... well, I'm not having him back ...ever."

"Really?"

"No ... he's made his bed. I've got to get on with the rest of my life now ... whatever that is."

"Well, I'll always be here for you, Anna, you know that. Any time, day or night, just ring." She looked at her watch. "I must go – I want to get through Bristol before the rush hour."

We walked together to the car park and said our goodbyes by the ticket machine. As I walked towards my car and it flashed its indicators at me, I felt more alone than I'd ever felt in my entire life.

Husband gone, son gone. Just my black friend waiting for me at home. I got in, turned on the radio, which was still on Radio One, at Adam's insistence. The loud, unrelenting jolliness of the DJ with his inane chat, managed to make me feel even more miserable than I already was. I turned over to Radio Four and caught that programme where they discuss people's lives who've just died. Some amazing woman who did charity work into her eighties was being discussed. As I listened to her life, she made me realise that I've got at least another twenty years of potential life to live (as long as I stay healthy) and I've got to go and live it.

Chapter Seven

Since the day David left until now, I have had precisely three conversations with him. You can imagine how strange this is for me. The man I have lived with forever and discussed every aspect of my life with, has simply disappeared from my radar.

Obviously, when I was at school I saw him every day, but I didn't have to speak to him. I had to watch him: in assembly; wandering around the corridors and drinking cups of tea in the staff room, if he deigned to come out of his den. Each time I saw him, my body would have the same reaction; my legs would shake and my heartbeat would quicken, as if I was in the first throes of love ... but I think it was a physical reaction to his betrayal of me. His mere presence made my body both angry and hurt and the end result was a feeling of sickness, nerves and hatred. Whenever possible, I would walk away from him; I'd find any excuse to leave the staffroom or turn around in the corridor. I'm sure everyone noticed, but I didn't care – it was the only way I could cope.

So, on the day I got a message, via my pigeon hole, to meet him in his office at 1.15 pm, it was with some trepidation that I knocked on the door. I had considered not going at all – why should I obey his command and come running? But then I realised I should go, even out of morbid curiosity.

His distant *Come In* sounded monotone from the behind the wooden door; I opened it and he stood up.. "Hello, Anna – come in ... take a seat."

I closed the door quietly behind me and walked towards him, thinking what a weird situation this was.

"What do you want?" I said, petulantly. "Why have you summoned me to your office like this? Couldn't you just come round to the house, if you have something to say?"

"I didn't think you'd want me to ..." he said, sitting down and looking sheepish.

"Well, get on with it ... whatever it is ... I've got marking to do." I stared at him with as much contempt as I could muster.

" ... I was just wondering ... I was wondering if you were okay?" he said.

"What? You've got me in here ..."

"Anna ... please ... I worry about you and I wanted to know if ..."

"Look David ... you lost the right to ask me anything, a week ago – on the day you left me for someone else. You can't expect to just summon me to your office like this. I have nothing to say to you." I could feel tears pushing out, but I was determined not to cry – I couldn't let him see me crying. I stood up and started walking to the door.

"Wait ... Anna ... wait. I feel terrible about what I've done ... I care about you ..."

I stopped in my tracks. I said, "How touching."

"I do care about you. I'm sure, in time, you'll understand ..."

My hand was on the door handle, but I stopped myself from storming out. I came back into the room, marched over to him, went round his desk and said in a low, threatening voice, right in his face, "I will never understand what you've done. Never. I thought we were happy. I thought we'd be together forever. I had no clue that you ..."

"I'm sorry," he said, leaning back. "I was happy with you, but then something changed ..."

"When? As far as I knew, we were going along the same as always ..."

"We were ... maybe that was it ...maybe we got too complacent ..."

"So now you're blaming *me*? I thought you simply fell in love ..."

"I did ... but maybe there was a reason ... maybe I was looking for something ... something you couldn't give me ..."

"So, this just gets better," I said, feeling myself getting hot in the face. "You're a bit bored with humdrum everyday life ... so you go looking for a younger model. You're so predictable, David. We all get bored ... God knows, I was pretty bored with washing your underpants and picking up your dirty socks off the floor but ... hey, that's life. I got on with it. I didn't think of looking for someone else to ...fall in love with. I loved *you* ... so I got on and did your washing." I had to lean on his desk, my legs were shaking so much. I felt drained of everything – as if all the love I'd had for him had suddenly trickled away, along with my self-esteem.

"I still love you, you know ..." he said, slumping forward, his head in his hands. His telephone started ringing and he looked up at me and then at the phone.

"You've got a funny way of showing it. Answer the damn thing. I've said all there is to say." I walked away and pulled the door open with force. I really wanted to slam it shut when I left, but saw his secretary glance up from her computer, pretending she hadn't been listening in to our conversation, and I decided not to give her the satisfaction. I closed it quietly, glared at her and walked out, into the adjacent corridor.

I had to get outside – I needed fresh air, like an alcoholic needs a drink. I stormed out into the car park, breathing the cool air down into my lungs as I walked in a confused state, past the bins, past the netball courts and round the back of the bike racks.

I stopped suddenly and stared across the open expanse of green playing fields. I've got to get away from this place, I thought. What the hell am I doing, even considering staying? Perhaps without knowing it, that was the first time I formulated that idea – before Lisa even told me about early retirement and lump sums. I just knew I couldn't stay in the same building with him. It was madness to stay. Not after this.

The second time we spoke was when I tried to persuade him to come and see Adam before he went – and we know how well that went.

The third time, he came round one evening without warning, just after Adam left. I was sitting, cuddling Gaz on the sofa, a glass of wine by my side. I was watching David Attenborough – wild life programmes always fascinated me and this one, in particular, was riveting – it was about animals that mate for life. I couldn't help marvelling at their straightforward devotion to each other and their utter lack of 'boredom' that David claims had pushed him into the arms of another. Animals are so much more honest ... and noble.

The door bell went – quite a few thoughts rushed through my head. Who the hell is that, being the first one. The second being, I don't know anyone who would call round at 8.30 pm.

The third one being: Would a mad axe man knock first? And the fourth one, I wish it could be like the film 'The Holiday' when Jude Law just happens to be standing on the doorstep.

This one really was wishful thinking. A) I don't look remotely like Cameron Diaz and B) I'm about thirty years too late and C) What would Jude Law be doing in Stowchester, anyway?

Putting that all aside, I went somewhat slowly to the door and slid the chain on. I opened it slightly, having turned on the outside light and there was ... David. I was acutely aware of the difference between Jude and David at that point and also reluctant to remove the chain. I drew the door open as far as the chain would go and said, "What do you want?"

"Can I come in?"

"No, I'm busy."

"Really?"

"Yes, I am. I have got a life, you know."

"Please ... Anna ... I need some more clothes."

"Why didn't you ring first?"

"Well, I thought it would be okay."

"Well, you thought wrong."

"Can I just pop in for a few minutes?"

"No, you can't," and I slammed the door. It gave me such satisfaction that I rather childishly did V signs at him from behind the door.

He rang the bell again and I could hear his muffled voice pleading, "Please, Anna ... just a few minutes."

I undid the chain and opened the door with force. "Come on then, get a move on."

I found it difficult to be normal with him. How was I meant to react? This was something out of my experience and I know I was behaving like a spoilt brat, but I couldn't stop myself.

He came through the door looking as if he was expecting me to lash out at him. Gaz got up and came over to David, wagging his tail. "Hello, ol' chap," he said, bending down to stroke Gaz' ears. Gaz looked up at him with such love in his eyes, I wanted to take him to one side and put him straight – but dogs don't have all our baggage. They just know who they like.

"So, how are we going to deal with everything then?" I said, slumping down on the sofa. "I don't want you to keep barging in here, whenever you want. I think you ought to come round properly and move everything ..."

"Hold on, Anna, this is my house ..."

"Oh, is it? I was under the impression that you'd just moved out to live somewhere else."

"Yes ... but it's still my house and I have as much right to be here, as you."

His face was grey – combining both anger and guilt, in equal measures. He sat down on one of the kitchen chairs and stared at me. I wanted to say something reasonable, not get involved in a cat fight, so I said, "Well, legally you're right, I'm sure, but morally ..."

"I realise that, as you say, morally, I have no right – but practically, I do need my clothes, Anna. Couldn't we just talk about arrangements, sensibly?"

I thought about this – Gaz was now sitting next to me – I felt as if he'd chosen an alliance with me – and drawing him closer for support, I said, "Look, you've made your decision. Any 'arrangements' as you call them, boil down to this – collect your things and – leave me alone."

"Anna, it's very early days, I know and there's no pressure, but ... Suzie and I can't stay in her flat forever ... at some point, we're going to have to move and then we'll have to talk about selling this and sharing ..."

"Over my dead body," I yelled, Gaz looking at me with shock.

"When you've calmed down, you'll see that it's the only way. There's 'no blame' in divorce now, you know – we'll just divide our assets fifty/fifty."

He was being so matter of fact about the end of our marriage. The word 'divorce' had never entered our vocabulary before and it hit me in the gut. I knew he was right, but I didn't want to face the reality of it. God, he'd only been gone a few weeks. What was the hurry?

"Is she pregnant or something?" I said.

"No, of course not ... but the flat's really small ..."

"Why didn't you think of that, when you left? It's hardly my fault, is it?"

"Look, we don't need to even think of it yet ... but as long as you know, this is something we will have to address sometime soon. In the meantime, Anna, I need some clothes. By the way, did Adam get off okay?"

"Yes, no thanks to you," I said. "Why didn't you insist on seeing him, before he went?"

"I thought it was better that way ... I know he's really angry with me ..."

"Can you blame him?"

"No, I know, but ... I didn't want to spoil his big moment. I'll email him and explain everything once he's settled over there."

"Maybe you could email me too – I'd be fascinated to hear your 'explanation.'"

We looked at each other across the chasm between us. Where had our relationship gone? It had been wiped out ... swept away on a flood tide of bitterness.

"One day, I'll try and explain it all to you, Anna. I'm not sure I understand it myself at the moment. All I know is – I had to go and I'm sorry for what it's done to you." He stood up. "Can I have a couple of black bin liners? I realise I haven't brought anything to carry my stuff ..."

I got up and went to the drawer where they live. I broke off two and shoved them at him. "Close the door on your way out," I said and turning up the volume on the TV, I sat down next to Gaz.

Monkeys were grooming each other, finding fleas and eating them. David left the room and I continued to watch, as a male monkey lorded it over a group of females. I suddenly saw myself as one of David's harem. I decided I was going to have to break free – not at all easy at my age and in terms of the animal kingdom, maybe dangerous, but I was going to have to try.

Chapter Eight

So, the summer holidays stretch in front of me. Six weeks of freedom – to do whatever I want. I've done my swim – my first bid to get fit and lose weight – now what?

Holly has suggested I go up to London for the weekend, which I'm looking forward to, but I've got five days to fill, in the meantime.

I sit up in bed – I've woken late on my first free weekday of the holidays – a luxury that we both used to enjoy. I grab my mobile phone that's sitting on the bedside table – it says it's ten thirty – I can't quite believe I've slept so long. I feel as if I've been drugged, my limbs are heavy and my eyes won't open. The bedroom is a mess and I decide today will be the day I'll clear out my cupboards, throw away clothes I've had for years and never wear any more. Shafts of sunlight are streaking through the closed curtains and I slowly get out of bed and shuffle over to pull them. The sunshine makes my eyes ache, the sky's a piercing blue and I watch a magpie as it lands on next door's willow tree.

I realise Gaz must be crossing his legs, as it's so late and I wander down the stairs into the silence of the hall. There is a pile of letters on the door mat, which I ignore, and go into the kitchen.

Gaz gets off his bed slowly and wagging his tail, he plods towards me with a hurt expression on his face as if to say, *you really are letting standards slip – I've been starving since seven o'clock.* I feel guilty as I stroke his head and reassure him silently that it won't happen again. I throw his unappetising dry biscuits into his bowl and place it down on the floor. Gaz hoovers the kibble up in about twenty seconds flat and then stands at the back door, waiting to go out into the garden. I let him out and watch him through the kitchen window, as he wanders off round the lawn, lifting his leg on various plants as he passes.

I TAKE A CUP OF TEA to the table, with my cereal, and sit down. Your presence flutters and drifts around, pervading my thoughts. You were always so bright and cheery in the mornings – not like me – you were a 'morning' person and whistled when you stood waiting for the toast to pop up and chatted animatedly about your forthcoming day. You'd joke with the children and read bits out of the newspaper you thought I might find interesting. You'd run back up the stairs to do your teeth and call out loudly 'See you at school!' when you left – we'd go separately, you leaving far earlier than me, most days. When you were in the house, there was always life and laughter and now you've gone, the house is quiet ... so quiet.

After what you've done, you'd think I wouldn't be able to look back with love, but I can. The moment I saw you that day, so many moons ago, I knew you were the man I wanted to marry. I was only twenty-one, just finishing my degree – a naive, young student, but I just felt I'd been waiting for you. They talk about love at first sight and it was definitely like that for me.

You were sitting on that bus and you had the only spare seat, next to you. I can still remember walking up the aisle, nearly to the back, transfixed by your face. You were totally unaware of me coming towards you – you were staring out of the window – and as I sat down next to you on the narrow bench, you turned and smiled at me and shuffled up a bit, to give me more room. My shoulder was rubbing up against your shoulder and I was sure there was some sort of electric current buzzing and hissing through our sleeves. I hoped you weren't going to get off at the next stop ... and you didn't.

I, too, pretended to be riveted by the passing scene, just so that I could look towards you. I studied your profile – your angular nose, your cheek bones jutting, your floppy hair with its hint of gold. You turned and spoke to me. I still remember those words; they weren't earth-shattering or anything, but they were the start of our life together, the beginning of a friendship that would go on and on. Because that's how I saw us, as friends. You were my best friend and my husband. I told you everything and trusted you with my life.

You said, *I'm getting off at the next stop* and on a whim, I said, *So am I* ...even though my stop was way further. We smiled at each other and I stood up and let you go first down the aisle. I hadn't thought it through, I had no idea what I was going to do when we both stepped off the bus, but I walked behind you, loving your back view, as much as your profile. You held onto a steel pole to steady yourself as the bus lurched forward and you looked back at me. Now I got the benefit of a face-on smile and my insides melted. The bus braked and I swayed forward and you caught me, as I was about to fall. We laughed and I could feel your hand burning the skin on my arm. After much hissing of airbrakes, the bus inched forward in the heavy traffic of the busy Birmingham road and slowed, more gently this time, as it eased its way into the bus stop. More hissing, as the doors opened and we both stepped out onto the pavement. I couldn't bear the thought of you just walking away and laughing, I said, *Thank you for catching me, just then.* And you looked at me and said, *Do you fancy a drink?*

In that moment, I knew I had met my soul mate. Such mundane words had been spoken, but it was as if I'd known you were there, somewhere in the world – and you'd just been trying to find me.

WE HAVE SOME FITTED cupboards in our bedroom – his remaining things are on the left, and mine are on the right. My heart sinks when I open the righthand doors – I have a daunting task. If I remove all the things I now hate, there would probably be only one pair of jeans left – every piece of clothing hanging there, appears to be either black, charcoal grey or light grey; dullness jumps out and strangles me with its dull dullness.

I get everything off its hanger and lay the clothes out on the bed; I start trying things on that I haven't worn for years. One pair of jeans, I can't get past my thighs; one grey skirt – I can't even do the zip up; one smart pair of black trousers, I can get the zip up, just, but the button pops off as I attempt to put it through the hole. My only evening dress, in red chiffon, floats beautifully on the hanger, but on me, looks like some frightful, cheap catalogue dress. I realise I've turned into my mother, as I stare at myself with utter amazement. When did that happen? I look just like I remember her, when she and my dad went out to a works do – nicely 'done up' in her eyes, but looking frumpy and unsophisticated, in mine. And now, here I am, looking like her, but worse.

I pull off the dress and throw it across the room in disgust, angry both at the dress, for making me look a fright and at myself, for allowing the rolls of fat to accumulate around my middle. I pull my rather large pants up over the rolls, in an attempt to disguise them, but to no avail. I vow to buy some magic pants that are said to be a wonder at sucking it all in and hiding it – but surely it's got to go somewhere? Maybe I need one of those all in one underwear garments, as seen on Gok Wan's TV programme, so there's nowhere for the fat to escape. No VPL (visible panty line) because the pants end below the knees and the corset ends above the boobs. It sounds like torture, but maybe it's the way forward.

The process of trying on things goes on for an hour and by the end, I'm exhausted and depressed with the state of my clothes and my physical shape. There's a huge pile of 'definite throw outs'; a small pile of 'possible keeps' and very few 'definite keeps'.

I'm going to have to go shopping or I'll have nothing to wear. Most women would love this prospect, but I view it with dread. I've never been good at buying clothes and now that I've confronted my body head on, I know buying clothes will be even more of a challenge.

LISA AND I ARRANGE to go shopping on Wednesday, in Bath. It's going to be a day out as well as a shopping trip – a chance for her to have a day away from her kids and for me to have some company. I don't like shopping with other people, but we agree we'll split up, do our own thing, and then meet up for lunch.

I pick her up and we drive to the Park and Ride. The buses go every ten minutes, so you never have to wait long, but it's annoying as one pulls out as we pull into the car park. It reminds me of my past, when I had to catch a bus to and from school every day; the bus drivers, I was sure, took delight in pulling away, as I ran like a maniac, shouting and waving my arms.

A queue forms and we appear to be two of the younger ones – only OAPs and teachers on holiday have the time to go shopping mid-week. I don't consider myself like those old people ... yet.

As we drive down Lansdowne, past all the Regency buildings near the bottom of the hill, I begin to wonder if living in Bath might be an option for me. It's so beautiful and it would mean I was in a city, with everything on tap.

"I wonder if I could afford to live here, with my half of the house?" I ask Lisa.

"What? Are you thinking of moving? I didn't realise you ..."

"Well, if I retire and we have to share the assets, maybe a whole new start would be good for me? I'm sure there's loads going on in Bath ..."

"I'd miss you ..."

"It would be a good excuse for you to come to Bath more often. Whenever I come here, I always wish I made the effort. It's so ... so ... civilised. I could probably only afford a room, though."

I stare out of the window. The bus is just turning into Milsom Street and we stand up to walk down the aisle. A fleeting memory of David on *that* bus, all those years ago, flits into my mind.

I must stop going back. *Forward.*

We walk down the street, past all the expensive shops which I would love to go in, but where the shop assistants are all impossibly young and glamorous and regard you with utter disdain. I usually come out feeling ancient and anyway, their clothes are out of my rather meagre bracket – so we ignore them and go on down the main street to the more 'normal' chain stores. Lisa and I part company at the Roman Baths and arrange to meet in Marks and Spencer in an hour.

As I walk on my own, I go past large groups of French kids shouting and running around; past stalls full of colourful scarves, pictures of Bath and jewellery; past a man holding a board saying *Sale, This Way,* with a large arrow; past a man dressed like a statue, standing so still, I momentarily wonder if he's real or not – and I look at everything with an objective eye and wonder if I would like to be so anonymous. Where I live now, I recognise people and people know me, either through school or the tennis club or just fellow dog walkers. At least I feel as if I *belong* somewhere. Here, I would be invisible – is that what I want? I should weigh up the pros and cons, before I make any big decisions. I mustn't rush into anything.

When I go shopping, I tend to wander around in a stupor, with what I'm sure is a glazed look on my face. I touch random pieces of clothing, as if I'm going to be able to get inspiration, by merely touching the fabric. I have to be in a certain mood to even *like* things, never mind try them on.

This day, I have a sinking feeling that I'm not in the mood and that I'm not going to like anything; the shops are full of autumn things, even though it's the summer holidays. I go into Dorothy Perkins, TK Max, BHS and River Island and walk around, fuming – does no one cater for the older woman any more? I don't want to look like mutton dressed as lamb, but I also don't want to look like my mother. Where do people of my age *shop*, these days?

A lot of the fashions are so difficult to understand – there are tops on hangers that I have to study – *are* they long tops or are they short dresses? I don't want to ask, for fear of looking out of touch ... and stupid.

Then there is the trouser issue – am I too old to wear jeans? I sometimes look at other older women wearing jeans and think they look frankly ridiculous, but somehow manage to forget I'm probably their age and wearing jeans, myself. Are black jeans more acceptable? (The denim is less ... denim). The shape of trousers is another huge issue – low waist, high waist, boot leg, slim leg, jeggings, treggings – the list is endless and they don't all look the same in different shops, either. You need to spend a week in just one shop, to find the right pair.

Cardigans – that's another problem – they're either too long, or too short. Too long, and they look as if you've gone out in your dressing gown by mistake; too short, and they leave your rather large bottom exposed to the elements. Why doesn't anyone actually ask us what we want?

I do what I always do, go to Marks and Spencer. I feel 'safe' there; it's part of our culture and I always feel as if I have more chance of finding something there, than anywhere else. I wander through the ladies clothing.

What is it with all the different brands within M and S these days? Per Una, Autograph, Indigo – I just don't get it. I think the powers that be, think it helps, but it just confuses me and makes things worse.

I look at my watch – I've already wasted half an hour, so I try to get to grips, shake off this negativity and grab some likely things off the shelves. I go into a fitting room with armfuls of stuff, strip off and look aghast at myself, from every angle. There's no discipline to the things I've got with me, nothing goes with anything else, but I start the process of pulling things either up over my thighs or down over my head. I begin to look as if I've just had a particularly active session in bed – red faced, hair tousled, underwear askew. I wish ...

"Can I help you at all?" the assistant says through the door, and I hand her a pair of promising black bootleg jeans, that are just a tad too small.

"Could you see if they have them in a bigger size?"

"A 16?" she says, loudly.

"Mmm," I say, wishing she could have said it a little quieter. I know the 'average' woman is a size 14, not the waif-like size 8 that models are, but still 16 sounds elephantine, to my ears.

She comes back with the right size and they actually look good on. I appraise myself in the mirror and I feel a lifting of my spirits, as I think I look acceptable in them. They slim me down and elongate my legs. I realise that I'm meant to be breaking out from my black/grey obsession, but I can always wear a colourful top, can't I?

I put on a loose fitting, black and white top (ignoring my own advice) and together, they look surprisingly nice. Perhaps I'm not past it, yet, I think to myself. If I'm going to find myself a new man, I'm going to have to start taking more interest in my appearance.

And then it hits me ... perhaps David was right. Perhaps we *had* both become too complacent, too relaxed. Maybe Suzie

Barton *did* give him something I didn't? I have to admit that for years, I've been wearing the same clothes, year in, year out, never really caring what I look like. I peer forward at my face – I hadn't even bothered to put makeup on, to come out to Bath, for goodness sake. *What's wrong with me?* I could at least make the effort.

I try on three other things; none of them are right, but I'm pleased with the jeans and top and go to find the payment desk. I pass the jewellery section and treat myself to a necklace and matching earrings and suddenly I feel buoyant and light, adding them to my purchases.

As I go up the escalators to the café, the store looks somehow different – full of possibilities. Lisa is already in the queue and I join her. We get some sandwiches and I order a large cappuccino and we find a table. She's clutching several bags – none from M and S.

"So, any luck?" she says, flopping down on her seat and placing her bags at her feet.

"Well, yes, surprisingly ... I've got some black jeans and a top so far. I couldn't find anything at first, but I suddenly started to enjoy it, towards the end of the hour. I even bought myself some jewellery. I've now got to find an excuse to wear it. Maybe when I go to London at the weekend. Holly's got us tickets for War Horse."

"Brilliant. There you are – you've got to start finding reasons to go out, get dressed up, start enjoying yourself."

I stare into my huge cup of coffee, lost in my own thoughts. Life seems so daunting sometimes, on your own. Looking up, I say, "How did you cope when you found yourself on your own?"

"It was hard, I won't lie. But I had the kids to keep me occupied and I was often so tired, I didn't have time to think. It's different for you, with both the kids off and gone. It'll get easier; you've just got to take every opportunity to get out there. You're doing really well, Anna. It's early days ... and already you're making plans for London ... and we're here today. You're doing much better than I did. I hid away for months."

"The school holidays seem so long ... I never even thought about the length when I was with David. We just enjoyed them, lived them ... and they always went far too quickly. This time, it feels like I've got to fill the time."

"Why don't you think about joining something, learning something completely new? You never know, you might meet someone nice ..." she says with a grin. "Play him at his own game."

"What do you mean?"

"Well, go out with other men; don't let David be the only one ..."

"Oh I don't know. Not sure I'm ready for that, yet. Maybe in the future ..."

"Yes, I suppose it's very soon but ... it did me the power of good when I started dating other people. I know I haven't found the right one yet, but it makes you realise that there *are* other people out there. When you get home, just have a look at a few dating websites ... it's quite fun, actually."

"I might ... I'll just *look* at this stage. I'm not ready for anything."

We finish up and spend the rest of the time in Bath, together. Lisa persuades me to buy a dress I wouldn't normally wear, but I have to admit, I look good in it. I'm not a 'dress' person normally, but she goes rushing out and brings me back some killer heels to wear with it, and the end result is sensational, even if I say so myself. The shoes will probably ruin my feet, but who cares?

"You don't look remotely fifty-five, you know. More like *forty*-five, to be honest."

"Well, you're very good for my ego, Lisa – where are your glasses?"

"Oh ha ha, I'm serious ... you look a million dollars in that."

I end up in the lingerie department and we have a giggle looking at all the different ways to hold your fat in. I go for a traditional corset in the end; I wonder if I'll be able to breathe, if I wear it for long.

We are both tired by the time we get back on the bus to go to the car park. I gaze out of the window, not bothering to make conversation. Can I see myself living here? More to the point, can I see myself internet dating, joining clubs ... meeting men for ... what? I'm sure they all know what they want when they go on these sites ... what all men are looking for ... but I'm not sure I want *that*. It would be nice, I suppose, to have a companion – someone to go out with, to go to the theatre or cinema with, to walk with ... but do I really want someone to have sex with? I silently shudder.

"Are you cold?" said Lisa, feeling my shiver, as we're crammed into a seat together.

"No ... Just thinking about ... my future," I say enigmatically.

Chapter Nine

As our wedding anniversary approaches, 1st August, I wonder what is going through your mind or whether you have even remembered, now that you have your new family.

I remember our day, as if it were yesterday. Twenty nine years ago tomorrow, you made me feel as if I was the only woman in the world.

It was a scorching day – and all our friends and family were packed into that pretty little village church, a cool haven from the heat outside. The women, with their ridiculous hats and you in your top hat and tails; me, in that meringue dress. I look at those pictures now and we look so fresh and innocent. You look as young as Adam does now, although you were quite a bit older. People were different then – we *were* innocent, less street-wise.

If I had my time again, I certainly wouldn't choose that dress but ... that was the fashion then, and I'm sure I felt good in it. Laura was my maid of honour – I can remember not wanting to have any children as bridesmaids and opting for one only.

We had the reception in the village hall – very unsophisticated, but that's what we wanted. We didn't feel the need for something flashy and we were proved right – everyone had a great time. Much to your mother's consternation, we had a buffet, not a sit-down meal, but it was great because everyone mingled and chatted and laughed and then danced the night away to the local disco.

Our honeymoon to the south of France was the best two weeks of my life; driving down there in our old car, which broke down twice. Camping on the coast, in forests, the heat accentuating the scent of the towering pines ... even now, when I smell pine, I'm straight back there with ants the size of bluebottles, dark pathways leading to the dunes and the distant sounds of the beach, beckoning us on the breeze. We had a tiny one-man tent which we squeezed into every night – the heat was almost unbearable – but we still lay entwined all night, ridiculously in love with each other, unable to be apart.

We ate French bread and cheese, drank cheap, warm, red wine and licked a hundred cooling lollies on endless beaches. We meandered along that coast from Montpellier to Sète to Angelès-sur-mer, loving each other on different campsites, on different beaches.

That's how I remember it. Do you ever think of it now?

OUR ANNIVERSARY PASSES with no acknowledgement from David. Of course, there wouldn't be, would there? He would hardly send me a card ... what did I expect?

To my Darling wife of twenty-nine years, whom I've left for a younger, sexier version. With all my love, David.

It wasn't going to happen, was it?

The only communication I had, was a text from Holly:

Hi Mum – This day must be awful for you. Thinking of you, as always. Can't wait to see you on Saturday. I've heard from Jed. Wha-hoo! Love you, Holly xxx

She's so good, Holly – so thoughtful. I wonder if Adam has even registered ... I get my mobile phone and click on the Facebook icon. I haven't heard from him at all, but I wasn't expecting to, was I? We'd said Facebook was enough (I'm beginning to regret this now.) I scroll quickly down my timeline ... a picture. There he is, with Jake, both with wet hair, the Pacific behind them, with the comment: *First surf. Shit, they're bigger than Newquay! Legs still in tact – no sharks.*

I study his face – already he looks tanned and healthy ... and I'm happy for him. He knows the shark reference is going to wind me up – he probably did it for that exact reason, so I don't rise. I simply write: *Amazing – you look so brown!*

I think this is non-committal and can't be regarded as embarrassing. Surely? I wish I could write more and then realise I could send him a private message; no one else need see what I say and he can private message me back. Why hadn't I realised that before? He might be prepared to write short messages here, even if emails are too much. I press Message:

Hi Adam – it's great to see your photos here. You look as if you're having an amazing time. Where are you staying? Do post some more photos, so I can imagine where you are. Are Jake's relatives nice?

Life here's pretty much the same. I'm going to stay with Holly in London next weekend, so that should be fun. Gaz doesn't know yet. He'll hate going to kennels. I'm enjoying the holidays; trying to get fit (swimming) and went shopping in Bath – so, getting out there! Haven't seen Dad but if I do, will tell him your news.

I'd love to hear from you if you can. Love the 'legs in tact' comment. Joking aside, keep safe, Love you loads. Mum xxx

I read it through and hope I haven't been like a pushy mother. I haven't mentioned our anniversary – it hardly seems relevant any more.

I hover my finger over the Send button – and then press it. If he doesn't want to reply, he doesn't have to, does he?

I WALK GAZ EVERYDAY; I'm quite boring with my routine, I go one way in the morning and another in the afternoon. He doesn't care, though, the smells are always different and the possibilities for finding balls in the undergrowth, are boundless. It means I don't have to think, I can just simply walk and let my mind shut down, something that I want to do a lot, these days. The weather is lovely and I become a sentient being – a bit like Gaz, smelling the air, breathing in the oxygen of summer.

I've nearly finished my walk, I'm on the homeward stretch. Gaz has chased hundreds of imaginary rabbits, widdled on a every conceivable bush and emptied his bowels twice. For him it's been a satisfactory walk and for me ... well, it's just been another one in a line of hundreds, stretching into the far distance of his future with me. I wonder if David misses dear old Gaz?

I see a familiar figure walking towards me. We're still on the rec, there are a few people dotted about, but I can pick out his walk and the shape of him, as if he's part of me. He's a way off yet – I consider turning and running away from him, as quickly as I can ... because I see a small child running just in front of him and ... Suzie, by his side.

This is like my worst nightmare. I've lain in bed and envisaged this exact scenario and now it's happening for real. My feet are rooted to the ground; I stare at their slow approach and know there is nothing I can do to stop it. He registers me – I can see the slight change in his stride and awkwardness of his head position; he's deliberately not looking my way. He's talking intently to Suzie. They're probably wondering what on earth to say.

"This is awkward ..." I say, as they are now within speaking distance. "What are the chances ... ?"

"Hello, Anna," he says, "we're just out for a breath of fresh air."

I look at Suzie and she looks at me. "Hi," she says. I deliberately don't reply.

Gemma, at that moment, comes up to her mother and clings on to her legs; Gaz is wagging his tail and is trying to lick her face and Gemma begins to cry.

"Don't worry, darling, the doggie won't hurt you – he's trying to kiss you." She picks Gemma up at this point, which I feel is the worst thing you can do with a child who appears to be frightened of a blatantly friendly labrador. Why doesn't she leave the kid alone and let her get used to him?

"This is Gemma," Suzie says, pointlessly. "Say hello to Mrs McCarthy."

The child refuses and buries her head in Suzie's neck. "Come on, Gemma, be nice ..." says Suzie, but now the child has her hands tightly wound round Suzie's neck and refuses to show her face.

"Will you come to me?" says David, reaching forward to prize her off her mother. "Come to David."

Gemma's face appears and she reaches both arms forward, stretching them towards him. He takes her and says, "Gemma's not used to dogs, are you? Gaz loves children, don't you, ol' chap? Come and say hello, then." Gaz obligingly comes over and David crouches down, showing Gemma how to stroke his head. "There you are, you see, he's nice, isn't he?"

All this conversation about Gaz is a wonderful diversion from the reality of the three adults having to face each other. I'm desperate to say something to Suzie, to show her just how much I'm hurting, but Gemma brings me to my senses. It's hardly her fault and I don't want to frighten the little thing. She's a beautiful child with rich, brown, curly hair, chubby cheeks and blue eyes; she's now patting Gaz confidently and he's beginning to regret his friendliness, as she begins to chase him across the grass, holding onto his tail. Suzie yells, "Don't do that!"

"Have you heard from Adam?" says David. "Has he got there okay?"

"There've been no reports of crashed airliners, so I assume so," I say as sarcastically as possible. Suzie gives me a filthy look. I feel guilty and add, "I've seen a couple of photos on Facebook and he seems to be having a great time. Have you got his email address?"

"Yes, I'm going to write to him," says David, apologetically.

"I think he needs to hear from you, David, so please *do* that," I say. "He was very upset, you know."

"I know ... but he's a grown-up now and he'll survive," says David. I can't believe how dismissive he's being of his own son. I feel my blood begin to boil but again, I stop myself saying anything.

"Holly tells me you're going up this weekend?" he says.

"Yes, I am."

Suzie is now chasing Gemma and Gaz across the green expanse – there seems to be a lot of laughter and whoops of delight. Then, suddenly, Gemma falls and the delight turns to crying and Suzie picks her up and starts walking back towards us.

"I think we better take her home, Dave, she's getting tired." She gives him a hard stare, a stare that cannot be denied.

David has now become 'Dave' – that just sounds ridiculous. If there was *ever* a David who was *not* a Dave, it's David. "Nice to see you, Anna," she says, stares at David again and starts walking away, holding Gemma's hand. I don't say 'nice to see you too' as it isn't.

"I better go, then," he says with a half-grin.

"Yes, you better." I couldn't resist adding, "You better do as you're told."

He just blinks at me and toddles off to join them.

Well, Dave, I would say you're thoroughly under the thumb ... serves you right.

I stay where I am, until they are out of sight. I call Gaz, who is now right over the other side of the rec. He looks up when he hears my voice, and to give him his due, he waddles back towards me, looking expectant.

The whole episode has left me wrung out. They look such a close-knit little threesome – Gemma's so pretty and young; Suzie, so nubile and sexy. Even 'Dave' has taken on a young look about him, as if she's given him a new lease of life. He may look guilty whenever I'm around, but to an outsider, he must look like an attractive and vibrant 'older' man with his young wife and newly-acquired child. They leave me feeling old, past it and boring ... and above all, alone.

As I walk home, I imagine them walking hand in hand back to the flat, cuddling on the sofa together with a bottle of wine, having bathed Gemma together and tucked her into her snuggly bed. I'm jealous of them, there's no getting away from it. Jealous as hell.

I open the door of the house, sit in its silence, and look around me. I don't even feel part of my own house any more. I feel like I've just been squatting here, with no past, no future.

Oh Gaz, what the hell am I going to do?

As if he can read my mind, he comes and sits next to me on the sofa, flops down, with his head on my lap and looks up at me with his big, brown eyes.

You've still got me, he says. *You'll always be able to rely on me, whatever happens.*

Chapter Ten

I hear a faint ping coming from my mobile, which is hiding in the depths of my rather large handbag. 4G is everywhere now and I realise I can use the internet sitting on the train.

I'm on the 11.30 am to Paddington – it's great to be going to London and I relish the feeling of rushing through the countryside, towards the metropolis. I've bought a coffee from the buffet car and I'm munching my way through a packet of nuts and raisins, convincing myself they're a healthy snack. Every time I reach into the packet, I try to hide the fact that I'm constantly nibbling, by not rustling the plastic bag they're in. The man opposite me, however, keeps looking up and staring at me, as if he disapproves, and if I'm honest, I tend to agree with him. I put them back in my bag and consciously bury them beneath all the other stuff.

I bring out my phone – the ping was different from the usual message – more of a *ding* than a *ping pong* – and I realise it's a Facebook message. Hoping it's a reply from Adam, I press the icon.

It is ...

Hi Mum. Thanks for your message. Didn't realise you knew about Facebook messaging – you're becoming quite techy in your old age! LOL! We're staying with John's cousin – he's called Bruce, would you believe? His wife isn't Sheila, it's Jo. They've got this mega house in Double Bay overlooking the ocean – it's bloody huge. Why can't we have relatives like that? They've got a yacht and some jet skis and we're staying in their self-contained apartment. Bruce does something to do with computers in the city. They're both awesome. They let us come and go – we don't see them much, as we're always out. We've met some really cool people out surfing – the waves are incredible. Favourite beach so far ... Bondi. Someone was attacked by a shark a few days ago – don't worry, it wasn't me. Ha Ha. Still haven't heard from the Dickhead that is my father. Glad you're getting out there – we've been to a couple of clubs in Kings Cross – mental! Have fun with Holly. Love, Adam. PS Don't message me too much, I haven't got time to reply – too busy drinking, taking drugs and having sex.

Well, that's reassuring, then.

I stare at my iPhone ... furious with David for still not writing to him ... worrying about sharks attacking people on jet skis – imagining dark nightclubs, with cocaine being snorted through Australian dollar notes and ... huge waves. I shouldn't fall for Adam's joke ending, but can't help wondering if there's an element of truth in it? Anyway, there's nothing I can do about it, I tell myself, so I turn away and watch the passing scene through the grimy window. It's getting more urban; I check my watch – only fifteen minutes till Paddington.

Holly's shown me an app that tells you exactly which tube to catch for any journey, so it's with a certain amount of confidence that I get out of the train and make my way down the platform. I'm surrounded my hurrying people, who all seem to know where they're going.

It's true what they say about big cities – I suddenly feel lonely and vulnerable amongst the hordes and my confidence wavers.

I'm dragging my suitcase on wheels behind me, my large handbag is digging into my shoulder and I'm clutching both my iPhone and my Oyster card in my left hand. I feel like a country bumpkin, compared to all these sophisticated people – I realise I haven't been to London for two years and have always had David to usher me about. I have no idea if my Oyster has any money on it. I'm just going to see what happens at the gate.

I 'pull in' for a while – rather like you would in a car, into a lay-by – I let everyone else rush past me; I look at my phone and study the tube app, so that I know exactly which line to head for.

Circle Line (Eastbound) to Liverpool Street. 23 minutes, 9 stations, No changes. I've read this at least three times on the train already, but I want to be absolutely sure. Yes, Eastbound, not Westbound. I set off again and follow the signs to the Circle Line.

Miraculously, my Oyster card works; I could've checked it on one of their machines first, but decide to live dangerously. Down the escalators, I stand to the left and let others go down quickly, while I study all the adverts, designed to make me feel even more an alien in a foreign land.

Following the signs to *Eastbound,* I go through onto the platform. The rush of hot, stale air hits me in the lungs, as I watch the back end of a train disappear. The maps on the walls indicate that I've at least come to the right place and indeed, Liverpool Street is on this line. Two minutes till the next train – it's incredible the frequency of the tubes. You're lucky if you can get to Cheltenham and back in a day on public transport, back home.

The platform's full of people – I notice how many are plugged into their phones. What are they all listening to? It's as if everyone is blocking out the reality of their lives with loud rock music or soothing classical music (or maybe they just have their headphones in, to stop people like me talking to them?) A lot of people are reading Kindles too, so their ears and eyes are occupied with something other than the thankless task of getting from A to B.

The train approaches with new stale air and we all surge forward to the white line which is designed to keep us back. Crowds disembark and we all push forward. I manage to get a seat, by studiously ignoring all old ladies and nursing mothers and put my case by my side.

The train pulls out and the rush and rattle soothes me as I look around me. The girl opposite me gets out a mirror and proceeds to put on her make up. How can you do that in a tube, with everyone watching? Mind you, she's beautiful, dark-skinned, with huge eyes; if I looked like that, I suppose I wouldn't mind people watching me enhance my already stunning features. I'm mesmerised by her and have to avert my eyes, before she thinks I'm weird.

I study the map above her head and count off the stations we stop at. All these names that are so familiar ... Baker Street, Great Portland Street ... Barbican ... Moorgate. You have to be pretty stupid these days to miss your stop, as the recording keeps saying *The next stop is* ... but for someone like me and foreign tourists, it's reassuringly repetitive.

Suddenly, we're at Liverpool Street and I struggle to get up and out, before the doors snap shut. I stand on the platform looking for the Exit signs. I'm meeting Holly at the Information Desk on the main concourse at 1 o'clock; I've made it in good time – ten minutes early.

When I get to the right place, I hang around, pretending not to be waiting, for fear of coming over as some elderly hooker looking for business. I watch the mayhem around me and think my life in leafy Stowchester is incredibly dull. Everyone here looks like they're going somewhere exciting, doing important things and simply being more dynamic than me.

At last, I see Holly's familiar face in a crowd of people coming down the escalators from outside the station. I'm so relieved to see her, I feel quite emotional as she flings her arms round my neck and squeezes me hard. Holly always cheers me up, just by being *her*.

"Well, I've made it!" I say, stating the obvious.

"Yes, you have Mum. How was it? The train, I mean? Find the right tube okay?"

"Fine! That app's a godsend."

"I know – I've just discovered another one, called Citymapper which tells you all the possible options – it even shows you when the bus is coming and where the bus stop is."

"Soon, you won't have to *think* at all. There'll be an app for that!"

Holly guffaws loudly and says, "Nice one, Mum ... come on, let's go. Let me grab your case and we'll head straight to the pub, for something to eat. Then back to the flat for a quick relax, before going out to 'War Horse'. I can't wait to see it."

We spend a couple of hours in a trendy pub that seems more like a restaurant; the food is presented in such a way that it makes me feel 'cutting-edge' simply for eating it. I choose a salad – baked avocado, nestling on a bed of rocket and baby spinach, with feta, roasted pine nuts, oven baked beetroot, pomegranate seeds and grilled lemon. It's all piled high, with a drizzle of this and that around it, served with a chewy brown, seeded roll. It's Masterchef meets gourmet pub grub – I can almost hear that woman presenter's dulcet tones describing it and see John Torode's mouth, opening to taste it.

How can a salad be so delicious? It makes my attempt to eat healthily seem somewhat pathetic – at home, I fling together a tasteless tomato, some limp lettuce leaves, a few cucumber slices and a radish, with a slice of slimy ham, and call it a salad. I vow to be more adventurous in the future, as I sink my third gin and tonic.

Being with Holly is always so much fun; I begin to feel more like a thirty year old, as we giggle through lunch, people-watching and gossiping. I manage to persuade myself *not* to think of David and the fact that I'm on my own; I'm fed up of him entering my thoughts and refuse to let him in. Holly has a theory that people make their own luck in life and that positive things happen, if you think positively.

"Honestly, Mum, it's really true ... this is just a small example, but it works. Yesterday, I woke up late and realised I was going to be really late for work, unless a miracle happened. So, I put out positive thoughts to the universe and instead of missing my bus, it was waiting for me and all the lights were green and when I got to the office, my boss was late herself, so didn't even know about my tardy arrival. So, all you've got to do is *think positive* about your situation and something good will happen. I've already started on your behalf – every morning when I wake up, I think of you on a cloud of single happiness – I'm getting definite good vibes about your future."

"That's really sweet of you, Holly. I'm glad someone has something good to say about me ... I haven't got past the dazed and confused stage yet. I'm trying not to think too much about the future at all. Your father and his paramour tend to stand on the sidelines in my imagination and laugh at me ..."

"Don't be daft, they're too busy being 'in love' to laugh at you. You've got to forget them, and think about yourself now."

"I know ... I do think I've come to a conclusion – I *will* hand in my notice at the beginning of term. And I *will* email Jane when I get home tomorrow and ask about visiting her next year. There ... positive thoughts! Did I tell you I got a message from Adam?"

"No – what did my wonderful brother say, then?"

"Well ... not too much to be honest, but they're staying in some amazing house, surfing, going out a lot and ..."

"What?"

"Well, he ended the message by saying he hasn't got time to write as he's too busy drinking, taking drugs and having sex."

"Ah ... brilliant. And I suppose you thought that was a double bluff and you're now worried sick?"

"Yes ..."

"Mum, don't be ridiculous. Do you honestly think if he was doing any of those things that he'd actually tell you in an email?"

"Yea, I suppose you're right ..."

"I *know* I'm right. For all his faults, Adam can be quite sensible when he puts his mind to it, you know. Jake's the more likely one to do something stupid ..."

"Really?"

"Yes, really. Come on, let's get out of here and go and have a nice cup of tea back at the flat."

We walk companionably along the streets of Shoreditch, past expensive shops and ultra-modern coffee shops.

Her flatmate is away for the weekend and so I have the use of her bedroom. She isn't the tidiest of people, Rosie – her clothes are strewn everywhere, there are piles of books on the floor, make-up is scattered on most surfaces and empty wine bottles line up by the waste paper basket, but it's nice of her to lend me her room and to be honest, it makes me feel young again, as if I'm a student again.

No ... no David memories, please.

'WAR HORSE' TURNED OUT to be one of the best theatrical experiences either of us have ever had. I never dreamt that puppets could be so hypnotic and entrancing; we were both mesmerised by them and the story they told. It was all I could do to stop myself blubbering loudly at the end and Holly and I left our seats, clutching each other, eyes shining, trying to pull ourselves together, before we went out into the light of the theatre entrance and the real world. We stopped at a bar on the way home and finished the evening off with some Prosecco, while reliving the previous two hours' entertainment.

When she walked me back to Liverpool Street the following day, I felt as if I'd put a wedge between me and my 'other life'. The weekend served to show me that I could venture out into the big wide world and enjoy myself ... on my own. I didn't need a man to complete me; I was quite capable of enjoying another female's company and tasting the London life, on my own. Australia, at this stage, was a far-distant adventure, but I was beginning to think I could do it.

I was going to heed my daughter's advice and think positive thoughts. I'd loved David for nearly thirty-five years, but he had chosen to love someone else and I had to deal with that, whether I liked it or not.

Is love, simply a state of mind? David could have chosen to ignore the feelings he had for Suzie and decide to stay in love with me ... but for some reason, which I can't as yet understand, he chose to act on them.

Maybe, in time, I'll understand, but in the meantime, I choose to be positive. We've got one life and if I choose to be miserable, I will be.

I'm going to choose happiness. Retire ... move house ... visit Australia. That's the plan. Onward and upward.

Chapter Eleven

Gaz regards me with a certain amount of hurt, when I pick him up from the kennels. He manages to convey his disgust – he curls up in a tight ball in his bed and ignores me all evening. I try to tempt him out with a biscuit; he eats it, but with a look on his face as if to say, *I know what you're trying to do, and it's not working* ... and goes back to bed.

I decide to take action regarding Australia and, sitting on the sofa with my laptop and the television keeping me company gently in the background, I start an email to Jane.

We were always close as children, with only two years between us; Jane was my 'little sister' and we did everything together. We started drifting apart when I went to uni and then she went to art school; she'd always been talented with anything creative – I used to envy her ability to produce something out of nothing. She got in with a group of artistic people who seemed outrageously bohemian to me and I was intimidated by her, and her friends – I didn't have anything interesting to say to them. I think Jane thought my choice of career was the ultimate in dreariness; I can always remember her saying to me, "But do you want to spend your life telling other people what to do? Don't you want to do it yourself?" But the trouble with me was, I couldn't work out what *it* was – what was that *thing* that I wanted to do?

So, I went down in her eyes and she went off, living her creative life, with her creative friends, leaving me feeling diminished by her 'vision'. She married Marcus, a graphic designer; he was very successful, ambitiously changing jobs every few years and she became a self-employed illustrator of children's books. They visited some friends in Australia one holiday and fell in love with the lifestyle; they just upped and left England, a year later. He walked straight into a fantastic job in Sydney and she was snapped up by an ad agency. Of course, we kept in touch, but over the years, we lost interest in each other; our lives were so different. I know the fact that they never had any children was a huge issue for them both and even though we were no longer close, I felt sorry for her; I couldn't imagine life without my two.

Now that there's Facebook and FaceTime, it's easier to keep up to date with each other. They've moved to Adelaide – I see pictures of them on boats and on beaches; Marcus looks as if he's put on a lot of weight, but Jane looks amazing – it's as if she's found the secret eternal youth. Her girl-like figure is tanned and sinewy, unlike my more matronly one.

We only FaceTime at Christmas and on birthdays, so I start the email with trepidation – I haven't even told her my news yet. There's part of me that feels guilty for burdening her with my problems, but another part feels if she was in the same situation, I would want to help *her* – so I press on.

Hi Jane,

Sorry I haven't been in touch for ages. How are you two? I saw some pics on Facebook the other day and you both look well, as always! Have you decided to sell your house? I know you were thinking of it?

The reason I haven't been in touch is because I've had a horrible few weeks. David's left me and set up home with a fellow teacher and her daughter. I know … it's a shock. David seems like the last person to do something like that. Anyway, it's happened and I've had a lot to deal with. Adam and Holly are upset, as you can imagine – Adam's now left for his gap year and is in Sydney! I didn't tell you before now as he and his friend Jake were very vague about their arrangements. Not sure if he plans to come your way – I'll warn you if he is! Holly's been brilliant, so supportive..

You can imagine how it is, working in the same school as them – I've decided I've got to leave. Holly and I have come up with a plan. I'm going to retire – I know you never thought much of my choice of career and to be honest, neither have I! I've never felt comfortable teaching; it's just a shame it's taken something like this to make me face reality. The one good thing is I've got a pension, which I can take early and I'm going to give in my letter at the beginning of term and leave at Christmas.

Ever since you went to Oz, I've dreamt of coming out and visiting you. What I would love to do, is come out after Christmas, maybe March time, when I've had a chance to sort my life out. David wants to sell the house, so he can get a bigger place (they live in a tiny flat at the moment - my heart bleeds!) and if I'm honest, I know we'll have to sell eventually to sort out the finances. I'm thinking of going to live in Bath – what do you think?

Anyway, if that would be possible, I'd love to come out for a few weeks. Have a think. I know you both work – you could just ignore me and I'll have a meal ready for you, in the evening?!

Let me know your thoughts. What's the weather like in Adelaide in March? It would be so lovely to have the sun, the beach and a change of scene to look forward to.

Love, Anna xx

I press send, before I can question myself. If I did, I'd agonise over every aspect of my plan and I don't want to. I email Laura and ask if I can come and stay for a few days down in Cornwall – I feel like I'm inflicting my single self on people, but the thought of hanging out at home until term starts, is rather horrifying. Laura suggested it at the airport, so I don't feel too guilty. It's only when you're on your own that you realise that unless you organise things you could spend days, weeks even, without really seeing anyone. As a couple, you're in a little bubble of companionship and if you don't see other people it doesn't matter; you have each other.

I slam the laptop closed and click the off button on the remote. The silence envelops me; it's as if the house itself has developed a dislike of the lifeless atmosphere within it. All the fun, all the laughter has drained away, leaving me with the buzzing of nothingness in my ears. Gaz has still got his back resolutely towards me; I call his name and my voice echoes round the room. He can't resist – he lifts his head and gently wags his tail. "Come on, old boy. I always said you couldn't ... but would you like to sleep upstairs tonight?"

He gets up and follows me around as I check everything – I think how David used to laugh at me for what he calls *shaking the electricity cables to make sure they're completely off*. Ha ha, David, you were always such a wag.

This part of being alone I hate – the TV is now a blank screen and is no longer companionably cheery; I check the doors are locked, wriggling the handles to double check. I turn off the downstairs lights and make my way up the dimly lit stairs, to the ever present silence that awaits me at the top. I'm grateful to Gaz as he pads up the stairs behind – he takes a running leap onto the bed and lies as still as possible, hoping I won't notice him. "Don't worry, you can stay," I say to him, as I go through my routine of cleansing and teeth brushing.

I love you, even if nobody else does, he says to me, pandering to my feelings of utter loneliness. It seems worse, being here alone, having been in London with Holly. I can't rely on her to provide me with entertainment – I've got to start enjoying my own company and making a life for myself.

I get into bed and put my feet under Gaz' big warm body; he starts licking his paws and I ask him politely to stop. "Could you do your ablutions somewhere else?" I say and he gives me a filthy look as if to say, *Did I complain when you were flossing?*

I check Facebook on my phone. Nothing more from Adam. I imagine him floating helplessly on a surf board, far out to sea, with just marauding sharks for company.

No email replies. I text Holly: *Thank you for a fantastic weekend. Loved it. Gaz sends his love (he's on my bed – both of us very happy with the situation!) Speak soon, Mum x*

I turn off my light and wait for sleep to come, feeling comforted by Gaz' rhythmical breathing. My phone beeps and I reach for it in the dark. Holly.

Loved the weekend too. Give Gaz a big kiss from me. Dogs are such good company – I wish he was on my bed! Sleep well, Love you. Holly xx

I close the phone, the darkness is even blacker than before. A distant car roars down the road; I imagine teenagers driving too fast, as the engine noise fades into the distance. Then silence ... except that Gaz is now snoring.

Chapter Twelve

The summer holidays plod on – how come six weeks feels like an eternity? There's only a certain amount of housework you can do; never one for doing much anyway, I realise that the house stays miraculously tidy when there's only you to mess it up. Gaz is a pretty tidy chap, apart from his black hairs that accumulate under chairs. So, having hoovered and dusted, there's no more to do; no more clutter that Adam's left lying around, no more stuff that David's just dumped on the kitchen table. I used to complain about their ability to make a room look as if someone had held a car boot sale in it – now I wish I had something to complain about.

Laura emailed back the next day and I've arranged to go there next week. One of the cottages is free and although they don't usually allow dogs, she says I can bring Gaz. I was rather hoping I could stay in their house, but as she didn't suggest it, I've got to be grateful. The thought of being in a holiday place on my own at night though, is daunting.

Jane's email also came the next day. This is what she said:

Hi there,

God, what a bastard! I can't believe it, neither can Marcus. You two always seemed so happy together. (We were, that's the whole point!) *All I can say is it must be a mid-life crisis or something –*

although it's a bit late for that, isn't it? (Thanks for reminding me how old we are.)

You must feel lost after so many years with him. And the kids gone too. Don't rush into anything but yes, I think retiring is a great idea. You've got years of life ahead of you to do something else, if you want. And sell the house when you're ready, not when he wants you to. Bath is a fantastic city – maybe a new start would be good?

We'd love to see you out here and March would be okay. The weather would be good for you, not too hot but mostly sunny – often around 24 degrees. That's cold for us, it's coming into autumn. We'll obviously be working, but we're so near the beach, you'll be able to loll around or catch a train to the city. When I know your dates, I'll arrange some holiday, so we can spend time together.

No, we haven't sold the house. We wondered why we wanted to, in the end; it's got everything we want and it's so much hassle to move, so we're staying put. Marcus is under a lot of stress at work and I didn't want to add to it.

I can't believe Adam is off on his gap year; I feel as if he's still a little boy. It must be awful letting them go.

Lots of love to you. Jane x

I read the email through several times, looking for clues – does she really not mind me coming or is she being polite? She said March was 'okay' – not exactly enthusiastic, was she? She's never even suggested before that Marcus is at all stressed – why did she mention it? But then she said she'd take time off; maybe I'm reading too much into it. I realise she doesn't know Adam and Holly at all – she's seen pictures and videos, but she's missed most of their lives. Maybe I should persuade Adam to go and visit, as he's now on the same continent?

Her email leaves me feeling unsure, although it was written in good heart. Are my plans crazy? Why do I think going to Australia will be the answer to anything? To visit a sister I've more or less lost touch with, that I have nothing in common with and who, in the past, used to make me feel inadequate.

I tell myself that it's at least a *plan*, we all need plans and hopes – and it's the only one I've got at the moment, so I may as well stick with it.

CORNWALL TURNS OUT to be the tonic I've been lacking during the holidays. The boys get their results while I'm there – they've both done surprisingly well and Laura, John and I have a toast to celebrate. Adam lets me know on Facebook – *B, C, C – WOO-HOO!* is all his message says and Jake writes equally succinctly to Laura on email.

The few days I've chosen to be here are hot – there's high pressure sitting over the top of the UK, making it seem like the Mediterranean. Laura and I go for long coastal walks and as my eyes stretch to the horizon, the aquamarine shimmer of the sea lightens my heart. The sea is as calm as I've ever seen it – hardly a ripple – and much to John's disgust, even the normal surfing beaches like Watergate and Fistral are wave-free. To someone like him, days like this are wasted days. His school holidays are for spending every hour possible chasing the illusory golden waves and now, he is forced into inactivity; you can almost feel his disappointment oozing from his pores. For me, however, the weather provides me with a glimpse of what Australia might be like and makes me more determined to pursue my idea.

Being here with them, without David, though, is perhaps the strangest experience I've had so far, since he left. His presence hangs over the beaches, and walks with us on cliff tops. None of us mention his name, although he is constantly on our minds and his name lingers on our tongues. I know Laura and John have talked before I came and decided not to mention him, unless I bring him up and as I refuse to, he is not mentioned, talked about, analysed or cried over. He is a non-person.

For them it must be odd; for me, it's good. I want to be here and enjoy the present day, not remember past holidays and mourn their loss. At one point, Laura says quietly to me, "If you ever want to talk ... you know I'll listen." But I just smile at her and say, "I'm fine ... honestly," and that's all that's said.

I *am* fine, I tell myself.

Gaz enjoys hanging out with Sally, their Springer, and Jody, the terrier. They form a little gang and terrorise the postman and passing tourists as they rush outside the gate, barking hysterically, for no very good reason. Gaz is the oldest of the three dogs and even though he is only a visitor, he takes on the role of leader of the pack, for a few days. I realise his life at home must be incredibly dull for him, the highlight being a walk to the rec. Here, he's free to wander across fields, chasing unseen rabbits; he comes with us on our rambling walks and takes frequent dips in rock pools. He eats all sorts of unsavoury bits of old crab and rotting fish carcasses, rolls in smelly seaweed and drinks sea water. He throws up frequently, fortunately never in the house, and has a look of beatific happiness on his face. I honestly think if I left him here, he wouldn't give me a backward glance. He reminds me of Adam when he talked about Jake's relatives – *Why can't we live in a place like this? The rec just doesn't compare.*

One day, we're sitting outside in the courtyard having coffee when Laura says, "Have you felt this?" She's running her hand along Gaz' back at the time. "Here, feel this."

I put my hand where she's indicating and feel a small lump. I let my fingers stay there. "No, I haven't felt that before. What do you think it is?"

"Not sure, but perhaps you should have it checked out when you get home. It's only small, but any lumps are suspicious. Sally had one last year – it was benign, thank God. When was he last checked over?"

"Not for ages. He's due his jabs soon – I'll have him looked at then."

I put my hand over the lump again; it feels small and I try to reassure myself that it's probably nothing. Dogs get lumps and bumps all the time, don't they?

LAURA AND I SPEND A couple of afternoons at her gallery. She has a young girl who sits there part-time, but Laura has to be there the rest of the time. I find it a peaceful place to be and I sit and stare at the paintings, finding solace in their vibrancy. Some are watercolours, some are oils ... I decide I like the ones with loads of colour and which are impressionistic. A lot of them are seascapes – there's one particular artist I love – his paintings are full of movement and light and you get the feeling that he lives and breathes the sea, through his paintbrush. I've never bought a painting in my life, but have a tremendous desire to have one of his.

At the end of the second afternoon, I make a decision – I'm going to do something completely out of character – I'm going to buy one. My eye's been drawn repeatedly to one entitled *The Dawning of a New Day*. It's a magnificent sunrise over cliffs and blue-grey seas; the cotton white waves are just picking up the pink of the sun, the sky is radiating a warmth and breadth that somehow feels peaceful and hopeful, and the waves crashing on the rocks look positive, not aggressive. The price tag of £500 doesn't bother me; this is something I'm going to buy, a symbol of my new life. It's a big painting, but it will fit in the boot of my car.

"Could you wrap that one up for me. I'm going to have it," I say, pointing to it.

Laura looks up from her computer and with a look of incredulity on her face, she says, "What? Are you serious, Anna? It's £500 you know. He's very good, but ..."

"No, I know it's a lot of money. But ... I want it and I'm going to take it home with me. It looks how I want my future to be ..."

She stares at me and I can see her mind working – should she try to put me off or should she just let it be? She decides on the latter course and says, "Well, if you're sure ..."

"Will you accept a cheque?"

"Of course I will. Is this the new you ... being all decisive and spontaneous?"

"I'm not sure who I am anymore, Laura. But, yes, it's the new me. Me – doing something for myself, for a change, without any thought for anyone else. It's about time I treated myself."

"Good for you," says Laura, laughing. "Can I tempt you with another one, while you're in the mood ... perhaps this one?" she says, pointing to another one with a huge price tag.

"No thank you, one will do," I say, smiling. "One will do nicely."

LAURA AND JOHN ARE completely un-technical and Facebook is something they disapprove of. "Why would I want to tell people that I've just had a cup of coffee, for God's sake?" is Laura's response to my asking her if she's joined, so she can see Jake's progress. "I think Facebook is a waste of time and ... dangerous," she continued. "I hate the way everyone seems to want to share their entire life with other people ... it just makes people fed up with their own lives because everyone else *appears* to be having an 'amazing' time, on Facebook. Anyway, what would I say if I posted something? *Sat in the gallery for four hours and sold nothing?*"

"I know what you mean, but since Adam left, it's been a godsend. I've seen pictures of him and even messaged him. If it wasn't for Facebook, I wouldn't have heard a thing. Have a look ..." and I get out my iPad and press the Facebook icon. Laura, despite her dislike, comes and sits next to me on the sofa and we scroll through my timeline. There's a picture that I haven't seen before – in some dark nightclub. The two boys have taken a selfie, with about six other kids pulling faces all around them.

"Oh my God, I wonder where they are?" says Laura. "They all look drunk to me." She grabs the iPad and enlarges the picture. "Jake looks red-eyed."

"That could be the camera, Laura. They all look as if they're having a great time," I say, secretly scrutinising the photo for evidence of ... white powder round Adam's nose. "You see, it's great – you can see them and feel vaguely in touch with them. Are you still unconvinced?"

Laura is still looking at the picture. "Can I see the other ones?"

I search for Adam's timeline and we scroll through all the pictures there. There are shots of parties on the beach, parties in parks, parties in clubs. The more wholesome pictures are of Adam and Jake holding surfboards, wearing board shorts and thongs, getting browner and browner in each shot. The sky is always a piercing blue and looks broader and altogether larger, than it does here.

"Well, they certainly look well. I feel as if we're spying on them ... but I can *sort of* see what you mean about Facebook. I don't think I'll be joining though. Email's enough for me; I would only be joining for Jake and he said he didn't want me as a 'friend'. I'll rely on you to pass any critical information on." She takes a last lingering look at Adam's page and hands back the iPad. "I've heard from Jo and according to her, the boys are being the very picture of well-behaved youth. Maybe they're pulling the wool over her eyes, judging by those pictures."

"At least they're staying somewhere savoury and safe. Jo and Bruce will keep an eye on them, I'm sure. How long are they staying there?"

"A few more weeks, I think, and then they're moving on up to Byron Bay. They're going to do some work on the site – cleaning and such like. That'll do them good!"

I laughed – the thought of Adam cleaning anything was a completely new concept to me.

"If I go out there after Christmas, do you think I should try and see them?"

"Well, Australia's a big place, they might be on the other side of the continent, but ... if it's possible, it could be good, yes.

Whether they would want to see *you*, is another matter," Laura grinned.

"I know ... but it seems daft to go all that way and not see them. I might tentatively put it to Adam and see what he says. Maybe if we helped with their fares, they could fly down to Adelaide for a week – would you be prepared to do that for Jake? They ought to see as much of the country as they can, while they're there and I'm sure Jane and Marcus would put them up. Jane was saying she can't believe that Adam's so old now. She'd probably love to see them."

"Yea, sure – let's see what they say, when you put it to them. Good luck with that," she said, implying by her tone that she thought the answer would be an emphatic 'no'.

Australia was becoming more 'real' in my mind now. Just looking at Adam's photos of amazing beaches and open spaces, made me more convinced that I should go. I needed to do something completely different and maybe, who knows, it could open up a whole new life for me. And seeing Adam would be a bonus.

I miss that boy, I really do.

Chapter Thirteen

Only a week and a half left of the summer holidays now. I feel quite nervous at the thought of handing in my letter, but it's got to be done.

After Cornwall, I feel better about myself and the house seems less alien; my seascape picture hangs in pride of place on the living room wall and I admire it and its message of hope, every time I see it. It's come to represent something to me – my single future – and even though it's just a painting, I feel it's helping me reach forward.

Gaz, however, is depressed about being back home. His normal walk to the rec is now of the utmost tedium, he tells me. After the freedom of Cornwall, his whole demeanour is designed to make me feel guilty. I try and make the walks more exciting by playing ball with him, but I can tell what he's thinking: *This just simply isn't good enough any more. I need water, I need smelly fish ... I need to feel the sand beneath my paws.* Still, there's nothing I can do. We live in Stowchester, old chap.

One evening I'm bored (I'm bored most evenings, but on this one, I'm particularly bored. There's sport on BBC One, a history program on BBC Two, a soap I don't watch on ITV, a programme about dwarves dating each other on Channel Four and an American detective series on Channel Five. I flick through all the Freeview Channels and there's literally nothing

I want to watch. I'm temporarily drawn to a re-run of Embarrassing Bodies, but when some guy gets his bits out, I decide it's a step too far. How come, if he's so embarrassed by his testicles, he wants to show everyone on telly?)

I turn off the TV and open my laptop. I start googling Internet Dating and am amazed at the number of sites that come up. Some look frankly dubious – sugardaddy.com being one; eHarmony.com sounds unlikely somehow – most relationships are not harmonious in my experience. "My online dating horror" jumps out at me on the first page of google, along with "Is Online dating destroying love?" – an article in the Telegraph. I have a quick look at Match.com and decide everyone looks far too young and then click on Encounters, the dating site with the Sunday Times. I feel if they are the sort of people who read the Sunday Times, surely they'll be older and wiser? I can't be bothered to create a profile, it's too late in the evening and I'd find it too depressing trying to make myself sound exciting, so I just go for the Search Now option, where I can look for a few randoms, without any commitment.

I am 'a woman' looking for 'a man' in the age range ... now that's an interesting one. Do I really want someone between the ages of 55 to 70. My GOD, that sounds absolutely ridiculous, but the reality is, I'm 55, so men are usually older than women, so ... but surely, I'm a young 55, aren't I? Maybe I could go for 50 - 65, that doesn't sound quite so decrepit. So I put this in and say twenty miles from my postcode. I press Search.

Up come five pages of these men – I look at them and think they all look old enough to be my father ... then realise that I'm ancient and if I put a picture of me up, I no doubt would look like someone's mother, which I am, of course.

I scroll through the first page. On this 'free' search, you can only click on three people before you have to do it properly and pay their subscription, so I pick carefully and only choose ones who look don't look like serial killers or Father Christmas.

I click on one – he has a nice smile, lives near and is 62, which doesn't sound too bad, I suppose. (I can't believe I'm looking at someone of 62 as a potential partner; surely 62 is someone with nose hair, slippers, an annoying cough and who makes 'old man' noises when they get out of a chair?) I read down – he's 'widowed' – ah, poor chap ... but then would I want to be permanently in the shadow of the paragon of virtue who is now dead ... but better than 'divorced' (Why did they divorce? Abuser, trainspotter?) Apparently, he's 'young at heart' 'romantic' ...'tactile' ... WHAT? What the hell does *that* mean? He likes groping women?

My heart is sinking, even as read. I don't think I can possibly even contemplate someone who considers the word 'tactile' as a positive trait. Against my better judgement, I read on ... his ideal match: Body Type: Slim. Well, that's me out, although maybe at a push, viewed from the side in a darkened room ... Looks – Very Attractive. Wouldn't we all, mate? You're not exactly Adonis, are you? Age Range: 45 - 55. WHAT? You're 62 and you're looking for someone Very Attractive, Slim and 45?? What world are you *living* in?

I click on 'Next' in disgust, and he's the same – a very ordinary bloke with a balding pate, glasses and wonky teeth, who seems to be looking for a cross between Juliette Binoche and Carla Bruni, who just happens to be living in Stowchester.

I have one more chance before I'm locked out – I click on someone who isn't even trying to smile. He's staring into the camera in bewilderment. He looks a bit like a mad professor and whoever took the photo hasn't even bothered to check if it's in focus first. I must be getting desperate.

He's 64. Likes reading, drinking fine wine and is looking for someone to enjoy country walks with. So far, so good. I read on and discover he's looking for someone with a GSOH (well, I've got one of those, a good sense of humour – I must have, otherwise I wouldn't be reading his profile). He's looking for someone who likes 'the good things in life', who's 'tactile' (that word again – this time, *he* wants to be groped, not the other way around) and who's financially well-off. He doesn't like animals and he wants someone of 48 - 55. I feel offended that he wouldn't like Gaz – even more than the fact that he looks about 84, and wants someone of 48.

If you don't like animals, then I don't like you. End of.

I close the lap-top with an angry bang. If that's internet dating, then you can stuff it where the sun don't shine.

There must be a better way of meeting people ...

HI ADAM – DON'T WORRY, this isn't the start of interminable messages; I know you don't particularly want to hear from me, but I thought I would just share my plans with you.

Before I start, I hope you're still having a brilliant time? I was with Laura recently and we looked at your photos together. I hear you're going up to Byron soon?

So ... I'm resigning from the school tomorrow – in fact, I'm going for early retirement – hurray! I've just decided I've had enough. Being in close proximity to Dad and 'her' isn't how I want to spend the rest of my life. I've had a lot of time to think ... and I've realised I've got to 'move on'.

Dad's just been over here, suggesting that he buys me out of my half of the house and much to my surprise, I've decided to let him. I don't feel any attachment to it now that you've all gone and I want to move to Bath. So ... big changes.

My other big news is that I'm going to visit Jane in Adelaide in March next year. No dates as yet, but I wanted to let you know. I hope you don't think I'm following you out there – Australia's a big place. If you wanted to, you could come and visit. I'd pay for your fare on Virgin Blue or whatever. Jane hasn't seen you since you were tiny, so it would be a good opportunity to meet up.

You don't have to make any decisions now, obviously, but just thought I'd tell you.

Your mother is going to become a free spirit in her old age – I think they call oldies who wander around Oz with a caravan 'Grey Nomads'. I'm not quite there yet, but my life seems to be unfolding in a new and hopefully, exciting way.

Your sister is well – have you been in touch? She's met someone, a barrister called Jed. They met here, in the pub, but he lives in London. She seems really keen and so does he. They're going out all the time – I know, we've seen it all before, but this time, it feels different. Maybe wedding bells ... it's early days, but you never know!

Love, Mum xxx

I MAKE IT ALL SOUND very light-hearted in my message to Adam, but when you came round last night and said you wanted to buy me out, I was heart-broken. I know that's a hackneyed phrase, but I seriously felt as if my heart had broken in two. You were so distant, so cold – what's happened to you? I feel as if I don't know you any more, as if all the years we spent together have just been wiped away with the flick of a cloth. A smear on a mirror.

Maybe I never knew you?

Have you forgotten how excited we were when we bought this house? The agent told us about a house that had just come on the market and was 'exactly what we were looking for'. He took us round straight away and do you remember the feeling we both had when we drew up outside it? We looked at each other – we were in the back of the agents' car – and I mouthed at you – *This is the ONE.* You kissed me on the lips and when we got out of the car, we walked hand in hand towards the front door, Holly skipping in front of us.

Don't you remember the feeling we had when we stood in the hallway? That weird sense that we'd just walked into our 'home' – that atmosphere of welcome and calm?

Holly loved 'her' room – it was already painted in pink – and then we showed her what would be 'the bump's' room. We said hers was bigger because she was such a grown up girl and she kissed my stomach.

The sale went through without any hitches and we moved in two months later. It was as if it was meant to be, we said ...

And now, you just casually want to buy me out. To replace me with a younger, better model.

I know it's the practical thing to do – I get it – you want a bigger place and all that – but ... how could you carry on living here, knowing our past?

You've got what you wanted – I've said I'll go and you and she can live here, happily ever after.

I'll be gone from your life, out of your thoughts, your conscience, your heart.

I hate you right now.

"SO, HAVE YOU DONE IT?" says Lisa, in the staffroom, on the first day of term.

"Yes, indeed I have. My letter should be sitting on his desk, as we speak. He came round a couple of nights ago to 'talk' but I didn't tell him about my plans – he was too busy making his own. So, I hope it's come as a massive shock – but probably not ... I don't think anything I do these days registers with him."

"Any more thoughts as to where you'll go or what you'll do?"

"I'm moving to Bath ..."

"Really? What ... definitely?"

"Yup ... I've even started looking ... only on the internet, but it's a start. I've got to finalise how much I'll have to spend first, but I've got a ball park figure ... you don't get a lot in Bath for what I'll have but ... maybe I'll start renting first and see what area I like."

"That's an excellent idea. Try before you buy."

"It's got to allow dogs ..."

" ... that might limit your choice a bit ..."

"I doubt I'll be able to afford to live in Royal Crescent or Queen's Square, but I'm sure I'll find something nice," I say, trying to convince myself.

Being back at school is strangely comforting; I'm relieved to be back in a routine, with a reason to get up in the morning. The school holidays have been testing – I tried to impose my own little routine on myself by getting up most mornings and going to the pool for an early morning pound up and down the lanes. I feel a lot fitter for it – I must try to go after school, now I'm back.

My new year seven's are cute – a weird word to use for pupils, I know – but they seem so innocent, angelic even. They haven't, as yet, had the edges rubbed off them at the 'big' school – they still have the childlike qualities of primary school, oozing from their sweet faces.

I feel motherly towards them as they look at me with their big eyes, drinking in my every word – if only it lasted past the first term. By the Easter term, they'll already be more knowing, more streetwise, more cunning. They won't be trying to please me, they'll be finding ways to wind me up and thinking up ever more inventive ways to avoid handing in their homework on time ... by the end of the Summer term, they'll be more like sweaty teenagers: chewing gum, texting under their desks and calling me names. By the beginning of year eight, they'll be seasoned professionals: strutting around, shouting, terrorising the newbies. And so it goes on.

With a sudden leap of my heart, I realise I won't be there to see it all. I'll have gone to that 'other place' where teachers become people again – never again will I have to pretend that *Tom's Midnight Garden* is the most fascinating book I've ever read ... never again, will I have to sit in a staffroom full of people I've got little or nothing in common with ... never again, will I have to negotiate my way through new government initiatives ... or Ofsted inspections ... or school plays ... or parent/teacher nights (oh joy) ... or assemblies ... or teacher training days ... or sit in the cafeteria eating with hundreds of noisy kids ... or watch boring netball matches, just because I feel I should.

Never again, will I have to watch Suzie Barton stride into the staffroom in her pristine white sports blouse and her short little shorts, with her long tanned legs, her blond pony tail swinging in a jolly, yet sexy way on her perfect little head ... and never again, will I have to watch my effing husband mooning after her, along with all the other pathetic male staff, who seem to worship the ground she walks on.

What is it with her? Is it the dimples in her cheeks, when she smiles? Her almond shaped green eyes? Her low, sexy laugh? Her long, beautifully waxed, brown legs? Her hair that shines like a shampoo advert? Her teeth, straight and white, like Cheryl Cole's? Or is it all of the above?

I think I've answered my own question.

It's definitely time I was gone. Bring on Christmas.

I HAVEN'T HEARD FROM Adam for a few days; I think I've blown it by even suggesting we meet up. Then, my computer pings and I see, with relief, a new message from him:

Hi Mum

Just got back in from a surf at Manly with some of our new Aussie mates. The waves were awesome and the rip strong. Found myself right down the beach. My surfing is really coming on now. We spend hours out there – I'm not as good as Jake, but even he says I'm a lot better. We've been working hard too, waiting at tables. I'm actually enjoying it, which has surprised me. The café's on the beach and half the tables are outside, so I'm in and out of the sun all day.

I love this place. Neither of us want to come home, but at least I've got the grades and can go to uni if I want to.

Adelaide sounds a cool idea – just what you need. Of course we'll come if we can (and if you pay, ha ha). It would be great to see you and catch up with Aunty Jane and Marcus.

You might be interested to hear that I've at last heard from Dad. He tried to explain things ... it's so difficult being in the middle of you two. I know I've had my differences with Dad in the past but somehow, being out here, and being away from home, has given me a different perspective. He seems to be genuinely in love with the woman.

Anyway, I wrote back and we've kind of made peace with each other. Probably good that there are thousands of miles between us though – easier to feel benevolent at a distance, LOL. I feel I'm changing out here. I've realised that my parents are just humans after all – I never realised that before!

Bath is a great idea. Go for it! When and if I ever come back to Pommyland, I'll love visiting you there.

Let me know when you're coming out. Jake sends his love.

We're off out now – more clubbing to be done. Adam.

I can't get over how different he sounds. How can my little boy have changed so much in such a short time? He sounds mature, thoughtful and, dare I say it, adult? He loves *working*? I can't believe it and the fact that he's really nice about Adelaide too – it makes going out there even more enticing ... to think I'll see him again.

DAVID'S REACTION TO my early retirement is as predicted; he offers to give me advice and help, but he's detached and professional and I get the feeling he's pleased to see the back of me. He says we must 'have a talk' (what, another one?) about finances. We must agree a price for my half of the house – *Of course I will give you the going rate.* Well, that's very decent of you, Sir, I must say.

I point out that I want sixty per cent of the value, for the inconvenience of having to move out of the family home and he doesn't quibble. Perhaps Suzie will have something to say about that when he tells her but ... it's between him and me and that's how it's going to be. I've decided to stick up for myself and stop letting people walk all over me. He says he'll have to speak to his solicitor and I say, of course, but *that's the deal if you want me to go.*

We're in his office at the time and before opening the door to leave, I say quietly, "Otherwise, you can see me in court," with a kind of benign smile on my face, and I glide through the door, feeling marvellous.

There you go, David, I too can be assertive. I think it's a pretty generous offer, considering what you've done to me.

I TELL GAZ ABOUT OUR move – he doesn't think much of it. He just stares from the comfort of the sofa and looks at me as if to say ... *Is there sea in Bath? The name sounds promising...*

He's feeling pretty sorry for himself at the moment as, following on from the discovery of the lump, I took him to the vets today, after school. I know, I know, I should have gone before, but I was putting it off. If I didn't take him, I wouldn't have to face whatever the lump is.

Along with all his other phobias, he absolutely detests going to the vets. The moment I pull up outside the building in the car, he knows where he's going and starts cowering in the back seat. I have to pull him out and drag him across the car park. At the entrance, I have to haul him across the threshold and pull him in; he slides across the linoleum floor like a cartoon character – every ounce of his body weight pitched against mine. We must look pretty funny to an outsider. I get sympathetic little smiles from fellow humans in the waiting room – the other animals look impassively on.

Having established that we've arrived – "Name?" says the receptionist.

"Mine or his?" I say.

"His will do," she says, in a rather deprecating tone.

"Gaz McCarthy," I say. She gives a knowing little smirk.

What's wrong with that? He's part of this family, he deserves a surname.

He then sits, shivering and shaking at my feet, slobbering spittle on the floor, as he whines and pants. He keeps getting up and flopping down with as much exasperation as he can muster.

When his name is eventually called by the vet, who comes out of his room looking like a doctor in a white coat, Gaz is positively suicidal and tries to make a dash for the door that will get him out of the building. He nearly pulls me over, with his sheer determination to make a quick exit; everyone laughs in the waiting room and then we walk slowly back to the other door of 'doom'.

"And how can we help you today?" he says, as Gaz and I stand against the closed door, both of us now anxious and wanting to vacate the premises.

"Well, I was stroking him recently and I noticed a lump ... just here."

The vet approaches Gaz, who tries to hide behind my legs. "Sorry, he won't bite you or anything, but he really hates vets ... a bit like me with dentists," I laugh, nervously.

"Come on, old chap, I'm not going to hurt you," says the vet, gently running his hand down his back.

Well, you sure as hell look as if you might, says Gaz to me.

"Have you noticed any other lumps or bumps?"

"No, I don't think so ..."

"Did it appear suddenly ... has it changed?"

"I'm really sorry ... I'm not sure ..."

"Don't worry ... let me just lift him up onto the table," he says and up Gaz goes, onto a shiny topped table, where he stands looking vulnerable and bewildered.

The vet slowly runs his hands all over his body, pushing and rotating his hands, not saying a thing. He takes his temperature and Gaz looks at me as if to say *Can there be anything more more humiliating than having some random person put that up my ...*

"Have you noticed a change in his behaviour ... eating, walking ... urinating?"

"No, not really."

I try to reassure him, whispering, "It's alright, you'll be okay." But there's something about the vet's face that's worrying me and I begin to feel that it's not all right, at all. The vet opens Gaz' mouth and looks at his teeth, lifts his ear flaps and examines his ear canals.

You have to admit, Gaz, he's being very thorough.

"Well?" I say, quietly. "What do you think?"

He doesn't answer at first; he lifts Gaz back down to the floor and then says, "Well, I'd like you to bring him in tomorrow, for a biopsy. His temperature is raised and I don't like the look of the lump."

My heart falls to my feet. I had been so hoping for a different answer.

"Oh," I say, and bend down to hug Gaz, hot tears squeezing through my eyelids. I stay down there rather longer than I should, hoping to dry my tears on Gaz' black coat, but I fail miserably.

"Don't worry, yet, Mrs McCarthy ... it may be nothing. It's always good to be sure."

He ushers me out and we make the appointment with the receptionist. I have to bring him in the morning, before school.

Gaz virtually runs to the door – I'm the one skidding on the linoleum this time, as we shoot through the door into the fresh air and freedom. We both breathe deeply and we get back into the car with relief. I take him for a little tootle around the rec, on my way home and as he sniffs his way around the periphery, I watch him with a heavy heart and a love that only a dog-lover can understand.

I sit on *the* bench and reflect on the things that have happened since that fateful day. I feel pleased with myself ... that I haven't let David defeat me. I've risen above the situation and started, slowly, to build a life for myself after marriage. As Gaz waddles towards me and nudges my arm with his nose, I wonder what he has in store tomorrow. Should I tell David about it? Would he care? He doesn't appear to show any interest in Gaz any more, so I decide he's lost the right to know what's going on.

"Let's go home, old bean," I say, putting on his lead and standing up. "You've got a big day tomorrow."

He looks up at me with his hazel brown eyes, so trusting, so loving and we walk off to get in the car, to go home.

I DROP HIM OFF THE next morning and as the nurse leads him away, he looks back at me as if he is being led away to the guillotine.

What's happening to me? Why are you allowing her to take me away?

I say, "See you later, Gaz," hoping he'll understand.

I find it difficult to concentrate at school and rush back at 4.30 to collect him. I sit and wait for ages in the waiting room. They know I'm here, but no one tells me anything and I begin to wonder if something dreadful has happened.

Then the door opens and out he comes, wagging and squirming – smiling, even. The nurse hands me the lead and says the vet will be out in a minute.

We wait patiently – I note the bare patch on his back where the lump was, with a small bandage covering the wound. "Come this way," the vet says abruptly and we are once again ushered into his room.

"So ... the good news is we've removed the tumour," he says.

I wait for the bad news.

"I'm afraid it was cancerous, but we think we've got it all. You need to be vigilant now – to keep an eye on any possible recurrence. It's very common in dogs like Gaz, I'm afraid."

I feel sick, pleased, worried and relieved, all at the same time.

What would I do without him? He's been my stalwart companion through all this ... he doesn't deserve cancer.

"So, do you mean he's all right now, then?" I say, willing my eyes to dry up. I really don't want to cry again – I understand how difficult it must be to be a vet. Not only are you dealing with animals in distress, but with their owners too. You have to be a scientist, surgeon, counsellor and friend, all in one.

"He should be fine ... but there are no guarantees, I'm afraid. I'd like to see him again in a week, just to check the wound and if you have any concerns, bring him back any time. Because of where the excision is, we don't have to worry about him biting his stitches, but keep an eye on it. He may try to roll ..."

We say our goodbyes and I go to settle the bill at the little window in the waiting room. As much as I love Gaz, I do a double take when I look at the total. We'd never taken out pet insurance – David never considered it worth it. I think of sending him the bill with a snarky comment ... but then I think, no, this is nothing to do with him any more.

Gaz is *my* dog ... my friend, companion and I'll deal with it.

When we get home, I give him a larger than normal amount of tea to try to compensate for his bad day. We snuggle down to watch Eastenders together on the sofa and I say, "Sorry, Gaz. What a horrible day you've had." I grab his head, holding his silky ears in my hands and kiss him on the soft patch on the top of his head.

Steady on, old girl. You're hurting my ears, but thanks for your concern. Not one of my better days.

Chapter Fourteen

We get two different estate agents round to value the house. We don't let on that, in fact, they won't be making any money on the deal, so they wander around, saying what a 'charming' property it is and how, with a bit of updating here and there, it will be lovely.

What a bloody cheek. One of them says the bathrooms are 'a bit tired' and the other one, that the kitchen would benefit from some 'modernising'.

When they've gone, I appraise the house and try to look at it with objective eyes. I suppose they're right ... we've lived here for years and done very little to it. It's funny how you don't notice after a while; it's just your home – you don't notice the shabby tiles in the bathroom, the mould around the window panes, the threadbare carpet going up the stairs, the boring garden. I thank God that we're not *actually* selling it – we really would have to tart it up. Everyone is so 'into' buying houses these days after watching too many programmes on TV – they expect Sarah Beeny to have personally designed the interior. Well, show home this is not ...

The agents' valuations are within £10,000 of each other, so David inevitably goes for the smaller valuation and I, for the larger one. But what's a few thousand when you're talking hundreds? We agree on a figure and I'm happy with it.

I start looking at Prime Location and Rightmove on the laptop more seriously now. It's funny how quickly I find myself looking at properties completely out of my price range – I wonder if I could knock them down a couple of hundred thousand? Maybe if I win the lottery, I could afford this Edwardian mansion with eight bedrooms and twenty acres ...

I swop between rented and for sale and can't decide what to do. Renting is just money down the drain, isn't it? Do I know enough about Bath to buy something there?

People in France don't have this obsession with buying houses. Why is it we British feel it's just not ... well, *British*, to rent? Surely it would be better to move somewhere temporarily first and see if I like it?

This all twirls round my head as I click on hundreds of houses and apartments.

David has agreed that I don't have to move until December (that's big of him). He and Suzie have got to sort out the mortgage situation and I've actually got to find somewhere. It sounds a long way away, but I suddenly realise it's only, in fact, two months. That's eight weeks to the uninitiated and that's not long at all.

I TAKE MYSELF OFF TO Bath most Saturdays and wander around various areas, trying to get the 'feel' of the place. I decide I like the area known as Bathwick – if you're going to be in Bath, you might as well be central, otherwise what's the point?

I've decided renting is the way to go – I can reassess after my trip to Australia.

I find several rented properties that I like the look of, but they don't allow pets. Gaz is turning out to be a stumbling block.

I turn out to be rather a troublesome potential tenant; it seems what I want is near impossible in Bath – two bedrooms, a garden, somewhere to park, all mod cons and it has to be pet-friendly. A lot of the agents I speak to, look at me as if I might be slightly insane, but bite their lips and go and look through their filing cabinets, sighing heavily as they do so.

After a few weeks of searching, both physically and online, an agent rings me on my mobile and says something has just come on that he thinks is perfect for me.

I rush over after work and he shows me round this ground floor, two bedroomed apartment with its own parking place and a communal garden. Pets are allowed (with restrictions like being kept on the lead in the garden etc, but that's fine). The street is a bit busy but – hey – it's central and I can walk to the shops and there's a park, just up the road. It's unfurnished, apart from the white goods in the kitchen, has gas central heating and it's painted in neutral colours.

I feel a flush of real excitement as he shows me round. I can't quite believe I can afford it, but I think I can, just. I can move in on 20th December, which is perfect. School will have finished and I will have finished with school.

I take it – sign all the papers and pay the deposit.

When I get home, I email David with the news – we hardly ever actually speak to each other any more. I find email can be wonderfully impersonal and cold.

David

I have found somewhere to live in Bath. I move on 20th December.

We need to discuss who has what, re contents.

Anna

I think that's cold enough, don't you?

I TELL BOTH THE KIDS about my flat and send them links, via the internet. Both approve and Lisa comes with me one Saturday to go and have another look at it. We take the opportunity to have a wander round the shops and it begins to sink in that this soon will be my local area. I'll be able to walk to the Bath Theatre Royal and the The Little Theatre Cinema – both places I love. I look forward to my future cultural forays.

Following on from my email, David and I exchange a chain of emails along these lines:

David,

As my mother gave us the canteen of cutlery and the cut glass wine glasses and decanter, I'll take those. I'll also have the double bed (you can have the beds in the kids' rooms). I'm leaving all the white goods, as the flat has them. I haven't got a dining room, so you may as well have the dining table and chairs – but I'll take the three piece suite. I'm taking the telly, as I'm sure you and Suzie already have one.

Anna

Anna

That's all okay with me – I would dispute the glasses and decanter though – I'm pretty sure my parents gave us those. It would have been nice to keep the three piece suite – I always thought you didn't really like it?

David

David

It was definitely my parents – they gave them to us when we first moved in. Re the sofa etc, what makes you think I don't like it? You'll be keeping the one in the kitchen, anyway. By the way, please don't lay on some big 'do' for my leaving at school. I'd rather slip away unnoticed, given the circumstances. No doubt people will want to buy me something – get me a M and S voucher and then I can either get something for the flat or clothes. Literally, no fuss please.

Anna

So there we have it – that's what our marriage has boiled down to – sharing out the spoils. In some ways, I would like to leave everything behind and make a completely new start, but I have to be practical and I can't afford to buy everything new.

I try to imagine the stuff from our house in the apartment and work out where I will put things. I realise I'll have to buy a small table and chairs to stick at the end of the sitting room; the kitchen's too small for one – hardly room to swing a cat. Talking of cats, where is Gaz going to base himself? It'll have to be the sitting room; the only other places are the rather narrow corridor or my bedroom. Perhaps I'll let him choose.

AS THE END OF TERM approaches, I get my removal company to deliver some boxes and I start slowly packing. This sends Gaz into a highly nervous state and he sits permanently at the front door or at the bottom of the stairs – that way, I can't escape without him. His wound has now fully recovered and the trauma of his days at the vet are in the dim and distant past. I check him out for lumps but as yet, nothing. Long may it last.

Our walks to the rec are now tinged with sadness as we both know that there won't be many left.

How odd it will be to leave this house – our bolt hole, our haven and yes, our love nest, for so many years.

DO YOU REMEMBER WHEN we brought Adam home, David? In those days, they kept me in hospital for four or five days – you'd been at home with Holly, waiting for the big day when I was allowed home with him. You'd surprised me – you'd painted the little room and hung up a Welcome Home banner across the top of the front door. The house was full of flowers and cards.

I remember you lifting him out of my arms, as if he was a Fabergé egg. I was sitting in the back seat with him (before the days of compulsory car seats) and you walked so proudly with him up the garden path. He was wrapped in one of those blue blankets with little holes all over it and you laid him down in his cot. We both stood there, gazing down at him, hardly believing he was ours, that we had made something so incredible, after years of trying. We thought we'd never have a second child.

He was calm and awake and staring up at us with his piercing eyes, his mop of black hair sticking up – so black against the white sheet. Holly put a little blue rabbit next to him that you and she had bought the day before.

I remember you saying to me, "Thank you," and me saying, "What do you mean?" and you saying, "Thank you for giving me a son."

You had tears in your eyes and we held onto each other, crying with joy.

Do you remember that?

THE TUESDAY BEFORE the end of term, everyone is summoned to the staffroom after school. I know what's coming and I'm dreading it. I'm secretly interested, however, to see how much people have coughed up for the voucher – I know when other staff have left in the past, I've rather resented having to give money. It seems you're always having to fork out for someone or something in that staffroom. I wonder how many people felt the same way about me and just chucked a fiver into the pot, without much thought.

Our deputy head quietens everyone down – David is standing to his left, looking embarrassed. I scan the room for Suzie and she's keeping a low profile right at the back, head down. Thank goodness David isn't going to do the little speech – that would have been excruciating.

"So, we're all gathered here today, to say goodbye to one of our best-loved members of staff – (certainly not best loved by your headmaster, I add) – one who will be sorely missed by both her pupils and her colleagues. She has been at the school for many years and her commitment and dedication has been second to none. Not only has she got hundreds of pupils successfully through hundreds of exams, but she has attended many extra-curricular activities and counselled girls and boys through times of trouble. She has been a truly wonderful teacher and I for one, will miss her ..." Pause for applause. Everyone does indeed clap and there are a few muted 'here, here's'.

I hate this sort of thing, and I'm standing there, looking as embarrassed as David.

"As you all may know, Anna is taking early retirement and we wish her all the luck in the world with her future. Rather than giving her a traditional clock to stare at from her bath chair – (loud titters all round) – we have all clubbed together to buy you a voucher from M and S – we hope you will buy something either beautiful or practical, which will remind you of your time here with us all. Hip, hip ... hooray. Hip, hip ... hooray."

Everyone cheers, as I come forward to accept the envelope and then we all stand around wondering when we can escape.

After enough time has elapsed, people start to drift off, some of them coming up to me and either hugging me or rubbing my back, saying things like, "Good Luck" or "Enjoy!". (Why have people adopted that annoying expression?)

Some of the wittier ones try comments like, "You're only as young as the man you feel" (which under the circumstance is rather inappropriate) or "Life begins at 55"; the head of French, whom I've hardly ever spoken to, says, "In the words of Groucho Marx, 'There's one thing I always wanted to do before I quit...retire!'" and with that, he gives me a big, slobbery kiss on the lips.

Quite honestly, I just want to bolt through the door; David is already heading that way, without a word, or a look. I'm beginning to feel slightly tearful. I'm not sad about leaving the school, not one bit, but I'm sad at what this day means: that I'm old enough to retire, that my life has fallen apart, that I live on my own and ... yes, I will miss this. The routine of it, the chaos of it, the noise of it, the smell of it, the *life* of it.

Have I made a terrible mistake?

Soon, Lisa rescues me and we go and sink a few drinks in the local pub. Some of the younger ones come too and it turns into a bit of a drunken do. I drink far too much and get slightly morose, so Lisa drives me home.

I fall into the house and lurch into the sitting room. I look around, my eyes only just focussing.

One more day at school, three more days in this house.

I flop onto the sofa and Gaz comes to join me and licks my hands, which are salty from the copious amount of crisps I've consumed. Through my somewhat tipsy haze, I realise I haven't, as yet, opened the card with the voucher in it. I tear it open. The card says *We're so sorry you're leaving* (oh yeah?) and there are signatures all over it. The voucher is for £300 which, on the face of it, is quite good, but then I work out there over a hundred staff and it doesn't seem so great, after all. £3 average per member of staff – the price of a lifetime of teaching. God, they must have had to actually find change – surely it would have been easier to chuck in a fiver?

There's something else – a voucher for the Theatre Royal, for two tickets. Nice – shame David won't be coming with me. Shame I've got no one to go with.

I throw both vouchers on the floor and reach for the remote. *Have I got News for You* is on – the audience finds everything Ian Hislop and Paul Merton says, hilarious. I'm afraid I don't – I'm too drunk to understand the jokes, anyway. I flick through about twenty channels: cookery programmes, Top Gear, dating programmes, My Great Big Fat Stupid Horrendous Gypsy Wedding ... has the world gone completely MAD?

I switch it off and throw the remote on the floor, too. I sit back and close my eyes ... the room spins gently round; when I get to the top of the circle, I open my eyes quickly, with a lurch. I feel sick. I also feel desperately sorry for myself.

Gaz tells me I should be more grateful.

You've got me, you know. Would you like to join me on the sofa for the whole night?

I lie down and put my arms around him; he breathes loudly in my left ear and I close my eyes, enjoying the comfort of his warm skin. This time, I drift slowly, slowly ... I should be grateful, shouldn't I? I've got a roof over my head ... sort of ... two beautiful children, who are hundreds of miles away ... no job ... All those with a job, step forward. Why are you moving Anna McCarthy?

Laugh out loud ...

You've got a big, black, hairy, friend, mouths Gaz into my ear. *Tomorrow ... is another day.*

That's true, Gaz. That's true. I fall asleep.

Chapter Fifteen

The final day at school goes by in a blur – some of the kids seem genuinely sad to see me go; I get lots of cards and little presents from them.

When it comes to actually leaving, I feel as if I'm in a dream, leading someone else's life. I'm there, but I can see myself, as if from above, walking down the corridor and going through the doors at the front of the school, for the final time. I wait for some kind of emotion – either a lift of my spirits or a sadness ... or something ... but nothing comes. I feel numb.

I was half expecting David to come and say something to me or wave me off the premises, but he keeps well clear. I can't say I blame him.

When I get home, I don't let myself dwell on it and start packing, in earnest. I make a point of taking all the family photos with me – I wrap all the frames lovingly in newspaper and it feels symbolic – as if I'm finally packing away my past. That phase of my life has gone and all I have left of it, is a few photographs.

David, what have you done? Do you feel any regrets at all?

I thought I knew you – the David I *thought* I knew, would surely miss his family? Miss ... *me*?

THE DAY ARRIVES AND I'm up at five; I haven't slept at all and it's a relief to finally get out of bed. I draw the curtains and look out onto the street below. Everywhere is still, the street lamps are on and I can see frost glittering on the tarmac.

I can't believe this is the last time I'll get up, in this bedroom; it's unreal. I go down to the kitchen to make a strong coffee and the hot liquid hits my empty stomach with its bitterness. It just adds to the feeling I have of nervous excitement mixed with fear, sadness and alienation. I'm at a crossroads that has been imposed on me, not of my own making, and I have to face it head-on, or sink like a stone.

Gaz stares at me from his bed. *Why on earth are you up so early? Not like you at all.* "You're going to get a big surprise today, Gaz – you're moving house, old chap," I say to him, but he ignores me and goes back to sleep.

I'm surrounded by boxes and I keep adding to them, until the removals company arrives at 8.30. I don't need a very big lorry, as half the stuff is staying – the reality hits me when I see it pull up outside and two rather jolly men come up the path, whistling.

I oversee the proceedings; I can't believe how quickly my life is packed away and put in the back of a vehicle. Stan and John are great workers and it all goes smoothly – soon we're ready to go. Gaz, by this time, has decided the best place to sit is by the front door; I asked him to move, politely, several times, as he was getting in the way, but in the end, I hauled him to one side and there he sat, making sure I didn't make a getaway without him. Stan, particularly, loves him and despite tripping over him on several occasions, he pats him every time he walks past him (when he's not carrying some huge thing.)

The guys leave and I do the final checks round the house. It doesn't feel like my home any more and of course, it isn't; it's soon to be invaded by my successor.

I've already got Gaz in the car – it's the only way to give him peace of mind and that way, I know where he is.

"Good riddance, then ... I thought I liked you, but I don't any more," I say to the house. The walls don't answer, they just stare back at me with off-white blandness.

"Goodbye, then ..." I say as I close the door, "thanks for nothing."

STAN AND JOHN ARE VERY discreet; they don't ask me what's going on, but in the end, I volunteer the information. It's pretty obvious that something pretty devastating has occurred, so I say as I unlock the door to my new abode, "Well, here we are ... my new home, having been superseded by a younger model ..."

The two guys look at each other in an embarrassed way and Stan, the more outgoing of the two, says sympathetically, "Well, I really like the look of this place ... I think you're going to be very happy here."

I hope he's right.

During the course of the afternoon, I tell them everything – Suzie, retirement, Australia, the lot – it feels good to get it off my chest to complete strangers. I suppose this is par for the course for them – they must see all sorts of happy moves, but also people like me, being forced to move for reasons beyond their control, be it financial, career or ... divorce. Maybe other people don't share everything with them but, it feels good and I'm sad to see them do their final trip out to the van.

"Good luck, then," says Stan out of the window from the driver's seat. "Have a great time in Australia ... I'd love to go, one day. The missus says we can't afford it but ... one day!" and with that he pulls away, smiling and waving.

I turn back and walk in the front door to my new flat. Gaz is in his bed, surrounded by boxes; he looks as lost as I feel. Stan and John's chatty presence is sorely missed. They've put all the main pieces of furniture in the right places and even helped me put the bed up, but it's now up to me, and me alone, to unpack everything and get it away in cupboards.

My mobile beeps. *Hi Mum. Hope it's all gone ok today? Have been thinking of you. Will ring tonight. Holly xxx*

Once again, Holly has texted me at just the right time, she seems to have the knack. It's almost like telepathy or something. Just to know that she's been thinking of me cheers me up and I start looking through the boxes marked 'Kitchen' for the kettle, instant coffee and the remaining litre of milk I rescued from the fridge. I make a mug of coffee and then settle down to unwrapping everything and putting it all away. I feel like I'm playing at life, rather like a young girl with a doll's house, placing things in the correct cupboards and on the perfect shelf.

Stan had helped set up the TV and after an hour of unpacking, I go through to the sitting room to see if I can get the six o'clock news. It works fine and I watch the normal depressing rundown of political unrest, bombings and murder and decide I need to get out for some fresh air. It's already dark outside and freezing cold, but I have Gaz for company and he definitely needs to lift his leg on a few lamp posts.

It seems so weird to be in the heart of Bath as I come out; I love that I'm surrounded by people and life. Cars whizz by us as we walk along; a group of teenagers pass, shouting and laughing; the amber of the street lights give a warm glow to the cold scene. Christmas lights wink and flicker from windows.

I head for some green space where Gaz can do his thing and then, on a whim, for the first time in my entire life, I go into a pub on my own. It's a completely impulsive thing to do – I can't face more unpacking, I'm cold and I think I deserve a drink after the day I've had.

I check it's okay to bring Gaz in with me and I order a large gin and tonic. There's a roaring log fire, a Christmas tree in the corner and tinsel, surrounding every picture. The atmosphere is welcoming and I even begin to feel the excitement I used to feel, at Christmas. Until now, I'd managed to ignore its imminent arrival.

I sit down at a table by the fire, warming up my toes and eating a large bag of plain salted crisps. The alcohol warms me from the inside and goes straight to my head. Gin often makes me feel a bit down, but tonight it has the opposite effect; I'm happy, buoyant even, and bend down to give Gaz a big hug. I can handle this solitary life, I think to myself, optimistically.

"Nice fire, isn't it?" a voice says and I look up to see a man – mid forties – standing there. He bends down to stroke Gaz and offers him one of his crisps, which Gaz takes, rather too hastily.

"Gaz, that was rather rude ... sorry, he's usually a bit more polite than that, aren't you? He's probably starving ... I've realised I haven't given him his dinner yet, have I?" and pull one of his ears.

"You poor old thing," the man says, offering him another crisp. "You'll have to have words with your missus, won't you?"

He'd now drawn up a chair and was cradling Gaz's head on his knee. He laughs and looks across at me. "New round here?"

"How do you know?"

"It's just that I come in here a lot and I've never seen you before, that's all."

"Yea ... I've just moved in round the corner, actually. Gaz and I thought we'd check out the local pub on our walk, didn't we?" I say, realising that we're conducting this conversation through the four-legged third party. Easier somehow, than talking directly.

I quickly appraise my new companion – paint splattered trousers and boots; warm, navy blue coat, black and white scarf wound round his neck and wavy brown hair, left to grow longish. He has an open, friendly face and I decide he has a look of Daniel Craig about him – tough, craggily good-looking, without the shaved head. I notice his eyes – they're large and cornflower blue. He has a small scar by the side of his mouth.

Rather nice, in fact.

He's drinking a pint of ale and downs most of it in one go, as if he needs it. He takes another gulp and says, "I'm going to have one more, can I get you one?"

"No thanks, this one's gone straight to my head – with all the moving today, I've forgotten to feed myself, too."

He wanders off to the bar, coming back with his drink and another packet of crisps – "I hope you don't mind, I thought I'd share them with ... Gaz, did you say?"

"Yes, that's fine. Gaz, after Paul Gasgoigne, aka, Gazza. Suited him when he was a puppy, he was so fast, but they've both slowed down a bit, since then."

"Alcohol's got a lot to answer for," he says, holding his pint up to the light, "although I can't really comment, standing here with the second pint of the day." He laughs loudly and raises his glass and says "Cheers!". He has a lovely, smile and his eyes crinkle up with laughter lines.

"Cheers! Do you live locally?" I ask, but immediately regret it. It seems intrusive, somehow, and I wonder if he'll think I'm trying to chat him up.

He's not phased at all and says, "Yes, a couple of streets away. I often drop in here on my way home – preferable to going home to a solitary evening. I hate my own company."

I wonder why someone so affable is on his own? He's nice looking, pleasant ... why hasn't he been snapped up?

"Same here ... but at least I've got Gaz. Dogs are great company ... always pleased to see you ... never let you down."

A silence ensues, apart from Gaz breathing heavily; he's staring at the packet of crisps, willing them to fall into his mouth.

"I know – I had a dog when I was growing up. So ..." he says, "why Bath? Do you work here?"

"No ... I've just taken early retirement, actually, and I've moved here for a new start."

"Wow ... early retirement ... I dream of that ... I can't see me ever being able to stop working at the rate I'm going."

"What do you do?"

"I've got my own painting and decorating business, as you can probably see," he grins, pointing at his trousers.

"Are you busy at the moment? Plenty of work?"

"Yea ... but let's put it this way, I'm never going to be a millionaire. It just about pays the bills. I have a daughter ... don't get me wrong, I adore her, but there's maintenance and my ex is always demanding more and more ... it never seems to stop."

"I'm sorry ..."

"Yea ... but that's life these days, isn't it? How about you?"

"What do you mean? Why am I on my own?"

"Well ... yes, if you want to tell me, otherwise, it *could* have meant, what did you do before you took early retirement, you lucky devil?" I like the way he gets around a potentially tricky question, with wit and skill.

So, I give him a brief overview – the second time in one day, telling strangers my life story – and he makes all the right comments and laughs at my jokes about Suzie. I know it's my way of coping, by making her out to be some sort of sex bomb, but it works for me. He says, "Poor old Dave, he's probably knackered most of the time ... serves him right." I should find it offensive that someone's laughing about my husband being shagged out by some nubile blond, but I don't – it's somehow cathartic to laugh along with him and I change my mind and go and get another large G and T.

He tells me about Daisy, his daughter, who's five and he shows me photos of her on his mobile phone. "That's when she was only three hours old ... here she is at two ... and look at her now ... all blond curls." She is, quite definitely, a beautiful child and I can feel his sadness. I ask the question.

"How often do you see her?"

"Not nearly enough. She lives in Cheltenham now – I'm one of those weekend Dads who wander around playgrounds and go to fast food outlets, wishing they weren't in this predicament. Sometimes, I bring her to Bath for the night but Grace, that's my ex, always seems to find a reason why I can't. I could go back to court, but I don't want to make the situation any more antagonistic than it already is. God, I hate it."

He takes another swig of his beer. "Sorry, that's really ruined the mood. You shouldn't have asked," he said, trying to smile. I don't even know the guy, but even I can see that he'd make that little girl a great dad.

"It must be awful. Thank God we split up when the children had grown up – at least they're doing their own thing, living their own lives. I'm not saying they haven't been affected by it all, but it's not the same ..."

We then proceed to talk about my kids and I tell him all about them and not to be left out, I show him photos of them on my phone and tell him my plans to see Adam in Australia.

I look at the time and am shocked when I see a whole hour has passed. "I really should go ... poor Gaz will be passing out soon, with hunger. It's been really nice to meet you – I don't even know your name?"

"Ben ... Ben Jones," he grins, "sole proprietor of 'Ben Jones Decorating Services' – very original I know, but I never was good at creative thinking. More of a practical person, me."

I extend my hand and say, "Anna McCarthy, nice to meet you, Ben."

"I'm leaving too, so I'll walk you home."

"Are you sure? I'll be fine ..."

"Of course ... I'm sure Gaz would do a fair job at escorting you, but I don't like the thought of you two wandering the streets of Bath alone, when you're both so new to the area."

"Well, that's very kind of you. And thank you for making my first trip to a pub on my own, so jolly," I say.

And I mean it. It had turned into a very pleasant evening, much to my surprise.

We walk along together, chatting away and soon we're at my door. "I live literally just round the corner," said Ben. "If there's anything you need help with in the flat, just let me know. Have you got your phone? Right ... tell me your number ... and I'll ring it and then you'll have mine." This is just like Holly and Jed, I think to myself.

Having exchanged numbers, I walk to the door. It did, momentarily, come to me that I could invite him in for coffee but no, that would be a bit much and I'm tired.

"Thanks again, Ben ..."

"My pleasure. And I mean it. If there's anything you need help with, give me a call. I can fix electrics if I have to and I'm a dab hand with dripping taps." He waves as he walks down the street and I wave back. I go inside.

Before I feed Gaz, I get out my phone again and go to Contacts, then Create New Contact.

Ben Jones.

"SO MUM, HOW'S IT GONE? Are you exhausted?" says Holly.

"Well, I am, rather ... I've just made myself poached eggs on toast and I feel a bit better now. First meal in my new place."

"And how is it? The flat, I mean? Is it all all okay?"

"I think it'll be fine – still got masses to do – but the bed's made, so I'm going to collapse soon. I've only just got back from the pub – Gaz and I wandered into our local, this evening. Men go to pubs on their own, so why shouldn't *we*? Ended up chatting to a nice chap, called Ben."

"Go Mum! That's very hip and modern of you, well done. Is that part of your new ..."

"Yep, I'm going to be doing all sorts of new things I've decided – what, I'm not sure ..."

"So, who's this Ben, then?"

"Oh, just a guy who made friends with Gaz, rather than me. We chatted for ages and then he walked me home."

"Oooooh, get you! Did you ask him in for coffee?" laughed Holly, not realising she was actually quite near the mark.

"No, I didn't, Holly. Stop teasing ..."

"Well, good on you, Mum. Onwards and upwards."

"So ... what time are you arriving on Christmas Eve?"

"I'll be in Bath by about five. I've got the afternoon off – I'll text you from the train when I'm on."

"Okay, can't wait. I've booked us into a posh place for Christmas lunch. Are you seeing Jed?"

"Yes, if that's okay with you, he's going to come over on Boxing Day."

"I'm looking forward to meeting him properly."

"Have a good sleep in your new flat, Mum. Love you. Bye."

Lying in bed, fifteen minutes later, I listen to the sounds of the city. I can hear a distant police siren, the swoosh of cars driving by and people chatting, as they walk past. It's comforting to hear life going on outside. I feel less alone, somehow, than I did back home.

I'm pleased with myself for making this move; I'm convinced it's the right thing for me. Good to get away from David, good to get away from everything associated with my past. Physically, I'm not that far, but mentally, I've come a long way.

Here, I can start again with a blank sheet of paper.
It's never too late, they say ... let's hope they're right.

Chapter Sixteen

Happy Christmas, Mum. Spending the day on the beach – seems wrong! A barby just isn't the same as roast turkey and all the trimmings. First time I've felt homesick. Jake says I'm a wuss but I really wish I was back home today. Hope all's okay with your new flat? Job in caravan park going well – have met loads of people. Hope you've bought me something for Christmas?! You can always bring it with you. Love, Adam x

"Hey, Holly," I say, handing her the phone, "read this."

After a few seconds, she says, "Oh, poor Adam ... he sounds as if he'd rather be here. Oh well, I'm sure he'll be okay tomorrow. Nice that he remembered to message you, though."

"I think this year's going to do him the power of good. It'll be the making of him, I think."

"Yea ... he needed to grow up a bit."

We're back at the flat having had a superb meal out. We're feeling far too full, even having taken Gaz for a long walk afterwards. We're now going to enjoy doing nothing at all, but sipping Prosecco and watching TV.

"I wonder if he's got a girlfriend out there and he's just not telling me?" I say. "Has he ever mentioned anyone to you?"

"We haven't texted much, to be honest, and I'm not sure he'd tell *me* anyway. I hope he's playing the field ..."

"He always had masses of friends at school ..."

"Yea, he's sociable – everyone loves him. Even though he's my little brother, I can say, all the girls love him. He's funny, sporty and good-looking – he won't be lonely out there, that's for sure. Have you relaxed a bit about him now? You can't worry about him for a year ..."

"I think I have, sort of. He's sounding more mature somehow, even in his short messages. I do miss him ..."

"Well, it won't be long till you see him again, will it? Have you booked your ticket?"

"No, as soon as Christmas is over, though, I'm going to. I thought around the beginning of March?"

"Woo-hoo, I'm *well jeal.* I wish I'd gone out there when I had the chance, especially as I've even got relatives out there I could have stayed with. Stupid."

"One day ... maybe you and Jed could take a sabbatical?" I laugh, raising my eyebrows.

"It's a bit early days to be speculating about future holidays with him, Mum, but I wouldn't say no."

"You're keen, aren't you?"

Her eyes light up and she makes a coy, girlish face. "He's special, Mum. He's so lovely to me – thoughtful, kind and ... he makes me laugh. We have such a giggle together. He teases me and ... he's gorgeous, as well," she laughs.

"I can't wait to meet him properly. What time's he coming over?"

"He's going to spend the morning with his Mum and Dad and be here for lunch."

"Shall we go to the pub?"

"Yea, cool. That would be great and then maybe we could take Gaz for a walk. I don't think Jed knows Bath that well."

I grab my phone. "I'll just message Adam back."

Hi Adam, Happy Christmas! Holly and I are envious of your beach Christmas. It's freezing here, but you're right, you can't beat an English Christmas lunch. Bath looks beautiful too with all the streets lit up at night. Glad you like your new job – still can't imagine you cleaning! I've paid some money into your bank account today – rather than buying you something, I thought you could do with the money. Holly, Gaz and I are having a lovely day – just chilling now in front of the normal Christmas telly – we can watch Downton this year, without you and Dad complaining! Am going to buy my plane ticket soon. Can't believe it! Love you, Mum x

I press send and wonder what time it is in Byron Bay. Will it ping into his phone and be read immediately or be waiting for him when he wakes up? The thought of him so many miles away momentarily makes me sad, but then I look up and see Holly lying on the sofa and I'm grateful she's with me.

I miss David too. We used to have such lovely Christmases all together.

DO YOU REMEMBER THE Christmas we spent down in Cornwall? The kids were little and we thought it would be fun to get away from it all, so we hired a cottage, right on the beach.

We took so much with us in the car – the back was full of presents and decorations. The cottage smelt a bit damp when we got there, but we built a log fire and the central heating came on and it soon warmed up.

We put up our decorations on Christmas Eve when the children were in bed – we even bought a small artificial tree with us and in the morning, the kids couldn't believe that Father Christmas had found them, even though they weren't at home.

We still cooked the full Christmas lunch and while the turkey was roasting, we went for a wonderful walk along the beach. It was windy and the waves were huge; Adam insisted on looking for crabs in rock pools and you and Holly played football. We flew a kite, but it was too windy and the kite dive-bombed into the water-logged sand and we had to try and dry it out.

We stayed until New Year's Day. We walked and walked, that Christmas, all wrapped up, breathing the sea air, coming back to the cottage for hot chocolate and warm baths.

Memories like that are so special, David ... do you remember?

ON BOXING DAY, JED arrives just before one and I can instantly see the bond between him and Holly. They do indeed make each other laugh all the time and they are constantly touching each other – Jed affectionately kissing her on the top of her head when they're remembering something; Holly, sitting on his lap, curled up like a cat.

He lives up to everything Holly has said about him – I can see his respect for her, he's a true gentleman in the old-fashioned sense of the word – holding the door open for her (and me); pulling out chairs for us – and really *listening* to us. He seems genuinely interested in me too, asking all the right questions, complimenting me on the flat and asking all about Australia. It turns out he's been there – to Perth and Darwin – much to Holly's consternation.

He's wearing the same leather jacket he was wearing in the pub the first time they met and as I look at him across the table in my local, I can't help thinking what gorgeous children these two would produce. A bit premature ... but you just *know* when two people are made for each other, don't you?

"So, will you travel around Australia, Anna ... you don't mind if I call you Anna, do you?"

"Don't be daft, Jed, of course ... call me Anna ... I don't think so ... I'll want to stay with my sister – Adam's coming to Adelaide ... so probably not ... but hopefully, I'll get to know that area well."

"You're going to love the lifestyle out there – everyone's so outdoorsy and sporty and the food's amazing. I couldn't get over the beaches. I know we have good beaches here but, when you've seen an Australian beach ... you get quite blasé about them in the end – oh, another thirty kilometre beach of pure white sand!"

"Did you swim in the sea? The sharks put me off a bit ..."

"I did but ... I know what you mean. In Darwin, you have to worry about crocodiles too – they can be on the beaches there."

"Oh my God ... I think Adelaide will be quite enough for me. Not sure which is more terrifying - crocs or sharks!"

"No, you'll love it, Anna, you'll see."

The more he talks about Australia, the more I want to go. It's just what I need.

By the time Jed leaves in the late evening, I've convinced myself that he's 'the one' for Holly. He's perfect for her in every way and I'd love it if they got married. I stupidly put this to Holly the moment he's gone – I say 'stupidly' as I know they haven't known each other that long and I don't want to give their relationship the kiss of death before it's started but ... Holly's always been so open with me about 'boys' and I want her take on it.

"Let's put it this way, Mum ... I always said that my future husband had to ...One, be GWP (good with parents). Two, love animals, particularly dogs (Gaz – what did you think?) Three, make me laugh. Four, be sporty and ... Five, be lovely looking. I think Jed fills all those categories, don't you?" she says, grinning in a love-sick way.

"And more," I say. "He's *really* lovely, Holly. You've got a good one there."

I thought the same about David many moons ago – it should make me cynical about relationships, the way *that* turned out ... but I have a good feeling about Jed. A really good feeling.

"I know, Mum. We haven't used the 'L' word yet, but I do ... *love* him ... and I think he loves me too."

"I think he does, too. I'm secretly getting excited ... should I start looking for hats?" I laugh.

"I'd say 'yes' in a heartbeat if he asked me ... who knows? I don't think you need to postpone your holiday or anything ... but ..."

We hug each other and I feel happier than I've felt for ages. "I love you, Holly ... it's been so lovely having you here. Two girls together. I've always loved our girlie time."

"Me too, Mum. Me too."

WHEN HOLLY LEAVES ON the 28th, I have to admit I feel somewhat devastated. I'm aware of being alone in the world again and I walk back to the flat from the station, with a heavy heart.

I went onto the platform to say goodbye to her – as the train pulled out towards London, we waved to each other through the glass, Holly pulling a 'sorry' face at me, knowing how I felt. She's always so sensitive and knows exactly how I'm feeling.

Her face slips away and I wait while the whole train slides past me – I watch it until it disappears.

Can there be a lonelier place than an empty platform? I don't begrudge her going at all, she has some big party planned for New Year's Eve, but I miss her so much, it hurts.

When I reach the flat, I do my best to get on, to sort out the remaining boxes. I didn't want to waste a moment while Holly was here, so now's the time. Gaz plods around after me, getting in my way; I notice he's limping a bit and sit him down and have a look at all four paws, in turn. I can't see anything obvious – maybe there's a thorn in a pad that my poor eyesight can't see? I tell him to stop 'putting it on' and he gives me a hurt look as if to say, *Show some sympathy, woman.*

He sits and stares at me and obligingly gives me his right front paw.

"What do you want? Are you trying to just get food off me?" *Well, yes, that would help a lot, actually.*

So I get up and give him one of his dog biscuits, which he hoovers down as if he hasn't been fed for at least a week.

THE NEXT DAY, I DECIDE to enjoy the novelty of being able to walk to the shops. I've got the whole day in front of me with nothing very much to do and after a lazy morning, I wander slowly round all the main areas, discovering little backstreets that, as a visitor in the past, I never had time to find.

I come across a quaint little coffee shop, where I sit quietly reading the newspaper that was left on a chair. My phone pings. I look at it quickly and go to messages. *Message Ben Jones.*

I do a slight double-take.

Hi Anna! How are you getting on in your new flat? Just thought I'd drop you a line to say I meant what I said about helping. Maybe see you in the pub again soon? How's Gaz by the way? Ben

I stare at the message, surprised that he's bothered to contact me. Nice of him, though. What on earth do I say back? So far, I don't need any help in the flat – everything's working fine – but if I say that, it sounds a bit unfriendly. I type quickly:

Hi Ben. That's so nice of you. Okay at the mo, but sure something will go wrong soon – life can't be that easy, surely?! Gaz is fine, but a bit limpy – not sure what it is. See you in the pub soon I'm sure. Anna.

I thought that sounded non-committal enough, but friendly. I start scrolling down through my Facebook timeline and see a picture of Adam and Jake. Somebody else must have taken it – or maybe it was a selfie – they're both facing the camera, heads together, as tanned as real Aussies, sun streaked hair now long round their ears, caps on backwards. Like two peas in a pod. They look happy, healthy, excited ... I'm so pleased for them; I can feel their zest for life pulsing through the screen of the phone.

My phone pings again.

Why don't you and Gaz come to the pub on New Year's Eve? There's a bit of a party going on and it will be nice to see you both there. That's if you haven't got a better offer? Ben

Well, I certainly haven't got one of those, I think to myself. I'd been dreading New Year's Eve alone in front of the telly, so it's tempting to think of wood fires, gin and tonics and someone to talk to.

It's strange, but since coming to Bath, I've begun to realise that I haven't got many friends – most of the 'friends' I've had in the past ten years have been 'our' friends and now that there's no 'our', I've had to come to the conclusion that people have drifted away, as if it's too hard for them to take sides. Lisa, of course, is a good friend, but she's so busy with her kids and I feel on a different planet to her now. Laura's such a long way a way ... and all my acquaintances at school have gone into the part of my life marked 'gone'.

So, I press 'reply' and say, *Good idea. No invites to parties forthcoming, so see you there. Anna.*

When the message goes winging off, I have a moment of panic – do I really want to go to a room full of strangers and be kissed by randoms, on the stroke of midnight? I've always hated that – why on earth did I say yes?

But then I think, why not? I've got nothing to lose. (Just my dignity).

I'm collecting up my things to leave the cafe, when the phone goes again. (Anyone observing me, would think I've got a social life).

Great. See you there. I'll probably go around 10, otherwise it'll be a long evening. Ben.

So, it's done. I'm going.

I go home soon after and tell Gaz about our outing. He shows no interest whatsoever, but at least it gives me something to think about.

What shall I wear, Gaz? I haven't got a thing ...

I'm sure you'll find something ... He gets up, turns around in his bed and slumps down again, as if it's the last thing he wants to discuss.

NEW YEAR'S EVE TURNS out to be remarkably good. When Gaz and I arrive, Ben is already ensconced by the fire; he greets us like long lost friends, kissing me briefly on the cheek and squatting down next to Gaz to give him a secret crisp.

He introduces me to several people – a mixture of ages and types – and we all shout at each other above the loud music. Gaz wags his tail congenially and ingratiates himself on people, doing his *I'm never fed and I'm beaten six times a day* act to get food off them.

I start off with a cider, vowing not to drink too much, but by 11 pm, I'm on the gin and tonic and can feel my head turning to mush. I hope I'm still making sense – I appear to be making perfect sense to myself, anyway.

"So, what's wrong with Gaz, then? You said he was limping?" says Ben, feeding him part of a bread roll.

"Not sure ... I can't find anything wrong, but it seems to be getting worse each day. He didn't want to come out tonight, but I forced him."

"Oh dear, Gaz, what's the matter? Maybe you ought to take him to the vet?"

"I think I might, if it doesn't change. He hates the vet, don't you, Gaz?"

I'm aware that our conversation is focussing on Gaz again – so much easier than talking about anything else. I still can't understand why this man is wasting his time on me – surely he has other friends he'd rather be with? I take a surreptitious look at him – he's not wearing his paint-spattered clothes of course – jeans, suede tan boots, checked shirt open at the neck and a dark brown leather jacket. I can't help thinking he's rather gorgeous – his eyes are mesmerising – and becoming more so, as the night progresses.

The alcohol is loosening my tongue and after a brief pause I say, "Anyway, enough of Gaz – why aren't you out clubbing or something? I'm sure you must have friends in Bath you'd rather be with? Don't feel you've got to entertain me or anything, I'll be off to my bed soon." (Why did I say that? It could be taken two ways: one, an invitation to join me in said bed or two, I'm the most boring woman on the planet, going to bed before midnight on New Year's Eve.)

"No, clubbing's not my scene at all – never was, even when I was younger. You can't leave before twelve, anyway – that's the whole point!" He swigged from his beer. "After Grace left, I've found people we knew as a couple kind of drifted away ... we had friends through Daisy who've disappeared ... so no, in answer to your question, and in the words of the song, there's no place I'd rather be. I love this pub and the company," he grinned, and in my slightly inebriated state, I imagine a smile of something more than friendship.

God, I really must get out more. There's no way ...

Before I could stop myself I said, "How old are you, Ben? Sorry ... that's rude, but ..."

"No, I don't mind. I'm forty-five. Mid-life, I think it's called. How about you? I know you should never ask a woman her age, you said you'd retired, but you look far too young ..."

"Well, that's very kind of you to say, young sir, but ... yes, I *am* retired – as a teacher you can take early retirement at fifty-five. So ... now you know!"

"I'd never have guessed, just looking at you. You keep yourself fit, I assume? Do you go to the gym or something?" Ben's flattery seems natural, not forced and I glow inside, thinking, maybe ... I don't look so bad after all.

"I try to swim as much as I can, which reminds me, I must start going again. I haven't been anywhere near a pool since I got here. And of course, I'm always walking Gaz."

"My job's pretty physical, so I don't do much else – that's my excuse, anyway. I love taking Daisy swimming when I can."

"When are you seeing her next?"

"Hopefully, next Saturday. Grace is letting me have her for a sleep-over. Perhaps we could meet up – she'd love Gaz."

I'm quietly thinking to myself that there's only a ten year age gap. Is it so improbable that this man is chatting me up? I can feel a connection, can't I?

Time drifts by ... the owner of the pub puts on the TV, so that we can all see the celebrations in London. The clock is saying ten minutes to go, people are standing up and going to the bar to collect a glass of bubbly that our ticket includes. There's a great atmosphere and the earlier thought of not wanting people to kiss me at midnight, has evaporated. As I look across at Ben, I quite look forward to it.

"Shall we go to the bar too?" he says. "We can leave Gaz here in front of the fire. He doesn't look as if he's bothered either way."

"Yea, let's," I say and as we walk over to join the others, I feel Ben's arm round my back. It's a good feeling.

Soon, the countdown begins and we all join in, shouting out the numbers and finally Happy New Year! As Ben turns to me, all smiles and openness, I have no qualms. He puts his arms around my shoulders, kisses one cheek, then the other and says, "Happy New Year, Anna! This is going to be a better year for you, I'm sure." I kiss him back and say, "Hopefully ... and for you too." I like the feel of his lips on my cheek, the tickle of his stubble and the smell of him.

Then we get whisked away by other people on a tide of good wishes and I surprise myself by actually enjoying it. We then all link arms and sing Auld Lang Syne and I find myself opposite Ben. We laugh at each other and his eyes twinkle through the pub's low light.

"Why the hell do we all sing this every year?" he shouts over the now even louder music. "Ridiculous song, isn't it?"

"Mad, but it wouldn't seem right without it, would it?"

"You're right! Do you fancy a dance? They've cleared a space ..."

By this time, I'm quite light-headed – euphoric even. The combination of all the drink, the friendly atmosphere and a good-looking forty-five year old taking an interest in me, combines to make me feel almost desirable again. I shout, "Sure!" above the music and he grabs my hand and forces his way through the throng. "Tonight's gonna be a good night" is playing and forgetting past inhibitions I dance, not caring what people think of me, for a change. Ben's a surprisingly good dancer (I see David dancing suddenly – he was never very good, but we always had a laugh and messed around).

"Are you okay?" Ben shouts.

"Yes, Fine! Why?"

"You suddenly look ... sad."

"Do I?" My memory must have surfaced to my face and I try to smile. "Sorry ... just thinking ..."

"Don't think," says Ben. "Just enjoy the beat!"

And he's so right. Enjoy the beat. Don't think. That's the way.

We dance to several more songs and then we go over to see Gaz. Ben rests his arm round my back again, as he ushers me through the people. Gaz is splayed flat out, looking for all the world as if he owns the fireplace.

"I think I better take him home, Ben," I say, making Gaz my excuse.

"Really? The night's still young ..."

"No ... I think I better ..." I say, not really knowing why I want to escape.

"Okay, I'll walk you back."

"Are you sure?"

"Of course. I wouldn't dream of letting you walk home alone." He gets my coat and helps me put it on. "I think I'll call it a night too, if you're going."

As we walk back, the city encircles us; it's a clear, cold night, the stars are shining brightly through the amber glow of the city's air pollution and the odd firework pops and sizzles above us. Ben takes my arm and we amble slowly, taking it all in. Gaz limps by my side and I feel an anxiety I haven't felt before about him. I look down. "Come on old chap, nearly home now," I say.

At the door, I hesitate slightly. I can't find my key, but then find it, buried in one of the many little interior pockets of my bag.

"Thanks for tonight, Ben. Thanks for suggesting it," I say, as I put my key in the lock.

I turn round and Ben puts his arms around me and we hug each other. "It's been a great evening, Anna," and he squeezes me hard. He pulls back and still with his hands on my shoulders, he leans forward and gently kisses my lips. They feel warm and soft on mine, but I don't respond. I pull back.

"Sorry," he says, looking directly into my eyes.

"No ... don't be ... I'm just kind of surprised, I suppose," I say, "you're younger than me ..."

His eyes stare into mine. "Does it matter?"

"No ... I suppose not ... I don't know ..."

He hugs me again. I like the feel of him, the warmth of another human being.

"Look," he says, "let's just see how it goes ... I like you, Anna. You like me, I think ... I hope. I love your dog!" He reaches down and strokes Gaz' head. "Let's go on a date."

My stomach does a small little flip of excitement. Am I really being asked out on a date by this man? "Okay ... you choose," I say. "Surprise me."

He kisses my lips again and says, "I'll text you," and walks away down the path. I open the door and we wave.

I close the door and lean back on it. I can remember his lips, as clearly as if they are still on mine. I try to remember David's lips, but I can't.

Can we go to bed now? asks Gaz. *It's way past my bedtime.*

Chapter Seventeen

"So, how was your New Year's Eve?" says Holly. I'm lying on the bed, still in my pyjamas and it's already midday.

"Really good. Surprisingly good, actually. What about yours?"

"No, you tell me first ..."

"Well, the pub was full and the atmosphere was great and ..."

" ... and, and, what about this Ben, though? Was he there?"

"He was, actually, and if you must know, he's asked me out on a date!"

"Oh my God, Mum, that's brilliant. I can't believe it!"

"Oh charming," I laugh, "you can't believe your old mother's capable of getting a date?" I catch sight of myself in the dressing room mirror. I look a bit rough, but decide I don't look so bad for my age. Nothing a good layer of make up wouldn't improve.

"No, I don't mean that at all – what I *meant* was, you've only been in Bath two seconds and you've already been asked out. This change of location has obviously worked wonders."

"He's ten years younger than me ... does that seem wrong?"

"No ... why should that matter?"

"That's what *he* said. Anyway, I said I'd go ..."

"Go for it, Mum. What have you got to lose?"

"Yea, you're right, as usual. Anyway, he's going to text me – I probably won't hear from him ever again. So, how was *your* evening? How's the lovely Jed?"

"Fantastic! We went to watch the fireworks, met up with loads of his friends and then went back to his place. I'm still there now. He's just bought me a cup of coffee in bed."

I can hear muffled talk and giggles in the background. "Sorry, Mum ... I was rather distracted!"

"Lucky you. Gaz and I are waiting for someone to bring us one. Talking of which, poor old Gaz is limping badly. I'm going to take him to the vets first thing tomorrow morning."

"Oh dear. Give him a kiss from me. What do you think it is?"

"No idea," I say and as I don't want to worry her, I add, "I'm sure the vet will sort it out."

I DON'T HEAR FROM BEN on New Year's Day. I don't know what I was expecting – a bunch of roses on the doorstep, a text declaring undying love? But as I go to sleep, I decide it's all too stupid. Why would I *want* to go out with someone so much younger than me, when I still yearn to be with you, David?

What did you do this evening? Did you kiss Suzie on the lips and say how the next year was going to be amazing, now that she is in your life? Did you both talk about the possibility of Suzie having your baby? Was it just the two of you, snuggled up in our house together? Did you tell each other how lucky you are, how you don't need anyone else to celebrate with?

Do you remember last New Year's Eve? Adam was with his friends, sleeping over, and we decided that we had no desire to go out. I cooked us a special meal and you bought us an expensive bottle of champagne. We watched Jools Holland, saw the countdown and the fireworks and kissed each other at midnight.

It was a peaceful, contented night ... or, that's how I saw it.

Perhaps you were already wishing you were somewhere else ...

I CONSIDER GOING BACK to our vets back home (yes, I still call it 'home') but then decide there must be plenty of good vets in Bath. I google 'vets' and find there's one just very near.

This morning, Gaz stays in his bed longer than normal and is only enticed to get out, with the offer of food. He sucks it up in his normal hoover-like fashion and then goes and flops on the sofa, not wanting to go out.

I ring for an appointment and they give me one at 4 pm. I feel as if I'm just filling in time until then, but I start googling flights to Australia and after much deliberation, I book my tickets. When I press 'Buy tickets' my heart's thumping – I check everything about ten times, to make sure I haven't booked to go to a place called Adelaide in some place I've never heard of before. No ... Adelaide, Australia. Definitely. Jane had said I could go any time, so I don't check with her before buying them. They are a good price and I just want to get on with it. I print everything out and stare at the A4 pieces rolling out of the printer. I'm really going. On my own. To Australia. My heart's still thumping.

I email Jane with my dates and ask her if there's anything she wants me to bring out from England. Then I message Adam.

Hey! Guess what? I've booked my tickets. 4th March to 10th April. Emirates, via Dubai. So excited. Do hope we can see each other, but don't worry if it doesn't fit in. How was your New Year? I went to a local pub and it was fun – probably not as fun as your night! Haven't seen any pics on Facebook recently – are you too busy working or something? Hope all's well? Love you, Mum xx

Although I say 'don't worry if it doesn't fit in', I'm really hoping he'll come. I couldn't bear the thought of going all that way and somehow not seeing him.

I miss him like crazy.

I'm going to tell David he's got to look after Gaz for me when I'm away. There's no way I'm putting him in a kennel for that long and I think it's the least he can do.

GAZ AND I WALK SLOWLY round to the vets. As he doesn't know this vet, he walks through the door quite happily, but the moment he's inside, he knows. It must be like us and hospitals – the smell gives it away.

I sit in the waiting room with him quivering at my feet; it's a big practice and there's more than one consulting room, so there are several waiting patients: a cat that continually meows in its carrier; a springer spaniel who leaps about like an excitable child; a dachshund, sitting quietly on its elderly owner's lap and a rabbit in a cage, which even Gaz keeps glancing at.

After about fifteen minutes, we're called forward by a girl that looks younger than Holly. I can't believe she's old enough to be a qualified vet and wonder if she's the veterinary nurse. My rather sexist and ageist notion is immediately dispelled, when she welcomes us into her room and is obviously the one in charge.

She's really sweet with Gaz, who's cowering in the corner, shaking. She gives him a treat out of her white coat pocket and he pushes his nose in for more. I explain his symptoms and his past problems and she spends a good five minutes examining him thoroughly. She's won his trust, by *not* putting him up on the table and continuing with the bribery – he gives into the process with calm resolution. She doesn't say much while this is going on and I find my heart is beating in my ears, waiting for the verdict.

She stands up and faces me, speaking quietly and seriously. "Could you bring him back tomorrow? We want to get to the bottom of this, don't we, Gaz? I'd like to give him a scan. I can't find any obvious reason for him being so uncomfortable."

Here we go again, I think. My heart sinks at the thought and what it may reveal. I thank her, she gives him one last little biscuit and we leave the room. I make the appointment for 8.30 the next day.

HI MUM – GLAD YOU HAD a good New Year's Eve. That's amazing about your tickets – I'm going to talk to the guy in charge here and ask for a few days off around the beginning of April. It'll be really good to catch up with you. I don't think Jake's going to come.

I've heard from Dad quite a bit – he sent me some money too! It's so weird to think of him at home, but not with you. I can't get my head round it, but I suppose it'll sink in, eventually. I feel so detached from real life here – I've almost forgotten what England looks like. I know I've got my uni place waiting for me but ... I'm not sure what I want to do any more. I need to talk to you when you come out. I love it here so much and I feel I can be myself.

Love, Adam

I'm pleased when I read that David and he are communicating properly again and that it wasn't just a one off, but I wonder what he means about uni. Is he thinking of *not* going now? What would he do if he didn't go ... and what does he mean when he says 'I can be myself'? Why's Jake not coming, too?

I resolve not to question him on the internet and wait until I see him, in person.

I drop Gaz off at the vets as planned and wander home. For some reason, I feel depressed today and I go back to bed. I have hours to fill before I can go back there and I'm overcome by tiredness. I snuggle down under the duvet and try to forget ...

I must have slept for three hours; I'm woken by a *ping pong* as a message arrives. Groping bleary-eyed for the phone I read: *Message from Ben.*

Hi, sorry I haven't been in touch. Grace has dropped a bombshell and I didn't feel like talking to anyone. I know I said about a date, but do you fancy just meeting me at the pub for a drink this evening? I need cheering up! Ben.

I worry what this bombshell is – obviously something about Daisy – poor Ben. The trouble is, I don't know whether I'll want to go out later, if it's bad news. I text back:

Hi Ben. So sorry to hear about the bombshell, whatever it is. Gaz is at the vet having a scan at the moment, so I'm not sure whether I'll be up for the pub. Can I text you later? Anna

I get up and shower and decide I'll go for a walk. I need something to occupy myself and feel that fresh air might be the answer.

It feels odd walking without my constant companion, as if I've lost something, but I try to power walk and not dawdle, as usual. I pass a leisure centre and go in to have a look at the pool and discover when I could go lane swimming. There's a session at two, so I go back home and collect my costume.

Swimming, as always, soothes my mind and as I swim up and down, I begin to convince myself that the news will be good and that Gaz will have many more years ahead of him. He's a strong old boy ...

I like the pool and as it's so near, I join the swimming scheme which means I can go as often as I like, for a monthly fee. They have a good selection of costumes in the reception area and on a whim, I buy myself a new one.

When I try it on, I stand if front of a long mirror in the ladies changing area and look at myself. Without realising it, I've lost weight. Even though I haven't been exercising much at all, my body looks less podgy round the middle and my hips don't look so wobbly. I realise that ever since David told me his wonderful news, food has lost its joy. I eat when I'm hungry now and don't really think about it, like I used to.

At school, I was always cheering myself up with bars of chocolate or eagerly accepting doughnuts that some kind soul had brought into the staffroom. David and I would plan menus and cook together; we'd look at recipe books together and shop for the right ingredients. I would also reward myself for any attempts at exercise, with a large piece of cake, immediately putting on the all the calories I'd burnt off.

Now it's just fuel ...

The costume is black with bright turquoise and white stripes; it has flattering, secret panels which 'support' you in all the right places.

I look at myself and can't quite believe the transformation.

IT'S TIME TO GO BACK to the vets and despite my efforts to be positive, my stomach feels twitchy and nervous and I feel sick. I try to read the receptionist's face, but I can't – she smiles and asks me to sit down in the waiting area.

To fill the time, I don't sit down, but go and stand in front of their notice boards. I look at the adverts for dog walkers, dog groomers, catteries and pet artists. I see one for 'professional, dignified pet cremation' and find my eyes brim over with unexpected tears. I look away and go and sit down, staring at the wall.

Soon, my nice young lady vet comes out of her room and ushers me in. Gaz is nowhere to be seen.

"Where is he? What's happened?" I say, unable to keep the panic out of my voice.

"He's just through there," she says, pointing to another door, "I'll get him in a minute. But first ..." I notice her eyes look away from me, her whole demeanour is awkward. "But first we need to discuss the result of the scan, Mrs McCarthy. I'm really sorry but ... but we found that Gaz ... that Gaz has an aggressive form of cancer."

Her words fall into the air like shrapnel, hitting me from all angles. I can understand the words, but my mind shuts off and even though the pain is cutting through my mind like a sharp knife, I feel numb.

"Mrs McCarthy, are you all right?"

"Can I sit down, I feel ..."

"Yes, of course, here ... sit down." She waits for me while I sit, and I look at her. Even though I'm not functioning properly, I can tell she's hating what she has to say.

"The cancer has spread ... he's limping so badly because ..."

"So ... what are you saying?" I almost shout. "Can you operate?"

She pauses for what feels like a lifetime and then says gently, "I'm so sorry, but I'm afraid there's nothing we can do. It would be kinder to put him down now, before it gets worse." She looks embarrassed and turns away.

The words float around my head. Put him down? Put my Gaz *down*?

"He must be in considerable pain," she says "and it's only going to get worse, I'm afraid. Obviously, it's your decision, I can only advise you."

I'm now openly crying and the vet hands me a box of tissues which she has conveniently on the side, for just such moments. I wipe my eyes and blow my nose loudly. Who can I speak to? What shall I do? Once again, I realise I'm totally alone and it's my decision. Mine only.

"What would *you* do, if he was *your* dog?" I say. "What would you do?"

"I think I would see that to put him down would be the kindest thing to do ... but ... it's got to be *your* decision. Is there anyone you would like to ring?" she asks.

"No ... yes ... maybe. Could you just wait a moment?"

"Of course. I'll give you some time to yourself." She leaves through the other door. I get my mobile out and dial Ben's number. He's the only person I can think of. I can't burden Holly with this and David is the last person I want to talk to. Ben's in Bath. He loves Gaz. He'll know what to do.

He picks up. "Ben, this is Anna," I say. My voice must give me away.

"What's the matter? What's happened?"

"Could you come round to the vets ... now ..." I'm trying not to cry, but my voice breaks. "It's Gaz."

"What's happened? Of course, I'll come round, in say, fifteen minutes. Is that all right?"

"Yes, that's good. Thank you, you know where it is, don't you? You know ... just at the end of my road?"

"I'll be there. Hang on." He clicks off and I'm left standing in the consultation room on my own. I knock on the other door and say, "Hello, is anyone there?" and the young vet comes back in again.

"My friend's coming round. Can we have twenty minutes? I'll go outside and wait for him ..."

"Of course, Mrs McCarthy. You take your time. I'll see the next patient and then we'll reconvene ..."

I leave and walk around outside the building, in a daze. Why have I called Ben? What can he do? It's *got* to be my decision. I know what I've got to do really ... I do ... but I can't face it.

Shall I give him a few more days ... take him home ... a few last walks?

But who would I be doing that for? Him or me? How would that benefit *him*?

I feel like an executioner ... what right have I to make such a decision, to end someone's life? He's only a dog, I tell myself, he's not a person ... but he's been my constant friend for so long ... he's helped me through this awful time ... how can I simply give the go ahead to something like this? But the alternative?

Ben walks up the drive and comes straight to me and I collapse onto him. He puts his arms around me and strokes my back.

"Oh Ben, it's the worst possible news ..." and I tell him what the vet told me.

"She won't decide ... it's *me* that has to make that call. What shall I do?"

"I think you know what to do, don't you?" he says, calmly, stroking my hair. "There's only one outcome ... you'll just be making it a better ending for him, Anna. He won't know anything ... he'll just go to sleep." Whether he believed his own words or not, I don't know, but I knew what he was saying was right. "You've got to be brave, for *his* sake, Anna. I'll come with you. We'll do it together."

I look up at him and he's smiling down at me, willing me to do the right thing. My heart is fluttering like a trapped bird, my legs are shaking; he walks with me, holding me under one arm, back into the building.

We sit together; I see he's holding me hand – it's comforting, but it's as if my hand doesn't belong to me at all.

The vet comes out and calls us in and once again, Ben holds my arm as we go into the room.

"Have you made your decision?" she says.

"Yes," I whisper, "I think so."

"Do you want to be present?" she says, understanding instinctively what I've decided.

The thought of Gaz dying without me is unthinkable and even though I dread it with all my being, I say, "Yes."

Ben squeezes my arm and then puts his arm round my back and pulls me into him, kissing my head. "I'll be with you," he says.

"Are you ready, then?" the vet says, looking me directly in the eye.

My voice won't come out. I nod. How is this happening? One day, I'm walking with him, he's sniffing lamp posts, cuddling up with me on the bed ... and now ...

She busies herself, with her back to us and then goes through the door. She comes back almost immediately, with Gaz. He's wagging his tail slowly and plods over to me, nudging my hand.

I can't speak and now tears are flowing down my face. He's alive ... and I have the ability to stop this. Ben strokes him, pulling his ears and running his hands right down his back to his tail.

The vet explains the procedure to us, in a quiet, authoritative tone. "He won't feel a thing. He'll just go to sleep," she says, repeating Ben's words.

How do we know what they feel? Is it wishful thinking?

She gets him to lie on the floor and shaves some of his fur on his front leg. "Right. You hold his head, Mrs McCarthy." My stomach is heaving, my legs quaking ... I kneel on the floor next to him and cradle his head on my lap. His lovely, honest, brown eyes look up at me with such trust. *Why am I lying here? What's happening?*

I whisper sweet words to him. "You're okay, old chap. You're fine. I love you."

I kiss his head and my salty tears make his head wet.

The vet looks at me and murmurs, "Okay?" I nod.

Ben kneels beside me. He puts one hand on Gaz' ribcage and one on my back.

"Goodbye, Gaz ol' chap," he whispers. I can't stop the loud sob that comes out of my mouth.

She puts a needle in his vein and begins to push the liquid down ... down. I see it in slow-motion – the fluid seems to hover in the tube. She's pushing death into him, with efficiency and calculation. I want to scream and shout, to pull the needle out ... to walk out of the building with Gaz beside me. But I sit there motionless, waiting and watching.

It takes so much longer than I thought it would. Slowly, his eyes close and I feel his head become heavy on my legs. She withdraws the needle.

His breathing is slow, very slow ... his side is heaving up and down, up and down ... up and down ... and then life leaves his body ... with a faint sigh. I close my eyes.

Silence invades the room – all I can hear is the humming in my own head.

I open my eyes, hoping that I'm, perhaps, dreaming. I stare down at him ... but he's gone.

I've lost my best friend. I have. I bend over Gaz, breathing in his wonderful scent, one last time. I touch his head, his silky ears and run my hand over his body. I'm tipped forward over him; if I get up, I'll leave him there on the ground, alone. He's still my Gaz – I can't leave him there, alone, on the floor.

A feeling of panic comes over me, as a vision of David or the children, lying dead, flashes into my mind.

I try to stand, but I can't; Ben helps me to my feet. The vet has quietly left the room and I once again, fall against Ben. He doesn't say anything; he just holds me and hugs me and I cry. At that moment, life is unbearable.

After a few minutes, the vet comes back in the room and says she will deal with everything. At the door, I take one last look at him, lying motionless on the floor.

My gorgeous Gaz.

We walk along the pavements – Ben holding me up. We don't speak. To a passer-by, we must look simply like a couple, out for a walk.

WE GO INTO THE FLAT and I see his bed. His spare lead is hanging by the door. His food is on the side, in the kitchen.

I sit down on the sofa, watching as Ben collects his things together and quietly takes them outside.

He comes back in. "What would you like me to do? Do you want me to leave you alone or shall I stay? I don't mind ..."

I can't answer. I have no idea what I want. I just keep thinking about how to tell Holly ... and Adam, of course. David has to be told, too.

I look up at Ben, this kind stranger, and I can't speak. Everything I've gone through in the last few months, lands on me, like a boulder. I have no husband, no home and now even Gaz has gone. It's all just too much.

Ben comes over to me and wraps his arms around me, saying, "You'll be okay ... don't cry ..." – even through my anguish, I can tell he's one of the good ones. Not many men would sit with a crying woman they hardly know, and offer words of comfort.

"I'm sorry, Ben," I manage to say, "I know he's only a dog, but ..."

"Look," he says, "there's no such thing as 'only a dog'. A dog is part of the family – Gaz was part of your life ..."

"It's just everything ... I feel as if I've lost everything right now ... I hate David. How am I going to tell the children?"

"You'll find a way ..."

"The flat's going to be so empty without him ... I can't bear it," I say, looking round and seeing the place where his bed used to be. "This is probably the last thing you want to be doing, I'm so sorry ... leave me, I'll be okay."

"I don't want to leave you like this, Anna, I really don't. I'm happy just to stay here, cook us something to eat ..."

"Are you sure?"

"Course I am. I didn't know him as well as you did, but I can imagine what you're going through. I'm going to miss him too. I'll stay. Why don't you go and have a shower or something and I'll look in the cupboards and see what there is to cook?"

He stands up and pulls me up with both hands, off the sofa. He kisses my lips gently as my face comes level with his. "Go on, you go. You'll feel a lot better afterwards."

I feel like a child being told what to do, but I go off, undress mechanically and run the shower. As I stand under the warm water, I try to imagine all my problems washing away down the plughole, trying to visualise a cleansing of both mind and body.

Afterwards, I remember Ben's bombshell. With all this going on, I haven't even asked him what it is and feel so selfish. I'm sure he understands, but ...

I enter the kitchen; Ben is stirring some pasta and making a tomato sauce. The smell is heavenly, but I have no desire to eat. I pretend I do.

"Ben, thanks for this. I feel better now and that all looks very impressive," I say, still towel-drying my hair, my voice flat.

"I've had to get good at cooking since Grace left ... some basic staples: spag bol, shepherd's pie, omelette ... even a roast, sometimes."

"Ben, I'm so sorry, I haven't even asked you about your 'bombshell' – I've been so wrapped up in my own misery ..."

"Don't worry ... it's ... it's that Grace is moving to Manchester with her new man. He's got a 'really well-paid job' there, according to her, and blow the fact that it's going to be near impossible for me to see Daisy. God, why's life so difficult?" He's standing at the cooker with a wooden spoon in his hand, my blue and white striped butcher's apron on, and the agony of losing his child to distance, oozes from his voice. I go over to him and put my arms around him. "I'm so sorry, Ben, that must be awful for you. Is there nothing you can do?"

"Dads don't have many rights, do we? If she wants to go off to the North of England and take my daughter, who am I to stop her? She says I can still see Daisy whenever I want, but how can I?"

"Could you move there too?"

It's an idea that pops into my head on the spur of the moment, but I'd hate it if he went.

"How can I? My business is here, all my contacts ... I couldn't just start again up there." He turns back to the tomato sauce; the droop of his shoulders exudes the misery he's feeling.

"When are they going?" I ask, hoping there are some months he can enjoy, before she goes.

"Well ... it turns out they've known for ages, but kept it from me ... they've even got somewhere to live up there. So, it's at the end of March."

"Oh God. That soon?"

"Yes, and there's absolutely *nothing* I can do about it."

I sit down at the table and watch him, as he busies himself in the kitchen. My head hurts from all the crying and my legs feel weak. I say, "We're a sorry pair, aren't we?"

He turns round and smiles at me – his eyes full kindness. "Come and sit down and we'll eat. Shall we drown our sorrows with some wine? I'll pop out and ..."

I go and look in the fridge and I find a bottle of Pinot Grigio. "No need," I say. I get out two glasses and lay the table.

We sit opposite each other. The absence of Gaz is palpable; I keep thinking I can hear his claws, clicking on the lino, or his faint snoring. My stomach lurches, but I force myself to eat the food Ben's made. We drink a toast to Gaz, touching glasses and smiling at each other, each remembering him in our own way. I gaze at a picture I have of him on the side – it's a close-up of his head; his hazel eyes shine out of the picture at me.

After the meal I say, "Do you mind if I leave you for a few minutes? There's something I've got to do."

"No problem."

I take my mobile and go into the bedroom and ring Holly's number. My tummy churns with each ring. "Hello, Mum, this is a nice surprise."

The phone call goes by in a blur of tears and comforting words. Holly is devastated, as I knew she would be. But, as always, she thinks of me, not herself, and says things like, "Oh Mum, it must have been awful for you." And "Are you okay, Mum? I hate to think of you of your own."

I don't tell her Ben is with me. It seems wrong somehow, as if I've been able to 'move on' from both her father and Gaz, and I don't want to upset her more than she already is.

"It's not long till Australia, Mum. You've got a lot to look forward to ..." she says, at the end of the call.

"You're right, Holly. I must message your brother."

"He loved Gaz, even if he didn't always show it."

"I know."

"I'm going to so miss him, Mum. I can't believe it."

"I'm sorry ... I love you, Holly."

"Me too ..."

I go back into the kitchen, pleased that I've told her, but drained. Ben doesn't ask what I've been doing, but just simply comes up to me and hugs me.

And that's how we start kissing properly. We both need that human touch ... and comfort. He takes my hand and leads me to the bed and the night that follows is one of making love, of finding someone to hold ... and sleeping peacefully is his arms.

When we wake, it's as if we've done this forever. I feel joy when I open my eyes and see his tousled head on the pillow. For two wonderful seconds, I forget how we've got here ... and I think I can hear Gaz whining to be let out. Then, the memory of his loss hits me in the guts and I roll over to stifle the tears.

"Anna, Anna, it's okay, I'm here. I'll always be here for you."

Ben knows exactly what I'm thinking. He knows I'm not crying about being in bed with him. He knows I've just remembered Gaz, as if he's in virtual reality, full 3D ... and woken to his total lack of presence.

He draws me to him and I lie against his chest, cradled in his arms.

Chapter Eighteen

"I thought you ought to know."

"Thank you ... but I wish you'd rung me, before you put him down."

"Look David, I had to make a quick decision. Anyway, I think you've lost the right to complain about anything I do."

"But he was my dog too ..."

"You haven't taken any interest in him for months, David. Anyway, I don't want to argue with you ... I just wanted to let you know."

It was the first time I'd spoken to him, since I moved to Bath. I felt honour-bound to tell him, but now I wish I hadn't bothered.

My message to Adam was hard to write. Even though he's thousands of miles away, I knew this would hit him hard. I got his reply this morning.

Hi Mum – I just can't believe the news. Gaz was part of my childhood and I'm so sad that he's gone. They plod around your house with their funny little ways and their awful smell and they become part of you. Do you remember the day we chose him? I was SO excited – all the puppies looked exactly the same, but it was him who kept coming up to us on the owner's lawn.

I bet you feel lost without him. Now I'm away, I realise how you must miss our family life and now, even Gaz is gone. I'm so sorry Mum. I love you xxx

Adam has never been one for expressing his emotions, but I can feel his sadness through the computer and it makes me sad, too.

I CERTAINLY REMEMBER the day we chose him – do you remember, David? We had talked about getting a dog for ages and we saw an advertisement in the local newsagents and it felt the right time. We said we'd go and 'just look', knowing full well that we'd never be able to leave without one. We took the children with us and of course, they wanted *all* the puppies. There were six jet black ones and the only way the owner could tell them apart was to put coloured wool round their necks. 'Greenie' was the one who kept coming up to us on that daisy-filled lawn. We'd said we wanted a female, but Gaz managed to wheedle his way into our hearts. We said we'd go away and think about it. The price was quite high, as he had a champion gun dog in his ancestry, but his mum was a lovely character, soft and gentle, and we knew the price didn't really matter. As we left to walk across the lawn back to the car, Greenie/Gaz ran away from the others, towards us and ... we knew. They say puppies choose you, not the other way around, and they were right, weren't they, David?

THE WEEKS AFTER GAZ' death have gone by in a bit of a haze. I've missed him more than I ever thought possible. The flat echoes with emptiness; I'm still finding the odd black hair when I tidy up – I pick them up and look closely at them, remembering.

But Ben has been wonderful to me and our growing happiness with each other has helped a lot. After that first night when he stayed, I wondered if it was a one-off and just something that 'happened' after the trauma of the vets and his news about his daughter ... but it hasn't been. We've tried to cheer each other up and made a pact not to talk about anything depressing.

We've been out together – to the little cinema that puts on unusual films; to the Theatre Royal to watch a funny play that made us both belly laugh and we've even been to the Comedy Club and seen three comedians – one of whom was hilarious; the other two were average, but we had a great time anyway, eating and drinking and enjoying each other's company. We've been swimming together, going up and down lanes, trying to outdo each other. We've gone for long walks and had pub lunches. It's been good.

We're taking things slowly – he doesn't always stay; sometimes I go to his. Each time has been better than the last – I'm amazed how he makes me feel. When you've been married for so long, it's difficult to start at the beginning again with someone.

I feel shy when I take my clothes off. David and I had got to a point years ago, when we'd walk around naked and not even notice each other's bodies, except for making jokes about his paunch or my boobs. Now, just revealing my body, with all its flaws, its wrinkles and its flab, is embarrassing. I'm aware of my age and even though I've lost weight, my skin looks saggy and old and it's true what they say, everything 'drops' with age. Ben, however, being ten years younger than me and a whole lot fitter from having an active job, looks great. Sometimes, I look at him and can't believe it. His body is taut and muscly; he has chest hair, unlike David, and although it's not a six pack, his stomach is flat.

He doesn't notice the things that worry me about my body; he says things like, "I love your body," and "I've never liked skinny women – your body is perfect." He boosts my confidence and says things like he really means it, and not only when we're making love. He'll come up to me when I'm cooking and put his arms around me, nuzzle my neck and say, "God, I fancy you ..."

I'd forgotten what it feels like to be fancied. David and I – things had become so routine, so 'unseeing' that we took each other for granted and never said things like that.

Now, looking back, maybe I'm beginning to see where it all went wrong. I'd let myself go, quite literally. I'd gone happily into the mist of middle-age and was utterly complacent about how I looked, how our relationship was and our future. I'd assumed David would always love me and I made no effort to help him. Perhaps he found what I have now with Ben, when he met Suzie. I feel as if my eyes have been opened – I'm not just sleep-walking into the rest of my life, like an automaton, any more.

I love just looking at Ben's face. I could drown in his cornflower eyes.

His daughter is coming to stay with him soon and we're going to meet up and go out for the day. We didn't meet up the weekend after Gaz died – I didn't feel up to it.

We're planning to take her swimming at the local pool and then maybe to the cinema afterwards, if there's something suitable on.

"DAISY, THIS IS ANNA, my friend," says Ben, holding his cherubic daughter in his arms. "She's the lady I was telling you about." They're standing at my door, looking cold. I usher them in and we go into the kitchen.

"Hello there, Daisy. And who's this?" I say, pointing to a cuddly rabbit she's holding tightly.

"It's Peter Rabbit," she says. "Daddy gave him to me. He used to hold a carrot, but I lost it."

"Never mind. He's lovely, anyway," I say, smiling up at her. Ben kisses her cheek and she cuddles into him. I gaze at her; she's just as gorgeous in the flesh as she was on Ben's mobile phone. She's got the most beautiful face – huge blue eyes, like her Dad's, a little button nose and hair like spun gold, framing her face with unruly curls. I begin to think that Grace must be a beautiful woman.

"So ... would you like a drink of ... orange juice? Or milk?"

"Mummy says I should drink water."

Ben pulls a face at me over her head. He says, "I'm sure you can have one drink of orange juice, poppet. I expect Mummy means not too much ..."

"Mummy says it'll make my teeth fall out."

"Well, just this once," I say, grinning at Ben. "Would you like a biscuit? I've got some chocolate ones here." I could almost predict what Grace would say to that.

"I'm allowed one biscuit. Mummy says ... biscuits fill you up and then you can't eat your dinner."

I feel like the indulgent grandparent, allowing the child to eat terrible things, but Ben seems very laid back and just says, "Mummy won't mind, Daisy. This is a *special* day and on special days, we can eat biscuits and drink orange juice. I may even buy you an ice cream later ..."

"Can I have a purple lolly? I had one with my friend Maisie ..."

"I'm sure you can. We'll go hunting for a purple lolly, after our swim." He strokes her hair and looks at her with such love, my heart breaks for him. "Now, where's your costume? Have you got your arm bands?"

"Yes, they're in my bag," she says, pointing. "Are we going now?"

"Daddy and Anna are just going to have a cup of coffee, and then we'll go, sweetheart," he says, putting her down.

"Come with me, Daisy," I say, " and we'll see if there's anything good on the telly for you," and I take her by the hand and lead her through to the sitting room. I can almost hear Grace, who I haven't even met, saying, 'no longer than twenty minutes'. I know you shouldn't plonk children in front of the TV but sometimes, when they're in a flat that has nothing of interest for a five year old, it's the only answer.

When I see her happily ensconced in front of something, I go back to Ben and say, "She's absolutely gorgeous, Ben. She's beautiful. I can't imagine what it must be like for you, only seeing her now and again." I put my arms around him.

"I hate it, I really do. And you've probably gathered, I get Grace's rules thrown at me all the time. It's not Daisy's fault, obviously, but I feel I can't escape Grace's hold, even when she's not here." I watch as he takes his coffee and goes to sit with Daisy on the sofa, a protective arm around her, as she snuggles into him.

We try to forget things and concentrate on giving Daisy a lovely day. Swimming is a great success – and the cinema too. I really love being with her; I'd forgotten how joyous young children can be. Her innocence, her laughter and her enjoyment of everything, brings back times I had with Holly and Adam and make me yearn for those times again.

If only life was as simple as a child's perspective.

I feel sad when they both leave to go back to Ben's place to sleep. Daisy's made me feel unsettled and I'm dwelling on the past too much. I've *got* to look forward, I've *got* to make a future. When I see Ben struggling with his present and his uncertain future, I realise that I'm not so badly off.

I've got Australia to look forward to ...

Chapter Nineteen

"Do you want me to take you to the airport on Friday? It'll be much easier than getting a train." We're in my flat, cuddled up on the sofa and he kisses my head, gently, and strokes my arm.

I hesitate. I'd love Ben to take me, but am I taking advantage? It would be so much more fun if he came and if I'm honest, a lot easier being taken in a car, instead of struggling with cases on public transport. Also, I want to spend my last few hours in England with him.

"Well? I'm very happy to, you know that. What time's the flight?"

"9.05. It would be an early start for you ..."

"I don't mind. Really. Early mornings aren't a problem for me. You know me, up with the lark, unlike someone I could mention," he smiles. "I'm going to miss you."

"I'm going to miss you, too," I say, and mean it. I smile at him and squeeze his hand. "It's come round really quickly. It's felt ages away for so long ..."

"You're going to have an amazing time. You deserve it, Anna. You've had a difficult few months and now it's *your* time. I'll still be here when you get back."

I look at him. It seems wrong to be leaving him when we've been together for such a short time, but ... it won't be forever and if it's meant to be, he'll wait for me. If it's not meant to be ... well ... that'll be the end of it.

It's Monday evening – four nights left to be with him. Our nights together are now much more regular and I'm sure that he'll stay for the next four.

"Okay, then, if you're sure. It would be lovely."

"That's a deal then. Have you done your online visa thing, yet?"

"All sorted. I had a horrible moment the other day when I suddenly wondered if my passport was in date – but it was, of course. I'm being super efficient – all the paperwork for this trip is in a special folder. I've even nearly finished packing my main bag – it's hard to imagine needing summer clothes in March."

"What will the temperatures be like then?"

"Well, around twenty-five degrees. Not hot by Australian standards, but a very pleasant English summer's day ... it'll get cooler as the holiday goes on, as it's going into their autumn ... so I've had to think of warmer things, layers and ..."

"Swimming costumes?"

"Yes, got three of those ... but I'm not convinced I'll go in the sea. Maybe a pool, if there's one."

"Have you heard from Adam about when he's coming?"

"Yes, he's even bought his ticket. God, I can't wait to see him."

My mind wanders off – I try to 'see' Adam as he is now. I'm sure I'll notice a huge difference in him. He sounds so much more mature in his messages. "He's going to stay for a few days. It'll be such a treat."

I show Ben the latest selfie of Adam on Facebook. "He looks so much like you, it's uncanny," he says, scrutinising the photo. "He's got exactly the same smile."

"Poor chap," I say, laughing. "Don't tell him, when you meet him."

The significance of what I say, hits me – implying so many things: that Adam will come back to England ... that Ben will be around in the future ... that we'll still be together.

"I hope I meet him, one day," he says, handing me back my phone. "And Holly. Do they know about me?"

"Well ... I've talked to Holly about you. She's always so funny about it. She's been egging me on, teasing me, asking questions. She thinks it's funny that you're younger than me. She seems to think you're my toy boy, or something. But I haven't said too much ... I wasn't sure where this was going and I didn't want to build her hopes up. She's so desperate for me to be happy."

Ben turns the volume of the TV down with the remote and stands up. I wonder what he's doing or what he's going to say. He goes out into the kitchen and comes back with two glasses and a bottle of champagne. "I bought this, this afternoon ... I thought we'd treat ourselves and celebrate your imminent adventure."

"Wow! That's so nice of you, Ben." He peels off the foil around the top of the bottle and after a few seconds, he pull the cork out, with a loud pop. Gaz comes into my mind – he was always terrified of corks popping, poor thing – I quickly grab a glass to catch the liquid pouring out and then he fills the rest of the glass and the other one. We stand, facing each other.

"So, a toast to ... Anna's Australian Adventure," he says, laughing and raising his glass to touch mine. "And here's hoping you have an amazing time." He leans forward and kisses me on the mouth. I can taste the fizz on his lips and savour the moment. We both swig from our glasses. It's taken a long time to get here, but at this precise moment, life is good. I've come a long way from that dark day in the park, when my world collapsed. I wonder briefly how Ben sees the future. Am I in it or is this his way of waving me off into the sunset?

"And I'd like to add something – sorry if I get sentimental, but that's me! I'd like to tell you how happy you've made me, Anna. That day I met you in the pub ... well, it was the start of a new phase in my life ... I think you're an incredible person and ... I'm just so pleased I met you that day." He touches my glass with his again and his eyes burrow into mine. I can feel flutters of excitement, joy ... desire, in my stomach. "I was so lonely till you and Gaz came along. You've made my situation with Daisy more bearable." My eyes water and I lean forward to kiss him.

We flop back down on the sofa, the TV picture still flickering mutely in the corner. We both put our glasses down and we kiss, the kind of kiss I'd forgotten existed, until recently. I draw back and lie against the sofa cushions and say, "Thank *you* for helping me in my new phase, Ben. I honestly don't know what I could have done without you. Especially when Gaz ..."

"Sh ... shh ..." he says and lifts my feet onto his lap and massages them. He bends my toes slightly and expertly rubs each one in turn. I close my eyes, loving the intimate sensation.

"You can do that all night, as far as I'm concerned," I say. "It's heaven."

"Let's go to bed ... and carry on there," he grins. "I think I'm falling for you, Mrs McCarthy."

"Why thank you, young Sir," I say, standing up and leading him to the bedroom.

ON THURSDAY, I RING Holly for a final chat before going. "So ... how's the lovely Ben, then? Any developments?" she laughs down the phone.

"Well, he's stayed ..."

"Wow, Mum! Get you! That's brill! So ... I take it, things have moved on a bit, then?"

"Yes, you could say that. I've even met his little daughter, Daisy. Did I tell you his ex is taking her up to Manchester to live?"

"No ... poor guy. That's awful. What'll he do?"

"There's not a lot he *can* do. He'll just have to do a lot of driving, I suppose."

"What was she like, the daughter, I mean?"

"Oh my God, she's so cute. It was great to be with a little one again. I hope you're going to hurry up and make me a grandmother soon?" I laugh. "How *is* Jed?" I add.

"Yea, he's great. Actually ... he told me he loved me the other day, Mum. I'm so happy, sometimes, I feel like I'll burst. You don't think there's a catch, do you? It just seems so incredible that two people can feel the same for each other – how lucky is that?"

"There definitely isn't a catch, Holly – I could see, right from the start, that you two were made for each other. I'm so happy for you. Don't get married while I'm away, will you?"

"Well, he hasn't asked me yet but ... if he does, I promise we'll wait till you come back! But, more to the point, when am I going to meet Ben?"

"You'll have to come down to Bath for the weekend and I'll introduce you, if we're still together after Oz."

"Of course you will be ..."

"It's early days, Holly. It's a shame I've got to go, really, as we've only just ..."

"I'm sure he'll be there when you get back, Mum. And if he isn't, then he's not worth having ..."

"Yes, you're right."

"Have you got a picture you could send me of him, just so I can see ..."

"Yes, I've got a couple. I'll send it when I put the phone down."

"Cool. Can't wait to see him!"

After we've said goodbye, I scroll through the pictures I have on my phone. There's one lovely one of Ben, posing with Gaz, their two faces together. I can't send that, it would upset Holly. There's another one of him holding Daisy. He's looking at her, laughing. I try to look at it objectively. What would Holly think of him, if she saw this one of him? He looks so devoted in this and he is a father of a young child – it would show him as he is. Maybe there's one, just on his own?

Then I come across a silly selfie we took on a walk – we're both grinning like loonies into the camera. The perspective's a bit odd, but it's a natural photo and I feel proud when I look at it. Proud of myself and proud that someone like Ben could be interested in me. I select that one and attached it to a message. *Here he is! Taken last week in a park. I think you'd like him ... Will text from departures. Love you, Mum.*

A text came winging back almost immediately. *Mum ... he looks SO lovely. Fabulous eyes. And you look SO happy. I KNOW I'll like him. Love you, Holly.*

WHEN WE GET TO THE airport, Ben insists on coming in with me. I tell him to drop me off, but he wants to come and wave me off, he says. We've ended up being really early. The traffic at that time of the morning was clear and there were no holdups anywhere.

We park the car in the car park and Ben gallantly carries my case for me. I can feel the excitement bubbling around inside me as we walk along the moving corridors, past huge advertisements. Being a slow walker, I get a buzz out of pretending I'm walking really fast as the conveyor whizzes me along towards the departures hall.

We join the long queue to drop off my large case. I read all the notices about things that shouldn't be in a case and start to panic that I might have inadvertently packed a knife, a bomb or a stack of drugs. The rather beautiful girl at the desk takes everything in her stride, quickly dealing with my paperwork and attaching the long sticky ID on my case and it jerks off, through the plastic strips. I find it hard to believe that next time I see it, I will be so far away.

"Have a good flight," she says and I take my passport and boarding pass from her. How can anyone look so immaculate, I wonder? Her make up looks as if it's just been applied, every hair on her head is in its place and her uniform appears to have just come out of the packet.

"She makes me feel thoroughly underdressed," I laugh to Ben, as we walk away with my hand luggage. There are hoards of people everywhere and we push our way over to a café. I haven't got to go through yet – I've got at least half an hour before I need to even think about it.

"That was all very straightforward, anyway," says Ben. "Let's hope the rest of the journey is that easy. It says 'On Time' on the board, anyway."

"I wish I could have got an upgrade. People say, if you're on your own, sometimes it's easy to ..."

"You should have asked."

"Oh, I'll be okay. I intend to watch lots of films and I've got a sleeping pill if I get desperate."

We order coffees and sit down in the corner. It doesn't seem long ago that I was saying goodbye to Adam and now it's me. I swallow the coffee, but when it hits my stomach, I feel sick.

"Will you text me when you get there?" says Ben.

"Of course."

We're both silent for a while. Then Ben says, "Will you miss me?"

"You know I will," I say and reach over the table for his hand. "You'll get bored with the number of texts and messages I'll send you ..."

He reaches into his jacket pocket and comes out with a small wrapped object. "This is for you. I thought you might find it useful."

I take it, looking in his eyes. "Thank you."

I unwrap it and discover a small, very high-tech camera. "Ben, that's fantastic. I was just going to use my phone. Now, I can take some really great shots. Thank you so much. That's so thoughtful." I lean over and kiss him.

"I thought, the smaller the better. I didn't think you'd want something big and heavy to carry around."

"No, it's perfect. I'll treasure it."

We finish our coffee and walk over to the gate, where we must say goodbye.

"Thanks for everything," I say. I don't know what else I can, or should say. He hugs me hard and we stand there, unable to leave each other. His arms grip me so hard, I can feel their strength around me. Why did I arrange this holiday now? I want to stay here ...

"Have a wonderful time ... and I'll be here when you come home." He kisses me on the cheek and squeezes my hand. "Off you go," and he grabs my shoulders and turns me to face the right direction.

Picking up my small case, I walk towards the tapes that make you walk up and down, up and down, until you reach passport control. I enter the zig-zag maze and when I reach the desk, I turn to see if he's still there. He's waiting, he smiles at me, lifting his hand, shoulder height, to wave.

I show my passport and then it's time to go behind a wall. I wave, he waves, and I'm gone.

Chapter Twenty

Being on my own in departures is strange. It's as if I'm in another world, which effectively, I am. I'm in limbo – not officially in England any more – and not in another country, either. I think that it's a suitable metaphor for my life at the moment (typical English teacher) – in a no man's land, where I wander, not knowing whether to go back to my homeland, or forge forward into new territory. My homeland has been denied me, though. No visa to get back into the life I had. I have no real choice. It's new territory or ... be shot, trying to breach the barbed wire back.

I lose myself in the duty-free, fending off over-helpful assistants, who try to spray me with the latest Dior product, as I walk past. I smile politely and keep my wrists to myself. I contemplate buying some high-priced face cream that claims it can miraculously convert my fifty-five year old face to one of a twenty year old, and then think better of it. Let's be honest, you can't hold back time; it marches on relentlessly and it's better to accept it. People who go that one step further with Botox or surgery, end up looking like freaks with blank expressions. Like most women, I want to look my best, but I don't believe the hype of these creams. You age – get over it, I say.

Having saved myself £70 on a pot of promises, I escape the shops and retire to a restaurant where I order an omelette and salad, an orange juice and a latte. I'm working on the principle that I don't know where my next meal's coming from, so I might as well stock up, while I can. I read the paper while I'm eating and relax into the situation I find myself in – enforced waiting.

I make my way down to the gate at the appropriate time and feel relieved I've given myself so much time – it's a huge hike, and I feel like I'm never going to get there. The moving corridors stretch on into what looks like infinity.

We then all wait in a holding area and I gaze out of the window at the plane I'm catching. It's the biggest plane I've ever seen – an A380. It's size and power are overwhelming – it's beautiful, I admit, but the thought of it actually being able to fly is terrifying – how can something that big, possibly take off? I take a picture of it with my phone and as there's 3G in the terminal, I upload it to Facebook. *My taxi awaits!* I write as a caption. It's not long before people are 'liking' my picture – Adam writes a comment – *See you soon!* Holly writes, *Byeeeee! Have a safe journey and an AMAZING time.*

Modern technology is so weird, sometimes – it really does make you feel connected.

We enter the plane through Business Class, which seems a bit mean – is it designed to put us mere 'economy' people in our place? Huge seats which lie flat and that appear to have their own space around them, sit there, flaunting their opulence. Only a couple of them are occupied and I consider sliding into one, thinking the staff may not notice me. I really regret not asking for upgrade now.

However, I'm pleasantly surprised when I eventually get to my seat. It's large, spacious, comfortable and a good-sized screen is in front of me. I'd booked myself into an aisle seat, with a view to easy access to the loo. I hate that feeling of being trapped by some large man, who looks as if he's dead, never mind asleep.

The plane fills up and I wait to see who will be next to me. The last stragglers come in and finally, I realise no one is coming – I've got the row of three seats to myself. I can't believe it. I look around and there are several empty rows. This is turning into a good flight.

All the stewardesses are as beautiful and well turned out as the one behind the desk in the terminal. I wonder how they get away with only recruiting slim, attractive people? They walk seductively along the aisles, checking we've all fastened our belts and making sure the overhead lockers are secure, and then we run through the farce of the safety film. I always think that if it's got to the point that we've landed on water, I will have died of fright by then, so putting on the safety jacket and blowing my whistle, won't be an option, so I try not to listen to the film – deliberately blocking it out, except for the 'brace, brace' bit, which somehow penetrates my brain. Will the 'brace' position really make any difference when we're landing on water (or land) in a thing the size of high-rise building?

I love the tone of voice of the pilot – they must all go on training courses on how to sound authoritative, confident and in complete control. He makes it all sound so simple – we're just going to cruise along at a certain height and have a jolly time. His voice convinces me that he's done this so many times, he could do it in his sleep, and as we taxi along, I do indeed, 'sit back and relax' as he told me to do.

As we surge forward down the runway, with what feels like enough thrust to get us to the moon, I realise I really *am* on an adventure. I can't remember ever going on a plane on my own – crazy to have got this old and be so inexperienced. The wheels leave the ground and our ascent is smooth and quiet. The 380 must have new sound proofing – it's positively peaceful. And I feel peaceful too – I'm in the hands of the airline. I can make no contribution to the outcome of the journey; I have no responsibilities, nothing to do. I have no one to worry about. It's just me. I've left Ben, David, Holly, school, Bath, my flat ... my *life,* behind.

I feel a release, as if for the first time in years, I can think about ... me.

THE QUIETNESS OF TAKE-off is replaced by the penetrating hum of the engines, as we settle down into the flight. The hours pass – I read my Kindle, a Hello magazine, The Times – and then I go through their entertainment system, which is full of hundreds of films, TV programmes, documentaries and music. Fortunately, Adam told me to bring my own ear-phones and I plug myself in and watch a good movie. Meals come and go, I wend my way down the aisle a few times and still there are three hours to go to Dubai.

Why is it that time on an aircraft grinds to a halt?

Even though I'm not particularly tired, I decide to take advantage of the empty seats and I get my travel pillow, cover myself with my coat (the air-conditioning is positively icy) and lie down. Sleep comes and goes – any little turbulence wakes me with a jump. I'm saving my sleeping pill for the Dubai to Adelaide bit. It will be through my night and I'll really want to sleep by then.

After a while, I sit up again feeling dishevelled. I decide to watch another film and by the time I've watched that, we're beginning our descent. David always liked to look out of the windows and try to point out things to me as we got lower, but I was never keen. The reality of what we're doing, hurtling towards a densely populated metropolis, looking for a straight strip of land to put our wheels on, is something I don't want to dwell on. So, I read my Kindle intently, pretending to myself that I'm sitting in my living room. Honestly, anyone watching me would think I'm the coolest traveller – no nerves on display at all – but when the wheels touch down, I secretly thank God for another miraculous escape from death.

We have seven hours to waste in Dubai, before we continue our journey. It seems a shame to be somewhere so new and exciting and only see the airport duty free area, but that's how it works. I *still* resist the pull of the face cream. I wander aimlessly, drink coffee, read, eat sweets, feel sick with tiredness, feel bored, frustrated and exist. I go to the gate too early, simply for a change of scene.

Back on a smaller plane – the 380's too big for the airport in Adelaide – still comfortable, but this time, I've got a couple sitting next to me. Let's hope they don't have my desire to go the loo every five minutes.

This part of the journey is a lot longer – five hours in and I feel as if I may grow senile and die on this plane. I've had a meal, a drink, a trip to the loo, a film and a sleeping pill and I'm wide awake. The couple next to me are snoring contentedly and everyone around me is in a comatose state – mouths open, heads at funny angles, headphones akimbo. I put my pillow round my neck, push my chair back into the so-called reclining position, cover myself with my coat and close my eyes. The hum is annoying. My neck isn't comfortable. I have an itch, which I can't scratch. My back aches. My legs have got jumpy leg syndrome. My skin's dry. I need a drink. I can't keep still.

Without noticing, I fall asleep. I wake up with a cricked neck, dry mouth and feeling like I've been asleep for hours. I look at my watch and my heart sinks – it says I've still got nearly five hours to go. How can that be? I could have sworn I'd slept for ages.

I go to the loo and splash my face with water and moisturise it with the hand cream provided. Perhaps that face cream was a good idea, after all? I could do with some serious help. I brush my hair and do my teeth with the little brush and tube of toothpaste we were given at the beginning of the journey. I emerge feeling a little more human and stand outside the door of the toilet, stretching my legs and flexing my ankles. The cabin is in near total darkness and I envy people I see, when I walk back down the aisle, who all are asleep. What's wrong with me that I can't?

I watch an American comedy that seems particularly unfunny with its forced jokes and canned laughter. I've decided I have no idea what the time actually is, either in England or Australia; all I know is that I'm watching something in semi-darkness, surrounded by sleeping people, thousands of feet in the air.

I must have drifted off, as I'm suddenly aware of light, movement and the smell of airline food. It's a bit like being in hospital, being woken up at some godawful time with a tray of congealed food for your breakfast. Still, the coffee revives me and I realise I'm hungry.

After another trip to the loo to cleanse and moisturise, it doesn't seem long till we are descending – we've reached Australia; I can't believe it. We have flown into the day and now it's night time in Adelaide. The pilot has kindly informed us it's going to be 20.05 when we land. I've lost the concept of time completely now; my body and mind are in a state of utter confusion.

I glimpse snatches of lights and buildings across my companions – we appear to be low over the suburbs of Adelaide. I look ahead, not wanting to see how close we are. The bump comes soon after and we screech down the runway, finally coming to stop.

I'm here.

"ANNA, ANNA," I HEAR, as I emerge, like a drunk, from customs. My head is fuzzy, my legs weak, but I'm so relieved to be able to walk on the ground. I look around the mass of people and see Jane, waving and beaming. Marcus is by her side. As I walk towards them, I find tears are on my cheeks – I've missed by sister, but I've only just acknowledged it. My life with David was enough for me, I didn't need anyone else. Now, without him, I understand how important my sister is.

We throw our arms around each other and hug and hug. It's been years since we actually touched each other and it feels like we never want to let each other go.

"Wow, you look amazing," I say. I've already taken in her short, cropped hair, her long slim arms and her skinny, boy-like figure. Her clothes are loose on her, fashionable and informal – she's wearing cropped trousers with a floral top with a low, scooped neck, showing off her bony chest and lack of bosom. She's wearing the obligatory thongs, her toe nails, bubblegum pink. She looks fresh and younger than her years. I feel a wreck beside her.

"So do you," she says. "You must be exhausted after the flight."

"Marcus, lovely to see you," I say, as he too hugs me. I'm almost swallowed up in his huge, bear-like grip. He's tall, 6'3" and as I had thought, is a lot larger all round than when I saw him last.

"Let me take your case, Anna," he says, wheeling it along and putting my small case on top of the large one. He strides ahead and Jane and I walk, arm in arm behind him.

"It's only twenty minutes to the house ... so tell me about the flight," Jane says, "was it okay?"

"Well, it's okay, now it's over," I say, "but at the time, it was tedious ... beyond tedious! I couldn't really sleep on either flight and we had hours to hang about in Dubai. I feel as I've been in a parallel universe."

"That's why we haven't been back to the UK. I don't think I could take it. Marcus does a lot of flying anyway, for his job ..."

"So, here's the car," he says. "Hop in and we'll get you home and you can have a nice shower, meal and bed. You'll feel fine in the morning."

"I hope so," I say.

We chat on the journey, but my mind is foggy and I feel I'm going through the motions. I gaze out of the window, amazed that I'm somewhere so exotic as ... Australia.

Soon, we pull into a drive and we head into the house. It's huge, with white walls, white painted wooden floors and colourful artwork on the walls, but I'm so tired, I can't take it all in. There are large picture windows and they tell me there are spectacular views over the ocean, but all I can see are some flickering lights. I'm disorientated and when they show me through to my bedroom, I stare longingly at the bed, wanting to flop down on it, there and then.

I feel considerably better after a shower in my own en-suite bathroom – again all white, with a large drenching shower head that pummels my tired brain with refreshing hot water.

Jane has poured me a large glass of white wine and she produces calamari and salad which we eat, sitting at a stylish long wooden table. The alcohol goes straight to my head and I can hear my voice as something detached from me. They tell me about their jobs, show me around the rest of the house, but I feel like a zombie.

"It's no good, Jane, I'm going to have to get some sleep before I keel over. Do you mind if I go to bed now? Sorry ... but ..."

"No, don't be silly. Go! We can chat properly in the morning."

"I thought jet-lag was a myth, but it isn't," I laugh. "I've never felt quite like this before ..."

"Go ... go on. We won't wake you in the morning. Sleep as long as you want."

I drag my feet to the bedroom. I can't face unpacking – David would have had everything hanging up by now and in drawers, but for once, I can do what I want to do, which is, go to sleep without any further interruptions.

I land on the bed. As Mum used to say ... a short portion of death, hits me like a hammer and I pass out.

Chapter Twenty-One

I wake at midday the next day, still feeling groggy, so I have another shower and wander out to see where Jane and Marcus are.

"So ... you've finally woken up!" says Marcus. "Feeling better?"

"I think so," I say, unconvincingly. The light's so bright, I'm squinting. I walk to the windows to see the view. I'm unprepared for the scene that greets me. Their house is overlooking the most amazing beach I've ever seen – it stretches for miles both left and right, with white sand and azure sea. Between the house and the beach is just a small road; there are a few cars driving slowly along it. Then there is a pedestrian way, with people power-walking, running and generally being energetic. I can see steps down onto the beach – there are a few people on the sand, but no one in the sea.

"Oh my God, this is amazing," I say, gazing at what looks like paradise. "No wonder you decided to stay. Why would you ever want to move from here?"

"I know ... we're so lucky, aren't we?" says Jane, coming to stand next to me. "The city's to our right. You can walk for miles, either way. I thought if you feel up to it, we'd go for a walk into Brighton, which is left, after lunch. It's full of cool coffee shops

– we could wander down there and sit and watch the world go buy."

"That sounds just what I need. Some exercise and a strong coffee."

"If you don't mind, I'll stay here," says Marcus, "I've got masses of work I need to do, before tomorrow."

"No, that's fine, of course," I say.

"It'll give you two girls time to catch up properly," he says and wanders off into his office.

"Poor Marcus, he's so stressed at the moment. He's got this huge project at work ..."

"Please ... you two must just carry on as normal. I'm just grateful to be here. Are you going to be able to take any time off?"

"Well, I've persuaded Marcus to take, not next week, but the next, off. We thought we could all go off down the Murray River for a few days. I hope you don't mind, but I've already booked it. Here, this is the brochure," says Jane, handing me a colourful booklet with this mammoth houseboat on the front.

"This looks amazing, Jane. How much do I owe you?"

"Nothing ... it's our treat. We've got a friend who owns a shack on the river and he says we can tie up one night at his place."

"It all sounds great. What else have you got planned?"

"We'll go out for day trips and I thought when we're working, you could either hang out here or take yourself off into the city. When's Adam coming? Do you know yet?"

"Yea – in about three weeks. He's coming on his own for five days. Is that okay with you?"

"Fine. I can't wait to see him. I was working it out the other day, the last time I saw him, he was four!"

"I'm so excited to see him. Actually, Jane, I must just text him and Holly and tell them I've arrived safely. I did promise ..."

"Yea, fine, you do that and I'll get a bit of lunch ready."

I go into my bedroom to find my phone and turning it on, I find that I have two new messages. One from Ben and one from David.

Ben: *I hope by the time you get this you're at your sisters and have recovered from the journey. Daisy leaves for Manchester soon – dreading it. Just got a huge new job, so busy. Seems odd here without you. Love Ben xx*

I feel a longing for Ben when I read his words ... I can't believe I've got someone who cares for me, like he seems to.

I'm so intrigued about why David has texted me that I don't reply immediately to Ben. I open David's:

I thought I ought to let you know that Suzie is expecting our child – Holly and Adam don't know yet and I wanted you to know first. She's due in October and we're very happy, as you can imagine. I hope your trip to Australia gives you all you hoped. David.

My heart lurches. I read it several times, not quite believing it. Does he really think that I can 'imagine' their happiness? Has he forgotten how we so wanted a third child and I was told I couldn't have any more? Is he just cruel or thoughtless; so wound up with his own present happiness that he's forgotten the past completely?

DO YOU REMEMBER, DAVID, the day I went for some tests, to see why we weren't having any luck conceiving, after Adam?

You were with me and were waiting outside when I came out of the consultation room. You stood up – you knew, instinctively, that it wasn't good news, and you wrapped me in your arms.

You took me home, telling me how much you loved me and assuring me that our life was complete and that we were fine how we were. I cried myself to sleep that night.

Maybe we weren't at all fine, David?

I SIT ON THE BED, MY legs feeling weak and trembly.

I press 'reply' to David and write: *Nice of you to let me know. No, I can't imagine how happy you are. Thanks for ruining my first day in Australia. Anna*

I press 'send' before I can change my mind. How dare he assume that his news is going to be welcome. Does he not realise that it's so hurtful? My heart is thumping in my chest and I go hot all over.

Should I have sent such a bitter text?

Still, it's too late now. I can't un-send it. If it was a letter, I perhaps would have torn it up and re-written it.

I write a quick text to Ben; I try to reassure him that Daisy going, isn't going to change anything, but in my heart, I know it is. I tell him I miss him too, which is true and then quickly text Holly:

I'm here! Journey was SO long, but I got here in the end. Their house is A-maz-ing! Will take some pictures this afternoon and send them later. Love you, Mum xx

I write something similar to Adam and then hear Jane call me.

"Is everything okay?" she says, as I enter the kitchen. "You look as white as a sheet." Even after all these years, my sister can read me like a book.

"Well ..."

"What's happened? Is it Holly?"

"No, no, it's not Holly. It's ..."

"What, Anna?"

"David ... there was a message from him ... kindly informing that Suzie's up the duff ..."

"Oh my God ... he's too old to be a father again ... what's he playing at?"

"I know ... he seems to think that I can imagine their happiness ... for God's sake." I slump down on a chair and Jane comes and stands behind me, putting her arms around me.

"He really has turned into a bit of a bastard, Anna. I thought I liked him ..."

"He's changed ... this Suzie woman has addled his brain. He's forgotten how badly I wanted a third child ... sorry, Jane. I know how awful it must be for you, me whingeing on about not having a third when ..."

"Don't worry ... I've got over that now ... I've learned to live with it and accept it. You have to – don't you? But it's a good thing he's thousands of miles away. If he was here, I'd want to sock him."

I stand up and go and look at the view again. The sun, sea and beach lift my spirits and I say, "Come on, let's forget him and his stupid mid-life crisis and go out into the fresh air."

"More like old-life crisis," Jane giggles. "Yes, let's eat and go. Life's too short to worry about men ..."

I wonder if there's more to Marcus' stress than she's letting on. I resolve to find out and say, "Yes, let's go out for a girly walk and talk."

And that's exactly what we do.

WE WALK DOWN ONTO THE sand, taking off our thongs at the bottom of the steps. I've got my phone in my pocket and I take pictures of the beach – it's so stunning, I can't believe it. I'll email them later to Holly, but I'm not sure she'll see how truly beautiful it is.

I run to the sea's edge and feel the temperature of the water, my feet tingling in the cool, salty water. It's considerably warmer than the Atlantic in Cornwall and I vow to go in properly, tomorrow. We walk the half hour or so along to Brighton, seeing the jetty in the distance the whole way. For a while, we don't appear to be getting any nearer it, but gradually it looms larger on the horizon. After the long journey, the feel of the sand beneath my toes, the wind in my hair and the sun of my face, is magical. To hell with David and Suzie Barton and their future sprog, I say to myself. Let them go procreate and live happily ever after!

I tell Jane about Ben; I show her the same picture I showed Holly on my mobile phone, and as I tell her about him, I wish he was here to walk with, along the sand. He'd love it and I'd love him to be here. A man walks past with a dog on a lead and for a brief moment, I remember Gaz. He'd love this too.

I wait for Jane to tell me Ben's too young for me, but she doesn't. All she says is, "You look very happy together," and I'm grateful to her.

We meander along the jetty, to the end. The black metal structure, jutting out into the ocean, standing majestic, surrounded by aquamarine water, is a world away from the piers of England, whipped by grey waves. The colour of the sky is piercing, jaw-dropping, mind-blowing blue and it invades my senses with its power, vibrating my mind, grabbing me by the shoulders and shaking me out of my previous sadness.

I feel young and new, happy and excited to be here, in this land of colour. The wind carries the smell of the sea on its gusts, my eyes are assaulted by the vastness of the horizon and my legs stretch and enjoy the breezy walk back along the length of the jetty. I stop and watch someone fishing and remember the fear of sharks, lurking in the deep. But I don't care, right now – life is different and I enjoy the novelty, the newness, the feeling of being somewhere I've never even dreamt of before.

We walk up to the row of shops and cafés and find a seat in the sun. As I look around at the people sitting near us or walking slowly past, I'm envious of Jane's life. This is like living in Bath with its café culture, but with the sea at the bottom of the road, glistening and inviting, and a large city a short train ride away. The waitress brings us our delicious coffees and I sit, soaking up the sun, turning to it, like a flower, opening its petals as it feels its warmth.

I've missed having Jane to confide in; we talk for a long time about David, the children and Ben. It's almost as if I'm talking about someone else; my English life is drifting away from me. She listens, nodding her head and smiling.

"Enough about me ... you must be getting sick of hearing about my soap opera of a life," I laugh. "Tell me about you and Marcus."

There's a small hesitation – she looks away and I wonder if she doesn't want to talk. "We need a second cup – hold on, I'll just go in and order them," and she disappears inside.

After a few minutes, she comes out and says, "They'll be out in a second. So ... me and Marcus. What do you want to know?"

"So ... well, all I meant was ... is everything okay with you two? I might be being too sensitive but ..."

"No, you're not. How does he seem to you?" The waitress deposits the second cups of coffee and takes away our used cups. We wait till she's gone and then I continue.

"Well ... you've mentioned that he's stressed and he ... does come over as being ... a bit uptight."

"That's putting it mildly," Jane says. I detect a sheen of tears in her eyes and reach across and touch her hand. "He's pretty difficult to live with ..."

"He's obviously been on his best behaviour for me," I say, "but he has put on quite a lot of weight and that can't be good for his blood pressure."

"I'm always trying to get him to lose weight ... and to drink less." She wipes her eyes and looks away again.

"Is drinking ... a problem?"

"You could say that."

"Is he violent ..."

"No ...no ... nothing like that ... it's just ... it's just that he drinks every night and often during the day too. He was very restrained when you were there last night, but normally it would have been at least two bottles of wine. He then falls asleep – or should I say, passes out, most evenings ... I'm so worried about him."

"Has he got financial worries or … I know you said he had a huge project at work?"

"I don't know anymore whether it's the work that's making him stressed or the wine making things worse … it's a vicious circle. We're okay financially, but over the years, he's come to hate his work and all the pressure it brings. I think he's basically very unhappy and he drinks to … forget. But of course, it doesn't help; it never does."

"Have you tried talking to him?"

"Yes, all the time, but he shuts me out. He refuses to go to the doctor, as most men do."

"How long has it been like this?"

"I suppose it's been building up for years …"

"Why have you never said anything to me?"

"I didn't want to burden you and it's difficult at a distance. It feels really disloyal, somehow, too. I shouldn't be slagging off my husband. I love him, I really do. I want to help him."

"Look, you're not slagging him off, you're just telling me about your life. It can't be easy for you and you need to share it with someone or you'll go insane. Have you talked to anyone else about it?"

"No … all our friends know he drinks, but they have no idea how bad it's got."

I smile across at her and say, "Well, I'm here now. You must talk to me whenever you want. I could try and talk …"

"No," she says. "That wouldn't be a good idea. He'd hate that."

"Okay … I won't say a thing. You and I will talk together and see if we can come up with some sort of plan. I don't know what, at the moment, but …"

"It's good just talking to you. I feel like a weight's been lifted, somehow." She runs her hand through her hair. "Life's complicated, isn't it?"

"It is. Who would have thought when we were children, that our lives would bring us here? I was always so envious of you, leaving. I thought you were leading this perfect life in paradise. My life seemed so dull in comparison. Yours was all creative and fun – I felt you'd 'escaped' from the mundane."

We both drink our coffee and are silent for a few seconds.

Jane says, "Wherever you are in the world, whether it's by the ocean or in a Regency city or in a country village, your demons are with you, aren't they? I was so sure I'd have children – I was envious of *you* – I longed for your life, being mother to two beautiful children. But it wasn't meant to be for me. Maybe if we'd had children, Marcus wouldn't be in the state he is now ... maybe he'd be happy?"

"You can't think like that ... you have to deal with the situation you have now and don't dwell on what might have been. I'm sure Marcus loves you very much and has just lost his way."

She stares into the distance and a look of sadness falls onto her face. After a while, she says, "Yea, you're right. That's a good phrase for him ... he's lost his way."

My heart goes out to her. I've been so wound up in my own problems that I didn't even consider what her life's really like. It's so easy to be fooled by a lovely house, an amazing view ... but we all have our problems, don't we?

"We're a right pair, aren't we?" I laugh. "What would Mum say about our situations, do you think?"

"God knows. That generation would just 'put up and shut up' I suppose."

"I think Mum would be very supportive to you, if she was alive," I say. "She'd probably give Marcus a right good talking to!"

"Heaven forbid. I wonder what she'd think of David's escapades?"

"She'd be horrified. She worshipped the ground he walked on. He could do no wrong."

"Come on, let's pay and walk back. Do you fancy an enormous gelato, while we're walking?" says Jane. "We don't need to worry about our weight, do we?"

"Speak for yourself! But today, I don't care ... I'm on holiday. When have you ever known me turn down an ice cream?"

We buy two huge cones with the most delicious flavours, piled high, and walk back along the beach.

My first day in Adelaide has been wonderful.

I feel I've found my sister again; we've confided in each other and just being together, has helped us both.

Chapter Twenty-Two

My first week passes in a flash. Jane has an office in the house, where she works every day. She too has a lot of work on at the moment and even though it's tempting to take time out while I'm here, she's very conscientious and refuses to slip out of her routine of working nine till one, and two to five. Unlike Marcus and me, she loves her job, so it's not a problem. She's so good at it too – she shows me the book she's working on at the moment and I'm amazed at her artwork and interpretation of the story.

So, I leave her to her endeavours and do my own thing. I walk on the beach, one day, down to Glenelg and back; another day, I catch a train into the City and explore. Another day, I go to the local sports centre and plough up and down the olympic size pool, which I love, as it's outside, and I can get some exercise and enjoy the sun, at the same time. Everyone here looks tanned and fit, unlike at the pool back home. No one hangs around chatting and getting in each other's way. It's as if everyone is on a mission to be more macho, more tanned ... more Aussie, than the next person.

Another day, I swim in the ocean, telling myself the sharks won't surely come into the shallows? I spot the helicopter shark patrol, which both worries me and comforts me, but I carry on regardless. If a shark eats me ... well ... I hope he chokes on my old skin.

I find I'm quite happy on my own, exploring the area. The day I go into the City, I positively enjoy finding my way around, using maps and apps on my phone. I go down to the river, I admire the wonderful buildings with their ornate balconies and relax in a park. I love its compact layout and relaxed, laid-back approach to city life.

I try to help Jane, by cooking supper on a few nights; I borrow their car and go to buy ingredients from the local supermarket. I've always loved exploring other country's food shops and I wander up and down the aisles admiring the choice. I thought we had a good selection of yoghurt back home. Here, you need to make some serious decisions.

I discover that liquor, as Aussies call booze, isn't sold in supermarkets, but in 'bottle shops' so I go two shops down the road. I don't really know what to do about wine – I buy some, not knowing if Jane will curse me or not, but it feels wrong not to. I try to choose local wine from the Adelaide Hills' vineyards, which Jane says we'll visit later. The guy serving offers me some 'clean skins' – bottles with no labels – and says what a good buy they are. I succumb and buy two.

I watch Marcus like a hawk, now that I know the truth. He tries to be friendly, but I can see he's distant and dismissive with Jane. He reaches for a glass, almost the moment he comes in from work and keeps it permanently topped up, during the evening. He does indeed fall asleep in front of the TV and I notice Jane leaves him snoring and slumped in a chair, most nights. I worry what to do, but think there's little I can do. It's got to be *him* who sees the light in the end.

The following weekend, they are both the perfect hosts and take me on a road trip with one night in a B and B. We go down the Fleurieu Peninsular, visiting places with exotic Aboriginal names. We drive onto the beach at Aldinga, even though we're not in a four by four and then we drive all the way down to Cape Jervis, where the ferry goes to Kangaroo island. The weather becomes positively English down there and we end up eating fish and chips in the steamed up car, as the rain pours down outside.

We drive along the coast to Victor Harbour and gaze down at Horseshoe Bay; we go to Port Elliot and finally Goolwa, the mouth of the mighty Murray. We walk to the barrage and see pelicans, black swans and even seals, basking quietly in the sun. The light down there is stunning and I take some great photos on my new camera. A bird with an amazing warbling sound, which Jane tells me is a Murray magpie, sits and poses for me. He lets me go right up to him as he sits on a wooden post and stays long enough for me to practise taking close-ups.

I love our native bird population and their familiar songs, but the thing that's struck me here very forcefully has been the beauty and difference of Australian birds. Virtually none of them are familiar to me – except the sparrow. I hear a constant cacophony of calls that I don't recognise and when I look up, I see flashes of bright colours - the iridescent pink of the galah, the bright green of the lorikeet and the red and blue of the rosella. I'm driving Jane mad by constantly pointing and asking for their names. To me, they are the defining thing that makes me realise I'm somewhere far away from the land of robins and blackbirds. Their voices and their colours dazzle me.

I feel guilty that Jane and Marcus are doing all this travelling – they must have been to these places many times – but they don't seem to mind and we have fun together, stopping for refreshments in pubs and cafés. I love the variety of the food and the unusual menus, even in the most simple of establishments. The Aussies certainly know how to eat well.

Marcus does most of the driving and I'm pleased to see he doesn't drink when we stop; I grab a little smile from Jane when he comes back to the table with a pint of orange juice, but can see that he eats huge amounts. I tend to choose the salads wherever we go – I look back at the salad I had with Holly after Warhorse and decide Australian salads are even better than that. They combine unusual flavours and textures, herbs and nuts.

I could get used to this.

The trip down the Murray is scheduled for Tuesday. Even though I've only been driven around all weekend, I'm exhausted on the Monday. I get up late and mooch about, catching up on emails and Facebook, read my book and swim in the mighty Gulf of St Vincent, which I learn is the official name of the sea off Adelaide. Ben and I are writing little emails to each other every day. It's strange, but just the process of writing to him, is making our relationship stronger somehow. We're sharing our innermost thoughts with each other, along with the more mundane everyday occurrences.

That Monday evening, things are particularly fraught in the house; I can sense the atmosphere the moment I get in from my walk. Marcus is already drinking and poor Jane is trying to get the food organised for our trip. There are no shops where we're going and so we have to take everything with us. I muck in and when we realise we're missing a few important items, I offer to go and get them, wanting to get out of the house.

I notice that there's a lot of wine in bottles and cartons in the bags, but I tell myself we're away for three nights, so that's fair enough.

We're up early the next day and drive quite a way to a place called Mannum, where we are to get on our houseboat. We park up near the boat we've been allocated and start to load our things. I'm amazed at how big it is and begin to get nervous – I wonder if either Jane or Marcus has any idea about driving the thing?

Trying to sound nonchalant, I say as I'm loading the fridge, "So ... who's going to drive the boat, then? I hope you're not relying on me!"

"Marcus and I have done this before, don't worry. We haven't gone from this Marina, but we've done the whole houseboat thing, further up the river. They look huge, but to be honest, they're easy to drive. They go so slowly ... you'll see."

After a long time, filling in forms and being told in minute detail how the boat works, we set off. One of the men manoeuvres the houseboat through a maze of other boats, but then, when he's got us out of the enclosed space of the Marina, he jumps off, waves and we're on our own.

Marcus drives and I begin to relax, as I see he's perfectly competent. It does, indeed, go *very* slowly – you could keep up with it, if it was possible to walk alongside.

As we 'set sail' Jane and I explore the boat – it's much bigger than we need as it sleeps six. It's luxurious; I test my bed and as I lie on it, I can see the river banks slipping by, outside the window. I decide to go up to the top deck and stand at the front, mesmerised by the slow passing scenery. I've got my camera round my neck and take pictures of pelicans coming in to land, in their comical way. There are hundreds of them floating past, oblivious to our presence; the river is a mysterious green colour and the sandy earth, on each side, makes for a beautiful backdrop.

We make sure that Marcus is okay driving the boat and get some coffee. "Do you want me to take over?" asks Jane.

"No, I'm fine," he says, "I find it relaxing. I can think about ... *nothing.*"

I think this is perhaps exactly what he needs. The slow pace of the boat forces us all to relax. There is nothing to do ... but drift.

I can only compare it to being on a canal boat in England – which David and I did many years ago. You feel cut off from the outside world, as if you're travelling vast distances, but in reality, you're covering very few miles. Here though, there are no locks to negotiate, no pubs to pass. There are just miles and miles of pre-historic looking trees, half-submerged in water, or clinging to the edge, with cormorants drying their wings, in silence, on their branches.

I feel as if I'm suspended in time: no past, no future, just the present, in all its glory and quiet beauty. I can't help but be 'at one' with nature here; it's just me, the gentle swoosh of the water, the sapphire blue sky and the red earth.

We see very few other houseboats; one comes by in the opposite direction and we wave languidly to the people on board. A speedboat with two water skiers behind it, drives past and shocks us out of dreamlike trance; we've almost forgotten that noise and motion exists.

Jane takes over the driving for a while. Marcus and I lie down on the sun loungers on the top deck and simply watch the world go by. It's so peaceful, I fall asleep.

I'm woken suddenly, by a distant noise I don't understand.

"What's that?" I say, sitting up.

"Corellas," says Marcus.

"What are *they*?" I say, now standing up, trying to see the cause of the commotion. And then I do. There are hundreds, or maybe even thousands, of white birds heading our way. They are all squawking and screaming – the sound is deafening. I grab my camera to try to capture the sheer numbers of birds speeding past us, but I give up and simply marvel at the phenomenon.

"Noisy bastards," says Marcus.

"They're amazing," I shout above the noise. "What are they doing?"

"They're going to roost in the trees."

"Wow! That was incredible," I say, sitting back down as the stragglers go past. "Thank you so much for this trip, Marcus. What an amazing experience. I'm sure I'd never have seen any of this if we hadn't done it ..."

"Yea, we thought you'd like it. I just wish life could always be like this – so laid back, so relaxed. I feel so ... so ... uptight ... most of the time, and today, for the first time in ages, I feel as if ... as if I can breathe."

He lies back and closes his eyes, but even so, I feel as if he wants to talk, so I say, "Life's too short to feel like that, Marcus. Maybe you should do something ..."

He opens his eyes and tilts his head towards me. "What can I do?"

"Have you ever thought of retiring? Like me. How old are you?"

"I'm only fifty-eight ..."

"Well, maybe you should think of ... changing your lifestyle?" I hope I'm not speaking out of turn, but I want to help. "Jane mentioned that you have a huge project on at work and that you're finding it all too stressful. Could you perhaps ..."

"Yea, she's right there. But, Jane doesn't realise how much money we need to run the house and ..."

"I'm sure Jane would ..."

"Jane doesn't understand, she really doesn't. Her job doesn't pay that well and we live in that huge house ..."

"I thought you were going to sell it, a while back?"

"We were, but Jane said she wanted to stay. I'd be happy living anywhere, but Jane loves the beach view and the ..."

"Have you told Jane how you feel, Marcus? I'm sure she'd move if ..."

"I've given up ... she wouldn't move before and now we're stuck there, getting into debt."

"Does Jane know things are bad ... financially?"

"Not really ... I do all the paperwork and I've tried to shield her from it."

"Marcus, I think Jane would be fine ..."

"No, she wouldn't. You haven't seen her for years. She's too used to spending money, buying clothes, going out, changing her car every five minutes. She's no idea."

I look across at him. His eyes are closed again, but now his hands are in front of his eyes and he's rubbing them. Is this all true about Jane? He's making her out to be some sort of spendthrift and that's not the Jane I know, or have seen. Maybe he's blaming *her* for his problems? All I know is, they need to talk to each other; they need to address whatever is at the root of all this. Are they really in debt?

I hear Jane calling from downstairs. I say to Marcus, "Look, I think you really need to talk to her about how you're feeling. She's worried about you ... I better go down and see what she wants."

I go down the stairs and over to Jane who's sitting in the chair, one leg up on the dashboard, steering the large boat with her finger. "Wow, weren't those corellas amazing?" I say, trying to move on from the conversation I'd had upstairs.

"Noisy bastards!" she says.

"That's just what Marcus said. Obviously, Aussies don't have the same feeling of awe I had," I laughed. "Shall I take over for a bit?"

"Are you sure you want to?"

"Well, it seems easy enough to me. Just stay with me for a while."

I take over, Jane explaining how I have to anticipate any bends in the river and take action early, as it takes so long for the boat to change direction. I settle down, looking ahead at the wide green river stretching on forever, in front of me. The large steering wheel hardly moves and I learn to adjust the course by simply moving one finger.

Jane wanders off and I marvel at what I'm doing. I'm in charge of this huge vessel; I'm navigating our way down this mighty river, now edged with high red cliffs.

I'm really on an adventure.

MARCUS TAKES OVER AGAIN and we look for a convenient mooring post. They said we had to find somewhere with two trees to tie up to and seeing a little grassy inlet with conveniently placed trees coming up, Marcus uses the loud horn to indicate that we're changing course and drives the boat in. This takes a certain amount of skill and I'm pleased I don't have to do it. There's a lot of revving and reverse thrust and then we're still.

Jane and I organise the ropes, throwing them out and tying them around the huge gum tree trunks. Marcus, meantime, is letting the engine idle, until we're fully secure. It's a perfect spot.

It's five o'clock and we're all hungry, so we set to and start the barby. Marcus, having stopped the engine, immediately opens a bottle of wine and starts drinking. We make the salad and he cooks the steak and sausages. We take it all up onto the top deck and eat round the table.

"A typical sausage sizzle," says Jane. "You're seeing how us Aussies live. The great outdoors, the river running by, the smell of cooking meat ..."

"It's brilliant," I say. "I never dreamt when I first planned my visit that we would do anything like this. It's perfect."

I look out over the water. Swallow-type birds are skimming the surface; the ubiquitous pelicans are still wafting by and little circles of water are appearing on the surface, where unseen fish are jumping.

We all sit quietly, taking in the silent paradise. I think about my earlier conversation with Marcus and understand how this holiday can only serve to emphasise his unhappiness. It's so tranquil here, that it makes you contemplate your life; your worries seep into your conscious and leak out again, without any conclusions. I think of Ben and Daisy and wonder what they're doing. I haven't thought about them for a few hours, I've been so enraptured by my surroundings, but now I miss Ben and hope he's okay. I can't communicate with anyone here – no internet. It's almost a relief to be so cut-off for once.

I have to admit, Jane and I have a few glasses of wine, as we sit watching the light fade. Marcus, however, takes things further and seems to be downing the wine quicker than usual. He goes downstairs to get a fourth bottle.

"Should I say anything?" asks Jane, in a whisper.

"No, I shouldn't. There's no point when someone is drinking. I think you should time your talk, when he's sober," I say, sounding as if I have experience of dealing with drunks. I haven't, however – David was never a drinker.

"Drink anyone?" says Marcus, as he slumps down in his chair.

"No thanks, I've had enough," says Jane, pointedly.

"I'm going to have this and then take the kayak out," he says.

Jane and I look at each other. "Is that a good idea?" I say. "The light's going and we've all had a bit to drink."

"I'll be fine; just want to paddle about a bit." He's not going to be persuaded otherwise, I can tell by the look on his face, so I drop it.

David downs his drink, as if it's water, and stands up. "Don't forget to put the life jacket on," says Jane.

"Nah, can't be arsed," says David, disappearing down the stairs.

"Oh God," says Jane, "do you think I should go out with him?"

"I think maybe you should, if he'll let you. I'd offer, but I've never been in a kayak in my life. I'd be more of a hindrance."

Reluctantly, she gets up and disappears. I follow her down; they're both in their bedroom. Marcus comes out in some board shorts and goes to the back of the boat, where the kayaks are stored. Without waiting for Jane, he gets hold of one, and puts it in the water. Even to my inexperienced eye, I can see that this is not going to be an easy manoeuvre, lowering himself over the edge, onto what looks like an unstable, plastic plank. His eyes have a glazed expression and I wonder if this is a safe thing for him to be doing.

Jane comes out in her costume and puts on a life jacket. "Here, take this, Marcus," she says, handing him another one.

"No ... I don't need one. I said. I can swim, can't I?"

"So can I, that's not the point. Why are you being so pig-headed?"

"Why are you being so *annoying*?" he shouts. "I wanted to go out on the water on my own for a bit. I don't want you following me."

"Well, I'm coming ... maybe if you'd wear a life jacket, I wouldn't, but ..."

"Oh for God's sake, I'm off." And with that, he lunges off the houseboat and with some miracle, lands heavily in the kayak. It seems that even when you've had a lot to drink, if you're used to this sort of thing, you can still do it.

"Good luck," I whisper to Jane. Marcus, by this time, is already on his way.

Jane gets on hers efficiently and starts out towards her husband. I stand, leaning against the rail around the boat, watching them as they paddle out into the middle of the river.

It's wide at this point, the red cliffs towering above us. The light is fading fast and I feel worried for them. No one else is anywhere near. What if one of them has a problem? What would I do?

I go to fetch my mobile to see if there's a signal and for some reason, there is. Well, that's good ... but who would I ring? I've told the kids that I'm out of internet range for a few days and I wrote a quick email to Ben, explaining where I was going, just before I left – but I don't know anyone in Australia who could help.

I look up from my phone and I can see the two kayaks far off now – they are not together. Marcus is faster than Jane and has not waited for her. They disappear from view and a feeling of sheer isolation descends on me.

I'll never feel alone again, when I'm in my flat in Bath, I think to myself. Here I am, on the Murray River, in this primeval place ... with no one. Somehow, though, I feel at peace. At that moment, a lone pelican floats by; he's like a ghost, appearing out of the gloom. The air is taking on a golden glow; the trees are turning into silhouettes, the ripples on the water, dark pulses. They'll be okay, I tell myself. They've done all this before.

Ten minutes go by; the stillness invades me and I'm almost in a trance. I watch the fish jumping, the concentric circles casting their shadows on the surface. Then, Jane and Marcus come into view again – their kayaks are still far apart, but they seem in one piece. They cut a sad picture though, the water separating them, like the gulf that appears to be in their marriage.

"Good time?" I shout across the water.

"Yea. You see I survived ..." Marcus says, heavy with sarcasm.

"Well, I'm glad you did," I laugh. "I didn't fancy diving in ..."

They both clamber back on board, Marcus going straight into the bedroom. "God, he was *not* happy with me for going with him. He hardly spoke," says Jane, in a low voice.

"I saw ... but I'm glad you went. He shouldn't have been on a kayak, after all that wine."

The sun finally sets, painting the river with a deep orange palette. Marcus doesn't come out of his room and we assume he's gone to bed. It's only 8 o'clock, but we're all tired. Jane and I read our books, with insects and moths buzzing around the lights, on the upper deck. We can hear owls hooting in the trees – it's completely black now. We stand up to observe the night sky.

There are so many stars, it's like our own planetarium. They shine so brightly; we both stare up at them in wonder. We can see all the constellations, pulsing and blinking, above us and stare for long minutes with our heads tipped back, trying to spot a shooting star, or a satellite. "It's at times like this when you realise how insignificant you are," says Jane.

"I know. I don't understand physics, black holes, infinity ... it's all beyond me ... all I know is ... we're just pinpricks, just grains of sand, in time. It makes me realise that our time on this planet is so short ... we've got to enjoy ... every minute."

"I know. Has Marcus said anything to you?"

I wonder how much I should say ... but I decide she has a right to know. "He did talk to me a little, when you were driving. He implied to me ... I think you should know ... that he has money worries, Jane."

"Really?" She seems genuinely shocked. "What did he say, exactly?"

"Just that he wanted to sell, but you didn't and he doesn't think you'd want to – that you're used to your lifestyle ..."

"When we talked about selling the house, it was him who seemed to reluctant ... I was happy to move, to downsize. God, what's going on?"

I look up at the diamonds above us and say, "Jane, I think he's really in need of a change. He said he can't breathe ... those were his words. He can't breathe."

"Oh God," says Jane and her eyes glitter like the stars, with tears. I put my arms around her.

"We need to do something, don't we?"

"Yes, I think you do."

Chapter Twenty-three

The next morning, Jane wakes me early. "Quick, get your camera, Anna. Quick."

I jump out of bed in a daze, wondering what's the matter, and then I see why Jane's called me. I pull back the cabin curtains and all along the river, a thick white mist hangs suspended, just above the water. It looks truly magical and I grab my camera and go outside.

"This is amazing ... it looks ... dreamlike." The early morning light adds to the magical luminescence of the scene. The pelicans shift in and out of sight, shrouded by clouds of whiteness. I take lots of pictures, but then stop and just simply look – I try to sear it into my memory. Cameras are great, but sometimes you need to look with your eyes and not through a lens. I can't see the river banks, apart from skeletal trees poking through the cloudiness. It's as if we're floating in cotton wool.

It passes, dissipating gently, so I go to shower and get myself presentable. I look at my reflection in the mirror – my cheekbones are more prominent and my skin has a healthy glow. I put on a bit of mascara and liner and even a bit of lipstick.

"Hey, look at you," says Jane, when I emerge. "Who are you trying to impress?"

"Myself," I laugh.

"We're going to go the same way for a few more hours and then we're turning round, so that we can moor up for the night at Dan's place. Do you remember those shacks we passed back there?"

"Well, they're hardly what I'd call 'shacks'."

"No, they're not shacks now, but they were, years back. It's 'Aussie' for a house by the river now, even though some of them are glass and metal monuments to modernity. Dan's place isn't showy, it's just ordinary, but it's not a shack."

"What time's he expecting us?"

"I said about four. But he's about as laid back as anyone I've ever met. If you want to meet an archetypal Aussie guy, Dan's *it*! Never been known to wear a proper pair of shoes, doesn't possess a pair of trousers and always wears an Akubra."

"What's that?"

"The hat ... you know, *the* hat. Oh ... and he'll probably call you 'Mate' all the time. So ... he wouldn't mind if we turn up next week. He'll have the tinnies cooling, that's for sure."

I was intrigued to meet this guy. So far, I'd only met 'real' Aussies, in shops. Marcus and Jane didn't count, as they were Brits at heart. I could hear their Aussie accent and upward inflection, but they wore their Britishness for all to see.

"He sounds like a cross between Paul Hogan and Steve Irwin. Does he wrestle crocs?"

"Not quite, but he loves the bush – every year, he goes to the Birdsville horse races in the middle of the bush, thousands of miles from civilisation. We've never been, but he's always telling us to go. Maybe, one day ... it would be an adventure." It sounded a bit too adventurous for me – would I be able to drive across dirt tracks for hundreds of miles, without worrying about the car breaking down? I don't know ... in my present frame of mind, I feel anything's possible.

Marcus backs us out of our mooring and we head off down river again. The weather's hot and Jane and I sunbathe on the top deck. The river is busier than yesterday – a few jet skis fly past, disturbing our peace and making the houseboat jiggle up and down. Then, in the far distance, we see a huge boat coming towards us; it turns out to be the Murray Princess paddle steamer – a huge version of our boat, painted in maroon and white, with a giant water wheel at the back.

As it passes us, we wave to all the people on deck and watch the water cascading and rushing like a waterfall, from the wheel. Our boat is then buffeted by some serious wake and we bob slowly up and down for a while.

"I'm glad we're on our own – I wouldn't want to be on that. Too many people," I say to Jane.

"It's expensive too ... we did look into it, but it's more fun this way."

"Certainly is," I say, as I drift, once again, into a light slumber.

WE ARRIVE AT DAN'S shack at about five; the current has made our progress even slower going back – it felt as if I could have hopped on one leg faster than the boat was going. Marcus manoeuvres it expertly in and as he does so, Dan appears, waving, as he walks across the vast expanse of communal grass that's in front of the line of shacks. Tall gum trees stand majestically on the land; Dan's wooden mooring platform, serves as our point of disembarkation.

He is exactly how I imagined; as he nears the boat, I can see his craggy features, his broad smile, his muscly physique. He's wearing khaki shorts, a white t-shirt, leather thongs and the Aussie hat. His hair, a kind of straw colour, straggles out. As he looks up at the boat, I notice his piercing green eyes.

"G'day mate," he shouts to Marcus. "Good trip?"

"Great. Looking forward to some beer," says Marcus, as he flings the rope over to Dan, who catches it expertly and ties it, in seconds, round a convenient trunk.

"Hey, Jane – is that yer sister?"

"Yep, Anna, meet Dan." I hop down the small gang plank and Dan throws his arms around me, like a long lost friend. His arms are amazingly strong and I'm squeezed, in a vice like grip.

I'm aware that I sound so English when I say, "Hi Dan, nice to meet you." He eventually lets me go and holding my shoulders at arm's length, he studies my face and says, "Yer look just like y'sister, mate, only prettier!"

"Thanks, Dan," says Jane, slapping him affectionately on the shoulder. "Nice to see you, too."

He then envelops Jane in his arms and lifting her up, he puts her over his shoulder and runs up the grass towards the house, with her screaming and banging his back with her fists. I look at Marcus to see how he's reacting, but he's totally unfazed, as he walks up the grass, carrying bags of booze.

There are a couple of other people and a dog on this open area; the dog comes bounding up to me and pushes his nose into my hand. It's a cross-breed – a labradoodle or cockerpoo or some such breed that used to be called a mongrel. I stroke its head and a longing for Gaz reaches out to me across the space of thousands of miles, as I feel the warm fur and cold nose. I've tried to bury his presence in my memory, to let him lie at peace there, but at moments like this, he rises like a spirit to lick my hand and wag his tail. Tears appear from nowhere and as I walk on, I try to brush them away, along with his face.

"Y'all right, mate?" says Dan. He has now put Jane down and he's striding back towards me to take a bag I'm carrying. He looks at me directly.

"Yea, I'm fine. Seeing that dog back there ... it er ... reminded me of my Gaz." Dan is more sensitive than he looks, I think to myself.

"What happened to him?" he asks.

"Cancer."

"Bummer," he says simply and squeezes my shoulder. I like the way he doesn't ask me any more questions. I'm sure I couldn't answer them right now.

"Yea ... bummer," I say.

THE BARBY IS ON, THE boys are clutching some cold tinnies and two glasses of white wine are sitting on the wooden table on the patio. We chat about life on the river and Dan regales us with stories of fishing and boats.

Jane and Dan wander inside, to do something with the food; Marcus and I stand next to each other, surveying the scene. Corellas are darting their noisy way to the trees, white streaks in the sky – the whole area alive with their screeching. The other people and their dog have disappeared; we have the whole area to ourselves. Our boat sits idly on the river at the end of Dan's plot, surrounded by little groups of pelicans; swallows are swooping low over the water and the sun is beginning to paint the sky a rosy pink.

"Wow," I say. "What a place. I feel so peaceful."

Marcus doesn't say anything for a while; he takes a swig from his beer and says, "It's beautiful. I could live here."

"What's Dan's situation? How come he's on his own?"

"His wife died about five years ago – cancer – and he's never appeared to want to find someone else."

Now I understand the empathy I felt – poor guy. I look back into the house to make sure Dan isn't within hearing distance; I don't want him to think we're talking about him, which we are, of course.

"So what's he do?"

"He spends a lot of time here, fishing and moseying around on the river. He's got a house in Hove too, but prefers it here. He owns three surf shops, but he's got life hacked – he's got good managers."

"Sounds like a nice life," I say, "but – don't forget ... he's lost his wife ... he may seem okay on the surface, but I bet he's lonely ... at least you've got Jane." I wonder if I've said too much, but he doesn't appear to mind.

"I know ... I just wish I could somehow get out of the rat race; I'd be perfectly content somewhere like this."

The corellas have stopped their screaming; the peace, however, is broken by a loud sound that makes the hairs on the back of my neck stand up – two kookaburras, one in a tree just near us and one further away, are calling to each other. It's the first time I've heard the sound since I've arrived, and I can't believe how deafening it is and how like a laugh it really is. They cackle to each other three or four times, their noise echoing around the whole area.

"That's brilliant! It's made my day," I say to Marcus, grinning. To an Australian, it's nothing I suppose, but it's such an alien noise to me. I wish I could bottle it and take it home with me, along with the sight and smells of this place.

"Okay, mate," says Dan, ambling out of the house, "Marcus, come and help me burn the snags." He has a plateful of sausages and behind him, Jane is carrying another plate of meat.

"We've got enough food to sink the boat here," she says. "I think Dan was expecting ravening hordes."

"Nah ... but I believe in having enough tucker ... I can always eat it tomorrow, when you've gone, mate."

The empty bottles of beer are steadily accumulating by the door of the kitchen. Dan and Marcus are cooking and Jane takes me inside and shows me around the house. It's homely, but lacks a woman's touch: things are strewn messily around and the bathroom looks like it could do with a good scrub. It has a balcony upstairs, so we go out and stand on it, looking down at the smoke drifting upwards from the barby; there are a few lit candles on the tables now and moths and insects are flying near the lights attached to the outside walls. The steady presence of the river rolling by, adds to the surreal feel.

"Marcus loves it here, you know, Jane. He was telling me how he'd be content (his word, not mine) if he lived somewhere like this. I hope I'm not being presumptuous but, here's an idea for you – maybe you could sell up and buy a small place near where you are now and something along this part of the river?"

"Maybe ... I'm not sure I'd want to live here permanently, though."

"No, of course not ... but it could be a compromise – a bit of sea and city life and then weekends, here. It might just be what Marcus needs. You can do your work anywhere, can't you?"

"That's true. It's a thought, Anna. Perhaps we could buy something that needs a lot of renovation. Marcus used to say he'd love to do something up."

"There you are, then ... you should suggest it." We stare ahead and I put my arm around her, pulling her in towards me. She puts her head on my shoulder.

"It's so good to have you here ... I'll miss you when you've gone, you know," she says.

"I'll miss you, too ... but now I'm a lady of leisure, maybe I'll be able to come again. We mustn't let distance come between us again. I'm realising all sorts of things while I'm here – I haven't made enough effort with you, or David ..."

"Don't go blaming yourself for David's ..."

"No, I'm not *blaming* myself, as such, but ... I was so ... so ... middle-aged, so boring ... so accepting of my life ..."

"There's nothing wrong with that, is there?"

"No ... as long as you're not blind to other people. David needed something from me that I wasn't able ... or willing to give. I didn't see how unhappy he was ... if I'd been a better wife, he wouldn't have felt the need to ..."

"Look, Anna, he *chose* to act, to fall in love, he ..."

"That's what I mean ..."

"What are you saying?"

"I mean, sometimes in life, you have to take drastic steps to change things. He chose to change things. And maybe he was right to ... did I want to continue living like we were? I thought I was happy, but looking back, I don't think I was. Hardly noticing each other ... what would it have been like, just the two of us, with Adam gone? Two people living in the same house ... that's it ... existing. Me, hating my job ... putting on weight ... him, resenting me ... maybe he's done us all a favour? Here I am, in Australia – reconnecting with my sister – he and Adam are now communicating, which they weren't before. I can see now, the change has been good. Being so far away from everything familiar, has opened my eyes.

I'm going to stop being bitter and twisted about Suzie. I've been jealous of her ... her youth and her sexiness. I've been horrible to David, but somehow, now, from a distance, I don't care so much, anymore. They're having a baby together ... and I want to be able to be happy for them. Maybe all those years we had together were our ... allotted time. Maybe there was a predestined time limit. Whatever it is, I can see that it's ... over. I've met Ben, I've moved to Bath. I'm going to enjoy my future, whatever it holds, without David. I was quietly sleepwalking into old age and I didn't even realise it, until now. Australia's woken me up.

Maybe it's time for *you* to make a big change too. Time to reassess. Do you want to continue on this path, with Marcus blatantly unhappy and slowly killing himself, or do you want to make your marriage work? For you, it's different – the thing that's coming between you two is Life, not another woman. Why don't you go to those races with Dan, in the wilds of the bush? Why don't you visit me, in England? It would be amazing ..." I turn to look at her and she looks back at me, smiling.

"When did you become so bloody wise and philosophical?" she laughs, leaning forward to kiss my cheek.

"I don't know ... it's just crept up on me ... I feel like a lifestyle guru," I laugh. "It's just that I can see things from a new perspective, I suppose, and I don't want you to make the same mistakes I did. You're my little sister and I'm looking out for you."

"What do you suggest I do, then?"

"Well ... I think you ought to say you want to sell your house; that you've 'seen the light' and that you both need a change. He thinks you want to stay and I know he wants to sell. It will take the pressure off him ... if *you* suggest it."

"Yea, you're right."

Looking down, I can see Dan walking to the table, carrying a tray of cooked meat.

"Hey, you girls up there ... get your arses down here, the food's ready," shouts Dan. "You sheilas, you're all the same ... leaving us men to do all the work ..."

"Yea, right," says Jane, smiling, and we turn to go downstairs.

WE'VE ALL EATEN AND drunk loads – I feel I don't have much right to preach about the amount my brother-in-law is eating and drinking, right now. My waistband feels tight and my head's fuzzy. We've talked and laughed for an hour – I've noticed how happy Marcus seems. He and Dan get on so well: Dan taking the piss out of him relentlessly and Marcus belly laughing, like I've never seen him do before.

Dan suggests we go for a walk – the whole river frontage belongs to the people in the fifteen or so shacks ranging along its length; everyone maintains and looks after their 'bit' and the end result is a massive area of manicured grass, with huge gum trees distributed around. The trees have a ghost-like presence now, silhouetted against the blackening sky; bats flutter through the air above us and a lone owl hoots, in the distance.

We wander past several shacks; most of them appear to be empty.

"Is it always this quiet, here?" I ask Dan. "No one seems about."

"People tend to come at weekends ... sometimes there's bloody people everywhere. Hate the buggers. I much prefer it when I'm here on my own."

"Thanks!" says Jane, trying to trip Dan up.

"Present company excepted," laughs Dan.

"Isn't it a bit lonely here, though?" I say.

"Nah ... just me and the pelicans. That's good."

In the looming light, the empty shacks look almost menacing. We've nearly reached the end of the grassed area, when I notice a 'For Sale' sign, sticking up in front of the second to last house. I nudge Jane in the ribs, not wanting to say anything and point to it. Her eyes follow my gaze and to my surprise she says, "Hey, Marcus, there's one for sale. Maybe we should buy it!"

I hope it's not the drink talking – maybe she's really taken on board what I said.

"Yea, the old guy who owns it, has just died and his kids don't want it," says Dan. "It's a bit of a bloody mess – he's had it for years and not done anything to it. In need on renovation, is putting it politely."

Marcus walks up to the house and we all start peering through windows, but it's too dark now to see anything. Even in the near darkness, however, you get the impression of a neglected house – bits of wood litter the front, tyres are piled at the side and a table is upended on the grass.

"How much do shacks go for, these days?" asks Marcus.

"Well, of course it depends on the condition, but I had mine valued six months ago and it was 350,000 dollars. I'm not thinking of selling or anything but, just wanted to know, as I've had it for so long. This one here ... probably about ... I don't know ... 200 to 250,000. It needs a shit load of work but ... it's got river frontage. You pay a bloody lot for that. There are houses behind us here, but they can't even see the river."

"Yea, there's no point being on the river, unless you're actually 'on' it," says Marcus.

"Why don't you find out how much it is, honey?" says Jane. "We could sell our house and buy something smaller near the city and something like this. We'd still have money left over."

"Really?" says Marcus. "Would you be happy to do that?" Even though it's dark now, I can hear the smile in his voice.

"Yes, I would. What's the point of us rattling around in that big house? We're always too busy to appreciate the sea, anyway, and this way, perhaps we could slow down ... it's about time you did. Maybe you could ask to do fewer hours?"

Marcus came over to Jane and hugged her; I realised I hadn't seen him show Jane much, if any, affection, since I'd been with them.

"Well, I think that's an amazing idea," I say. "Maybe next time I come out, you'll have your River Murray shack up and running and we'll be staying here, near Dan!"

We walk back along the grass, but nearer the river, this time. When we get to the wooden jetty near our boat, we all sit down and savour the gentle lapping of the water and the night sounds.

The stars are out and glowing brightly above us and we're silent, as we all just simply look and listen to the night around us.

"I'll give the agent a ring in the morning," says Marcus. Jane takes his hand.

"This could be our life," she says, as another owl hoots.

Dan grins. "Bloody hell, mate, does that mean I'll have to put up with you two more often?"

I quietly pat myself on the back. I may just have played a small part in them saving their marriage.

Chapter Twenty-Four

When we get back to Adelaide, their large house with its ocean views seems too civilised, almost too urban. The Murray, with its slow, sleepy existence, its magnificent red cliffs and its abundance of nature, has seeped into my brain. I miss its beauty and plethora of bird life.

I'm jolted back into the modern world, with its quicker pace. Cars are everywhere, joggers run past the house and groups of cyclists in lycra, scream down the road at lightning speed. Even though we've only been gone three days, I feel disorientated. I think Marcus and Jane feel the same, but I sense a calmness about them.

I don't want them to come back and forget what they were thinking when they were away from here, so I bring the subject up again the next day, when we've all had a good night's sleep.

When Marcus has left for work, I say to Jane, "So, how do you feel, now you're back?"

"How do you mean?"

"Well, any regrets about what you said to Marcus, about the house?"

"No, not at all, funnily enough. I think this house is too big for us – I've often thought it, but didn't want to move, because it's so much hassle. But you've made me see the truth and I'm looking forward to a new phase ..."

"That's so brilliant, Jane. I know it'll make Marcus happier and you'll be able to sort out your finances. Why don't we look on the internet and see what you could get round here? What would you want – a small house or a flat?"

"I don't know ... let's have a look." Jane gets out her laptop and we browse through loads of properties in Brighton, Hove, Somerton Park and Glenelg which are located back from the sea. If Marcus is going to continue going into the city, they should buy something that makes his commute easy so we look at places near the station.

Soon, we're perusing places in Willunga and Aldinga down the coast and Stirling and Strathalbyn up in the Hills. It reminded me of my search in Bath – how easy it is to end up miles away in both location and price, from your first search.

"We need to get this valued, so we know how much we've got to play with," says Jane, "then at least we'll know. The houses on the sea front here go like hot cakes – I don't think we'd have any problems selling it."

Jane closes her laptop and says she must start work. I take the opportunity to catch up with emails and Facebook. I open my laptop and there are several emails I need to answer, two of which are from Ben and Holly. I decide to download some photos I've taken to attach to an email in reply so Ben can see how much I've enjoyed using his present and Holly can see what I've been doing.

Ben's email reads:

Hi Anna – I know you're on the River Murray, but thought I'd write this anyway. I hope the trip was good? I'm assuming you're back, as you're reading this. I'm really beginning to miss you – I've missed you all the time, but ... time seems to be dragging now and there's still ages till you get back.

Grace and Daisy left yesterday, so I suppose I'm feeling sorry for myself. I hate the fact that my daughter is going to be so far away and there's nothing I can do about it. I'm going to go up there next weekend and check it all out. I still haven't met Greg (the new man) – he's always been deliberately absent when I've gone there, so I've told Grace that when I come up, I want us all to go out together and she's grudgingly agreed. I want to feel confident that Greg is a good bloke, which Grace assures me he is (but she would, wouldn't she?)

Anyway, enough of me. I hope you're having a fantastic time ... you deserve it. Maybe one day, we'll be able to visit Oz together ... if you'd like me to come with you, that is! I know we haven't spent much time together yet, but I feel great when I'm with you, Anna, and I'm hoping you feel the same about me?

When you get back, why don't we plan a few days away together? Maybe somewhere new for both of us, with no history? I'd love that.

Anyway, enjoy the rest of your time. It must be soon that Adam's coming over? I hope it goes well.

Can't wait to hear from you. Ben xx

I get out my phone and look at the pictures I have of him. I find myself smiling, as I scroll through the photos and realise that even though I'm having the time of my life out here, I really miss him. I don't know how anyone would describe our relationship – is it love? I don't know any more. All I *do* know is that, like him, I feel great when I'm with him and you can't ask for much else, can you? He makes me feel young again, which can't be bad ... we make each other laugh, we enjoy the same things ...

I tell him all about the trip and my hopes for Marcus and Jane. I try to reassure him about Greg and tell him I miss him. I end like this:

I know it's early days for us, Ben, but I feel the same ... I think of you a lot ... I often find myself imagining you and me together, on these beautiful beaches, walking hand in hand. Soppy, I know, but that's how I feel!

I've got Gaz to thank for bringing us together, that night, in the pub all that time ago. I'm sure if I'd been sitting there on my own, without him, you'd never have come and spoken to me – it would have seemed too much like a pick-up! He was our go-between. We've got a lot to thank him for. God, I miss that dog. Maybe ... one day, I'll get another one, but it'll never 'replace' him.

Yes, Adam's here next week. I'm so excited and for some reason, a bit nervous.

Will write very soon.

Miss you, Anna xxx

I feel guilty that I read Ben's email first, before Holly's, but knowing her, she'd say 'Go for it Mum.'

I open her email.

Hey Mum, I know you're back today. I'm going to ring you, your time around 7 pm. BE THERE!!! Love you, Holly xxx

I stare at her words and wonder why she's going to ring me – it doesn't sound as if there's a problem, somehow. We'd said we'd only ring if there was an emergency – what's so important that she can't tell me on the internet?

I spend the day walking on the beach and even have a (very shallow) swim in the sea. No one else is in the water and I begin to wonder if they know something I don't. I constantly look for shadows and jump when a piece of seaweed brushes against my skin. I get out, vowing to go to the shark-free environs of the pool tomorrow and then go back to the house to have an afternoon nap.

As seven o'clock approaches, my stomach begins to churn. I've prepared spag bol for our supper and Marcus has just got in. When the phone rings, I grab it and go to my bedroom. I fumble to press the green phone icon to answer it.

"Holly! Hi! How are you?"

"Mum! I'm fine. More than fine, actually!"

"What? What's happened?"

"Jed proposed and I said yes!"

"Oh my God ... that's fantastic. I'm so happy for you. Tell me everything ..."

"Well, Jed suggested we go for a walk at the weekend. It was quite cold, but we both like walking, so I didn't think anything about it. He wanted to catch the tube to Camden and walk on Primrose Hill. I've never been there before, so I thought it was just about that. We walked past all these amazing houses worth millions and wondered who on earth can live there. I dragged him into this gorgeous coffee shop – he didn't seem to want to at first, and looking back, it was probably because he was on a mission to get me to the top of the hill. He seemed a bit distracted, but we had coffee and cake there and then wandered on. I had no idea what a wonderful place it was, Mum – we went to the top and gazed out at the view, right across London in all its glory, with its stunning skyscrapers. And then he did it, Mum – he delved into his pocket and opened this ring box and asked me to marry him. He completely took me by surprise ..."

"How romantic, Holly. Did he get down on one knee?"

"Well, he said he'd planned to, but then sort of forgot, as he was so nervous. I'm glad he didn't, to be honest, I think I would've laughed."

"So ... have you set a date?" I ask.

"Not yet ... but he says he doesn't want a long engagement and neither do I. When you know it's right, what's the point of waiting?"

"Exactly ... has he told his parents?"

"Not yet, I wanted you to be the first person to know and Jed was cool with that. He'll ring them tonight. And when I get off the phone, I'll call Dad. I'll email Adam too. You're seeing him soon, aren't you?"

"Yes, in a few days. Wow, Holly ... I can't get over it. What brilliant news. What's the ring like?"

"It's beautiful – if I'd chosen it myself, I'd have picked it. It's white gold and three diamonds. I don't know how he managed to get exactly the right size for my finger. I'll have to ask him. Anyway, I better go now – God knows what this is costing on the mobile, but ... I wanted to talk to you, in person."

"Thanks so much. Lovely to hear your voice. When I get back, you two must come to Bath and ..."

"Okay, Mum ... will do. Love you! Byeee. Byeee."

I stared at the dead phone. Holly would make such a beautiful bride.

I found tears in my eyes – why do women cry when they're happy?

"SO ... WHAT'S JED LIKE?" asks Jane.

"He's lovely – perfect for Holly. I couldn't be more pleased for her. He's got a really good job – he's a barrister, so they won't be short of a bob or two and ... more to the point, he's a really nice person. I *knew* they'd get married, I just knew it." I'm grinning, I can't stop.

"Do you think they'll live in London?"

"I'm sure they will. That's where they're both now, anyway. Maybe in the future, they might move out but ..."

"Do you think you'll stay in Bath?"

"I think so. I'm enjoying being in a city, for a change. It's nice to be able to walk to the theatre ... any more thoughts about you two?" I don't want to nag, but I really want to see some sort of movement before I go home.

"Marcus rang about the shack today. They haven't had any offers yet and they implied the kids are keen to get their hands on the money. It's 210,000 Aussie dollars. They're waiting to see if they get offers, if not, they'll hold an auction. But even if that one goes, we can look at others – it won't be the end of the world. We can't do anything till we sell this. We're going to ring an agent we know and get him round."

"That's great, Jane. I hope you don't think I've interfered ..."

"No, don't be daft ... I needed a kick up the backside to see what was in front of my eyes. All I need to do now is gently persuade him to give up the wine," she laughed.

"Well, tread carefully. One step at a time."

I GET THE OPPORTUNITY to talk to Marcus alone, a few days later. I've noticed that although his mood has lifted, he's still swilling back the wine, like it may run out.

One night, Dan came over and we all went to Grange to a restaurant on the beach. The sunset was amazing and I spent at least half an hour wandering around taking pictures, after we'd finished the meal. When I got back, he and Dan were on their third bottle and poor Jane was looking out to sea, with a look of desperation on her face. I resolved then to speak to Marcus.

Jane went out early evening to visit a client; she apologised, but said there was nothing she could do. I assured her that I'd survive without her and ushered her out of the door, knowing that now was my chance.

"It's all looking very positive on the house front, then?" I say to Marcus, who is sitting reading The Australian on the sofa. He looks up, a bit distracted momentarily, but then pulls himself together. He has a glass of red, by his side.

"Yea ... this guy I know, Richard, is coming over at the weekend to take a look at this."

"That's great, Marcus. Jane seems to be well up for it now ... we were chatting today and she's really keen ..."

"I hope she doesn't chicken out this time ... we've been here before, as you know ..."

"No, I'm sure she won't. She understands how important it is for you – she really loves you, you know." I'm building up to bringing up his drinking and I'm trying to play the psychological card. My heart begins to quicken – I wonder if I'm overstepping the mark? Jane did warn me not to say anything.

"I know she does," he says with a smile. "You two are so alike ... I'd never realised before."

"Are we? In what way?"

"Oh, everything ... your looks, your laugh ... the way you put your finger on your chin when you're thinking about something – like you're doing now."

"I hadn't even realised I was doing it," I say, and stop. I pause for a while and then say, "I was thinking how crucial it is to be honest with people ... looking back, I realise how important it was for David to tell me the truth. He could have carried on seeing Suzie behind my back, but he didn't, he faced me – it was hard for me to hear, but I'm glad he did."

"So ... why are you thinking about this now?"

"Well, I want to say something to you, Marcus, which you might not like to hear." I stare at him with a little smile. His eyes cloud and I wonder what he's going to say.

"When I said you were like Jane, I didn't say I wanted you to turn into a nagging wife."

I'm not sure whether this is said as a joke or if he really means it. His expression doesn't help me. "Well?" he says. "Spit it out."

"It's difficult ... Jane's actually told me *not* to say anything to you, but I'm going to ignore her."

"Sounds ominous. You better just say it, now. I'm all ears."

"Well ... Jane's really worried about your health ..."

"Really? Why on earth is she worried about me? I'm fine, as far as I know. I get stressed, I know, and grumpy, but ..."

"She ... she worries about the amount of wine you drink. There, I've said it."

There was a long pause. Marcus stood up and, deliberately to my eyes, went and topped up his glass. He knocked it back and then took the bottle over to the table by the sofa and sat down.

"She shouldn't discuss my so-called health with anyone but me ..."

"Look, Marcus, you can be angry with *me* if you want, but don't blame her. Obviously, she's going to discuss it with me. She has to live with you, throwing wine down your neck every night, falling asleep on the sofa. She can see the affect it's having on you, on her and your marriage. She's bound to want to talk about it, to her only sister. I wanted to tell you because you've both made such a great decision over the house and you're trying to sort your lives out. This is just one more piece of the puzzle. I thought I'd tell you, so that you could think about it and work out why you drink so much."

Even to me, I sound like some kind of annoying therapist. I look at him to see how he's going to react and all I can say is, he looks a bit defeated; as if the fight has gone out of him.

"I don't drink *that* much ..."

"It depends how you look at it," I say. "Yes, it's wine, not spirits, but ... you drink enough to obliterate the day – every day. It *can't* be good for your blood pressure and you've put on a lot of weight ..."

"Don't sugar-coat it, will you?"

"As I said, I'm trying to be honest. Because I care for *both* of you. Jane's worried you're going to kill yourself. She doesn't want to lose you."

He puts the glass down and puts his head in his hands. I decide to sit down next to him and put my arm around him. I pull him towards me. "I don't think I'm saying anything you didn't know already, am I?"

He lifts his head and says, "No, I suppose not. But it's hard ..."

"I know, I know it's hard, but it's worth trying to change, isn't it?"

"I've tried to cut down in the past, but ... I always revert. Work stresses me out."

"Do you know what ... I think you should address the work situation first. It seems to me that work is at the bottom of *all* your problems. Have you ever considered cutting down your hours? Is it possible?"

"I've thought about it, but never actually asked ..."

"Well, why don't you ask if it's possible? You'll never know, if you don't ask. You're going to sell this – it must be worth a fortune – and when you've bought the two small places, you'll have some left over, won't you? You could maybe live off that, to top up your salary for a couple of years ... maybe Jane could do some more work ... there are *options*, Marcus, you know. You mustn't feel stuck on this treadmill. You *can* make changes."

"Yea, you're right." He looks tired, so I don't say anything else. I've sewn the seed and hopefully something will have gone in. "Don't forget we've got debts. I'm not sure if there *will* be anything left ..."

"Well, these are all things that need to be sorted out ... but at least you've made a start. I hope you don't mind me saying something ..."

"I won't hold it against you," he says, with a little grin. "Now, if you don't mind, I'm going to retire to my bed," and with that, he gets up and leaves the room.

I sit and reflect on the conversation and feel I can do no more. Hopefully, they will at least move closer towards each other now. Things aren't going to happen overnight, but maybe my little nudging of them both, will have helped, just a tad.

I feel like I've played Gaz' role as a go-between, without the silky black ears, brown eyes and waggy tail.

Chapter Twenty-Five

Facebook message from Adam:

Can you or Jane pick me up from the airport? I get in at 18.15 your time on Thursday. Can't wait to get away for a few days. Jake's driving me nuts (will explain when I see you) and the cleaning is doing my head in. I thought I was messy – God, the state some people leave their vans in. It's disgusting.

Anyway, I hope you've got lots planned for me? Can't wait to have a look at Adelaide. I'm not bringing my board, you'll be pleased to hear. Thought it would be good to give surfing a rest for a few days. If there's time, I'd love to go to some of the wineries up in the Adelaide Hills. A mate told me about them and they sound cool.

I'll text if I'm delayed but hopefully, see you soon. Adam xxx

I haven't heard from him for ages, so it's a relief to get this. I write back.

Hey – I can't believe it. So excited. I think Holly's told you her news? Brilliant isn't it? I think you'll really like Jed. Sorry there's issues with Jake – maybe a year is too long to be with someone, even when they're your best mate? Yes, we'll defo go up to the Hills. Glad you're not bringing the board, not sure I could stand the strain of actually watching you, knowing there are sharks around! Seems years since I last saw you, not months. See you soon, Mum xxx

Jane and I set out to pick him up – it's odd to be returning to the airport already. Seems like minutes since I was here, being picked up myself and it dawns on me that I've only got just two weeks left.

We park the car and make our way to arrivals. We wander right into an area that would normally be out of bounds, but this is a domestic flight – so it's a bit like catching a bus and turning up to the bus station.

I catch sight of Adam as he walks purposefully towards us, in amongst loads of other tanned people. He looks different, even from here, older and less like a boy.

I start to wave like a banshee and rush towards him. If I'd done this in the past, he would have been embarrassed, but he seems to be genuinely pleased to see me, wrapping his arms around me and squeezing me, till I laugh.

"It's so lovely to see you at last Adam," I say, breathing in his smell – sweat and Paco Rabanne, mixed with coconut sun oil. I don't want to let him go, but I do, and he kisses my cheek loudly.

"You look fab, Mum – you look younger, somehow. What have you done to yourself? Botox?" he grins.

"Cheeky. It's just the sun, this beautiful place ... anyway, Jane, meet your grown-up nephew!"

They hug each other and Jane says, "Wow! I really *can* say it – you've grown a bit!"

I look at him. He's filled out, got taller; his hair's longer, blonder. His face is browner than I've ever seen it and it makes his eyes stand out and his teeth look whiter. I can't believe what a handsome devil he is.

"Well, you look *older*," I say. "You look so ... well ... so ... Aussie."

"Yea, I suppose I do – I can even hear myself doing the upward inflection, but all my Aussie friends laugh at my accent. They think it's quaint."

"Come on," says Jane, "Let's go to the car and get you home. Supper's waiting ..."

Adam swings his rucksack onto his back and we walk across the concourse together, Jane with her arm through his. He's chatting away to her and when I look at him, I'm so proud of him. What a brilliant boy he's turning into.

"SO, MY BIG SISTER'S got herself a lawyer, then?" he says, as he tucks into supper. He's eating as if he hasn't eaten for a week, rolling spaghetti expertly round his fork. "Any date for the wedding?"

"Not yet ... but I don't think they'll hang around. I'm so pleased – he's perfect for her. I think you'll really like him when you meet him, eventually. What are your plans, anyway? Have you got any?" I laugh.

"Well, I did think for a while I wanted to stay here. But it's not that easy, there are so many rules and regulations and anyway, I'm coming round to thinking I *will* go to uni. Dad'll be amazed. I got the grades, so I may as well. What the hell!"

"What are you going to study, Adam?" asks Jane. I'm sitting quietly smiling to myself, realising that it means that he'll be home soon. I'd thought he might be planning to live here forever.

"Sports studies. It's all about the psychology and coaching ... and I can specialise in water sports. When I was applying, it was the only thing I thought I could possibly do – I saw the course at Solent, and that was it. Then I went off the whole idea – I thought I wouldn't get the grades. But much to my amazement and my parents', I did." He laughed, looking over at me with an ironic grin. "I know Dad thought I ought to do something more worthy, but ... it's what I want to do."

"It's good to know what you want, Adam. It's brilliant news. What's Jake going to do?" I ask.

"God knows."

"Oh. Doesn't he talk about it much?"

"I'll tell you later, Mum. I'd rather forget him for now."

I leave it there, but I'm intrigued. I'm worried for Laura's sake and am determined to find out the truth.

"So ... what do you think of Australia, then? Do we measure up?" says Jane.

"I love it here, I really do. I've had an amazing time, made some great friends. Your TV's crap, though. God, how do you watch it?" he laughed.

"They've forgotten what decent telly's like," I say. "I couldn't believe how many adverts they have. I lost the will to live when we watched a film the other night. It feels like they interrupt it every five minutes."

Jane laughed. "You get used to it, in the end. Or, you do what we do, and download things off the internet."

"That's one thing I won't miss when I go back to the UK," says Adam, "but there's loads I *will* miss. The weather. The beaches. The people. The laid-back attitude. The food. There's so much to like. But there's one more thing I hate, Auntie Jane, and that's their attitude to the Aboriginals. I hate the way they've been treated. I didn't know anything about it until I came here."

"It's a very complicated area," says Jane. "I hate it too, but when you live here, you realise it's not something that can be easily sorted out and in the end, you kind of accept the situation. It's awful, I know. We've got some friends who went and worked with Aboriginals in the bush for a while, and some of the stories they told ... it's hard to believe what goes on. They were here thousands of years before us and we took their land and now they're ... lost, really but ... it's so difficult to help them. The Government try to bring in all sorts of initiatives, but they just seem to make it all worse." Jane looks wistful and continues. "One good thing is that at least some of their artists are paid for their wonderful art work now. One of my projects I'm going to be working on is a children's book that's going to have some Aboriginal illustrations, alongside mine. It's going to be really exciting."

"You didn't tell me that," I say.

"No, well, it hasn't come up ... but I'm going to be working with the Aboriginal artist next year. We ought to go to this fabulous gallery in the city where there are masses of paintings – would you be interested in going, Adam?"

"Definitely. I bought a book about their art, as I love it so much."

This is a side of Adam that is completely new to me. He did Art GCSE but has never shown any real interest in it.

"That's brilliant, Adam. Let's go tomorrow," I say. I realise I know very little about it, but suddenly feel the need to learn. The picture I bought in Cornwall somehow represented my future. Perhaps I could take something back home, that would remind me of my time here.

That night, when Adam has gone to his room and I'm in bed, I remember he said he wanted to talk to me about something. I lie awake for a long while, worrying what it is. I know it's not his future as he's now told us about uni. Perhaps it's just this issue with Jake? I'm going to have to make it possible for him to talk to me, alone. We're all going to go to the city tomorrow, but maybe in the morning, while Jane's working, we can walk and chat.

I fall asleep with images of Adam and Holly swirling round my head. Ben and Gaz walk around my brain too, leaving me eventually to fall asleep with a feeling of love and sadness intertwined.

Chapter Twenty-Six

"Do you fancy a stroll along the beach?" I say to Adam. He's sitting on the balcony, drinking a strong expresso. He used to hate coffee.

"Yea, cool. Just give me a minute ..."

We cross the road and go down the steps that lead to the beach. The Life Saving Club stands above us, its yellow and red flags fluttering in the breeze. Norfolk pines range along the road, standing tall and proud, as if patrolling the seashore. We set off towards Glenelg.

Adam seems distracted this morning and we walk in companionable silence for a while. Passing a few dog walkers, he says, "I can't believe I'll never see dear old Gaz again."

He's now walking with his head down, looking at the sand. I put my arm around him. "I know ... he was such a ... friend." I watch a girl jog past, her pony tail swinging like Suzie's. "And you've heard about ... Dad and Suzie?"

Adam grunts. "Bit ridiculous at his age. Silly sod. The poor kid'll be laughed at when he's at secondary school, with a father who looks ancient."

"Yes, I know ... but I've decided to wish them well. I can't continue being a bitter old woman for the rest of my life, can I?" I nudge him and he eventually looks up and smiles.

"Why not?" he says, "I think I'd be bitter, if I was you."

"Life's too short."

"Yea. S'pose so. What's this Ben bloke like, then? Holly says he's younger than you?" He bends down to pick up a small pebble. "Do you like him?"

"I do, yes. We haven't spent much time together but ... he's been really kind to me. I was worried about being a bit older than him at first, but when you're our age, it doesn't really matter anymore. If *you* went out with a girl who was ten years older than you, that *would* be odd. I don't know what I'd have done without him when Gaz ..." He gives me a sideways look.

"So ... are you going to carry on, when you get back?"

"I hope so. But it's early days. We'll just see what happens." There's a long silence as we pick up the pace a bit and stride into the wind. "Let's walk by the edge of the water," I say and veer off to the sea. We're carrying our thongs and we splash through the crystal water, simply enjoying each other's company. He throws the pebble into the sea; it lands quite far out, with a plop. I take a few snaps, trying to catch the water droplets that are jumping from the Adam's feet, as he sloshes about and kicks the tiny waves. I know that I'll feel nostalgic for this time, when I look at the pictures, back home.

"It seems odd to be in the sea, without huge waves rolling in. Have you seen any surf here?"

"No, not since I arrived, although Marcus says it gets rough here, in the winter. If you want to surf, you go to Goolwa or somewhere. Still, you're not here to surf this time, are you?"

"Na ... good to have a break, if I'm honest. I'm surfed out!"

After a few minutes, I decide now's the time to ask him what it is he wanted to talk about. I have a feeling he's waiting for me to bring it up. He's ambling by my side and I feel a tension – maybe it's mine, maybe it's his, I'm not sure.

"Adam ... while we're on our own ... you mentioned that you wanted to talk about something. Perhaps now is a good moment?"

He turns his head and stares at me; I can see embarrassment pass over his face and he looks away. He doesn't say anything, so I add, "Is it about Jake?"

"No ... although I do want to talk about him, some time. No ... it's something else. Something personal ... about me."

I go up to him; both of us are still in the water and I get hold of his arms and turn him to face me. "Whatever it is, Adam, you can tell me. You know you can." I look into his eyes and will him to say it, whatever it is.

His face flushes red – I can see it through his golden tan. "Don't worry," I say. "Just say it. It's best, that way."

"Okay then. Here goes." He looks straight into my eyes. "Mum ... there's no easy way of saying this ... I'm gay." He doesn't look away, but his eyes flicker and I can see tears shining in the whites.

I'm so taken aback that I don't say ... anything. My heart does a somersault. Thoughts flash through my mind like lightning – this is the last thing I had thought he was going to say – I don't know what I was expecting – drugs, getting a girl pregnant ... illness? Is this as bad as those things or something that doesn't change anything at all? My mouth sparks into action; I know I must say something – and quickly.

"Oh. Well, that's okay, Adam. You're still my son and I *love* you, just the same."

Is this the right thing to say? What are you meant to say in this situation? Of course I still love him. What a stupid thing to say – why wouldn't I still love him?

"I've known since I was about twelve."

"Really? That young?" I can't believe it.

"Yes."

"Why didn't you ... say anything before?"

"Why do you *think*?" he says, angrily. "I didn't want to let you and Dad down."

"But Adam, you're not letting us down. Why would you think that? You know we would've supported you."

"Maybe you would, but what about Dad?"

"I know you've had your differences with Dad, Adam, but he would've been okay about this, I know he would."

"Well, anyway ... I didn't want to admit it to *myself*, never mind you. I just hid it; all those years at school. I hated the way all the other guys at school always asked me why I wasn't with any of the girls ... I had to make up stories about sex, just to keep them from always going on about it. Girls liked me at school ... I never was short of girlfriends. Some of them would try it on with me and I'd have to either fake interest or say I had a girlfriend in another town. By the end of school, I was sick of it. I was so relieved to get away. I wish I'd told them all. It's not such a big deal any more, but it's still so hard ..." His face looks racked with emotion and I simply put my arms around him.

After a few seconds, we draw apart and I say, "Look, Adam. You've told me now. That's the worst bit. I know how difficult it must've been for you to tell me. But, I'm fine with it. I can't lie, I'm a bit surprised, because I had no idea. Once again, I've missed something so fundamental in my family. I must be ... so self-absorbed or something."

"Mum ... you're not. How were you meant to know? I did a pretty good job of hiding it, I think."

"But surely I should have had an inkling? I did wonder why you never had any girlfriends, but you were always surrounded by girls ... "

"Gay people don't wear a big G on their forehead, you know ..." he grinned, sheepishly.

"But isn't there something called gaydar?" I ask.

"No, Mum ... that's just between gay people, not between mothers and sons," he pushed my arm, laughing. "It wasn't as if I was ..."

"But I should have *known*. Mothers are meant to understand their children. I could have helped you."

"I think ... I think I was too young then, Mum. It's only since I've come to Australia that I've been able to face ... the reality. I've come to terms with it now. It's just ... who I am. I'm glad I don't have to lie any more."

"Does Jake know? Surely he knew at school?"

"He knows *now*, but even he didn't know then. I was denying it to myself, so ..."

"What did he say?"

"Oh, he was cool about it. Pulls my leg, calls me names – but it's all lighthearted. I was fed up of going to clubs when we got here and him trying to pair me up. So I told him. There's a great gay scene in Sydney so, we'd go our separate ways in the evening."

The thought of my son going to gay bars and clubs on his own, made me feel strange. But I wasn't going to say that. "Have you met anyone out here, then?" I say, hoping, for some reason, he hadn't.

"No ... well, there have been some great guys, but no one special. Jake's even been to some gay clubs with me – they're not as bad as they sound, Mum. I know what you're thinking ..."

"I'm not thinking anything, Adam. I just want you to be happy."

"And I am now, Mum. It's not an easy road to follow. However 'modern' life is, being gay isn't an easy option, but, it's getting better all the time. People are much more understanding and I've discovered that people of my age, simply don't care what you are. It's *your* generation that care and call it 'not normal.'"

"The trouble is with our generation it's not long ago that it was illegal to be gay and that had implications, so that's why my age group are sometimes so narrow-minded."

I try to analyse my own feelings and I realise that I've had very little experience of gay people. I've never had strong opinions one way or another, but now my own son is gay, I realise how little I know.

"So ... what are you thinking, Mum? Are you going to be embarrassed telling people? Or are you going to do what I did, and pretend I've never met the 'right girl'?"

By now, we've nearly reached Glenelg and we're walking away from the sea, back up to the road, to where all the cafés and bars are. "I'm sure it will take a while to adjust ... but I'll get there. I definitely won't be pretending ... if I've learned anything out here, I've learned that being honest is the best thing. Come on, let's go and have a coffee and if you're lucky, I'll even buy you a gelato."

We sit down at a table outside, facing the ocean and look at the menu. I go inside to order two flat whites and I buy two large pieces of carrot cake to go with them. I think we deserve them.

I carry it all out on a tray and sit down next to Adam. I sip my coffee and break off small pieces of cake. The sun is so bright I'm wearing my sun glasses and I can feel the heat burning my cheeks. "I'm going to miss this weather. It's been perfect for me – around 25 degrees the whole time. Not too hot. By the way, have you told Holly?"

"No. I wanted to speak to you first."

"Do you want me to tell her? I will, if you want me to."

"Yea ... yea ... do that. I'm not good at saying things in writing and she's got to know soon. She'll be surprised, I think."

"She'll love you just the same, you *know* she will. So ... what's this about Jake? You may as well tell me that, as well."

"Yea. Well ... Jake's always been a bit wilder than me. He likes risks – he goes out that much further to catch the bigger waves. He drives that bit too fast. He drinks a bit too much – vodka shots, flaming sambucas – you name it, he drinks it. When we were at school, he often wagged off, didn't care if he got caught. He's slept with loads of girls. I've known he was like that but ... he's gone too far, now." He sips his coffee, blowing across the top, to cool it down.

"Why? What's he done?"

He puts his cup down on the saucer with a clatter. "He takes loads of drugs."

"Oh my God. Does he? What?"

"Coke, ketamine, weed ... anything he can get his hands on. Not heroin ... yet."

"Is it since he came out here?"

"We all did a bit of weed at school ... but it was always just weed. He made friends with some guys I don't like out here and they do it. Now he's doing it all the time. He misses his shifts, he's not surfing ... I've even caught him stealing from his uncle. It's a nightmare."

My thoughts turn to Laura. What on earth am I going to tell her? She'd be worried sick if she knew. What would I do if it was Adam? It puts Adam's announcement into perspective and I thank God he's not doing it. Or is he?

"You're not doing it, then?"

"No, Mum, of course not. I hate drugs and I hate people who take them. It's so pointless. You get high and then you feel like shit. And then you do it again. Why would I want to do that? For God's sake, Mum, give me a break."

"Sorry. I had to ask. It must be really hard for you. Have you tried saying anything to him?"

"Of course I have. He just doesn't want to know and tells me I'm a gay twat." He drains his cup and puts his finger in it to scrape the foam off the edge. What a horrible thing to say, I think, even if Jake *is* joking. That's what Adam's going to have to put up with in life. Taunts and bullying. I shiver.

"Does Laura's brother know?"

"God no, but the way things are going, he'll soon find out. Are you going to tell Laura?"

"What do you think I should do?"

"Christ knows. Jake would kill me if he knew I told you. But ... I felt I had to tell you. It's too big a responsibility for me to handle on my own. I'm so worried for him, every day."

"Is it getting worse?"

"Yes. As much as I hate to say it, I think you should tell Laura. She needs to know. They need to come out and rescue him, before it's too late."

He sounds desperate but, at the same time, mature, and I'm so impressed with him. I hope he's exaggerating – perhaps it's not quite as bad as he thinks? But when I think of Jake, I can imagine him being swept away by other kids and the 'glamour' and 'excitement' of drugs.

"Look, I'll think about what you've told me. I've got to work out how to approach it. I don't want to frighten Laura, when Jake's so far away. What's he thinking of doing? Is he coming home with you?"

"I doubt it. He talks about applying for a second year out here. As he's got rich relatives, he can. They could sponsor him or something. But I really think someone should step in before then."

"Have you thought of talking to his uncle?"

"Yes, I did ... but I chickened out."

We pay and wander back to Somerton Park with two cones piled high with gelato. The morning has been full of revelations. I feel closer to Adam than ever; the fact that he's gay hasn't changed a thing for me. I think I love him even more.

Funny how something so big, can be small, in the grand scheme of life.

WE GO, THE THREE OF us, by train, into Adelaide. We forget the morning's conversations and just enjoy the outing. We have a late lunch in a trendy little restaurant and then go to the gallery. It's not a huge space, but it's dedicated to indigenous art and the walls zing with colour and patterns. It's not something I've been much aware of before – we've all seen representations of this kind of painting, but to be confronted with it, in reality, is an eye-opener.

I start reading information about the different patterns, the dots, the dreamtime stories and the culture. Every painting is made up of symbols – concentric circles, which can mean campsites and rock holes; straight lines can be routes; wavy lines can be water or rain, I read. I understand that they are full of meaning – from people who had no written language. Before, I've always thought they were just pretty patterns.

I read that the dots are often used to illustrate native berries and stars – I see the native people painting the wondrous world around them – the colours of the desert and the multitude of stars above them. I can't believe how ancient their culture is – the Dreamtime stories are maybe 50,000 years old. It's only forty years ago that they started painting on canvas and board, apparently; before then, they painted on what was available – rock, bark and even themselves. When the white man came along, they started using the dots to hide meanings and stories from them.

Adam, too, is reading all the plaques on the wall. He stops reading and turns to me and says, "I love them all, don't you, Mum?"

"Did I tell you – when I went down to Cornwall to visit Laura, I bought a painting from her gallery? It was the first time I'd ever bought a painting. I have to admit, I'm tempted to get one of these. I think they're all stunning. So primeval somehow, so ... thought-provoking. But I'd have to buy something I can fit in my case."

My eye is drawn to one in particular – its title is 'Dreaming' and it's a mass of colour and dots in circles. I don't know what it means, but I love the 'feel'. It's on unstretched canvas and I decide, on the spur of the moment, to buy it. It's 250 Australian dollars, but for some reason, I feel the need to have it. The title is appropriate. I know their Dreamtime is about when the world was made, but my dreamtime is about my future, my life. Me against the universe; me against the stars.

I arrange my purchase, Jane and Adam looking on, somewhat aghast at my snap decision.

"Go, Mum," says Adam. "What a great choice. I love the colours."

"You've inspired me, Anna," says Jane. "When we get our new place, I'd like some indigenous paintings on my walls."

"I hope it looks okay, once I've got it home to Bath," I say, losing my nerve.

"Of course it will. It sort of sums up Australia, doesn't it?" says Adam.

"You're right. It does. And we can all dream, can't we?" I say.

Chapter Twenty-Seven

The next day, we go up into the Adelaide Hills, as requested by Adam. Jane has decided to take a couple of days off, while he's here. "I shouldn't really, but I can't sit in my office when you're here, Adam – God knows when I'll see you again."

I've told Jane about Adam being gay and let him know that I've told both her and Marcus. Adam's relieved that it's out in the open and that he hasn't had to tell them. Their reaction was great – "It really makes no difference to us – what people do in the privacy of their bedrooms, is none of our business," says Jane. "Good on him, for having the guts to tell you."

"Could you say something similar to him, if it comes up?" I ask. Adam's gone to bed and Jane and I are drinking tea in the kitchen. "It would be so nice for him to have a positive reaction from what he considers to be us oldies!"

"Of course. I'll think of something. I hate the way our generation deals with it. For God's sake, love is love, isn't it?"

What a brilliant thing to say. She's so right. Love between two people, whether male and female, male and male, female and female, black and white, should be equal. Look at me – love between Ben and I, ten years different. Between David and Suzie, twenty years different. Who cares? I wish everyone had the same attitude. Love is a connection of minds – not just bodies.

Jane was great – when we were travelling up the road to McLaren Vale, she said, "So, have you met any nice Aussie boys, while you've been here?"

Adam is in the back seat of the car and I turn round. He grins at me and says, "Yea, a few. They're all so ripped and fit. Puts me to shame. No one special, though."

"Oh well, it's good to play the field, at your age," says Jane. "Well done for coming out, Adam. I know it takes courage. Now you've done it, life will get better."

"Thanks Auntie Jane. Yea, I feel better for telling Mum."

I smile at him and Jane says, "Look, Adam, I think you're too old to call me 'Auntie' Jane. Just Jane is fine."

"Thanks, Aun... I mean, thanks, Jane."

And that was all that was said. Perfect. Well done, Jane, I say inside my head. I look at him again and we share a conspiratorial smile.

WE MEANDER THROUGH the stunning landscape, where perfectly manicured vines flow like emerald rivers across the land. As far as the eye can see, line upon line range up hills and into valleys. Long straight driveways stretch up to beautiful farmhouses and barns, which are now dedicated to producing wine and entertaining visitors with food and wine tastings.

We choose one particularly promising one and drive along the long tarmac road which takes us up a steep hill. We park and survey the scene.

The panoramic view falls away from us, the multitude of vines, too many to imagine. The brown of the earth, the vines' green and the sky's piercing blue assault my eyes with their vividness. We see wooden barrels lolling around the car park, roses in flower beds and a large wooden archway, inviting us through.

It's warm enough to sit outside on the decking and we opt for the cheese platter, the olives and the tasting. Jane has done this all before so to her it's no big deal, but Adam and I relish the taste of the different wines and eat our fill. Jane's driving too, so she has just one small glass.

With the sun beating down, the air clear and pure, the far-reaching views and the wine, I realise that at this precise moment, I'm happy. It's not often that I am aware of happiness – it sometimes just happens to me and it's only when I look back, that I realise that I *was* happy. But as I sit here, with my wonderful sister and my brave son by my side, I know with absolute clarity, that life is good. That life is worth fighting for ... and that I'll be okay.

I'm sure I will.

I know I'll look back on this day with love and gratitude.

I take lots of pictures of us sitting there, with the view around us. Precious times, forever remembered by clicking a button. But my own digital memory, my mind, has placed these images in my archive, filed them away to be restored, when necessary. I know that one day in the future, I'll be able to click on the folder marked 'Happiness' and open the memories I've stored there.

Australia – sub-folder – family – sub-folder – Happiness.

It might be the wine going to my head, of course it may be, but ... I'm proud of myself. This is me, post-David, a new person. Bold and ... happy.

JANE AND MARCUS HAVE definitely decided to put their house on the market – the agent valued it at even more than they thought, so the photographer's been round and taken all the photos and the brochure and web page is being prepared. Together with Adam, we've been scanning the internet for smaller places round here and we're going to see one – it's a two bed house, back from the ocean, but in the same location. We've looked at a couple of others, but they haven't been right.

It turns out to be in a quiet road – the house is set back a little, with a front garden overflowing with flowers. The owners aren't in and the agent shows us round – in Australia, houses on the market are stripped of all personal things for inspections – so when we go round, there is nothing out cluttering up the worktops in the kitchen, no knick-knacks in the sitting room, no bottles of cream or perfume in the bedrooms. It's sterile, but at least it means that we can see the house clearly and imagine their stuff in it.

It's about a sixth of the size of their present house, but the layout is good, the garden's north-facing (a good thing in Australia if you like the sun and gardening) and it's bright and cheerful.

"I like it," says Marcus, quietly to Jane and me, not wanting to give too much away to the agent, who is hovering by the front door, clipboard in hand.

"So do I," says Jane. "What do you two think?"

"I can see you two here. It will be so much less work for you and the good thing is, you're not really moving as such, as it's just round the corner from where you are now."

"You don't need all the space you've got," adds Adam. "This is perfect for you two, although you'll have to get rid of most of your furniture. Jane can use the second bedroom as her office most of the time. One thing I've discovered is that Aussies hide away in their houses when it's hot, pulling the blinds down. It's weird. But I'm assuming you two aren't like that? This house lets in all the sunshine you could want and the patio will be in the sun most of the day – you two are surely still Brits at heart, rushing out to soak up the sunshine?"

"Definitely," says Jane. She turns to Marcus, "What do you think?"

"We'll just have to hope ours is snapped up and this doesn't get any offers," he says with a grin. I can't get over how he's changed in the last week or so. His face looks younger and smoothed out and I'm sure there's been a reduction in the alcohol intake too.

When we leave, the agent gives us his card and all the details of the property. When we get back to their place, its sheer size hits us all. True, the view is magnificent, but ... it's not worth it for the angst it's caused Marcus.

AS I SAID I WOULD, I've emailed Holly about Adam and also asked her advice about Jake. Her reply comes winging back:

Hi Mum, Well, it seems like you've had an eventful few days. I have to admit I didn't see that coming about Adam, although with hindsight, it all makes sense. I did wonder why none of those pretty blond friends of his, ever seemed to be singled out. I wish he'd felt able to confide in me, but it sounds as if he couldn't tell anyone. Poor Adam, I feel so sorry for him – all those years at school must have been awful. Still, at least he's 'out' now and can start enjoying his life. It must be terrible carrying something around with you for so long and not be able to unburden yourself. I'll write to him after ~~*I've finished this.*~~

As for Jake, what a nightmare! I knew he was a bit stupid sometimes, but I never thought he'd be this stupid. I honestly don't know what you should do. My only thought is that you should contact his uncle and talk to him ... you're going to have to tell Laura, Mum – she'd never forgive you if you didn't.

Let me know how it goes. Not long now till you come back – boo! I bet Ben can't wait to see you, though. More news! We've been discussing weddings and we've come up with a date – December 23rd! I know it's rather soon, but who cares?! I love Christmas and it seems the perfect time. What do you think? We've already contacted the vicar at Stowchester (as we both come from there, we thought that was the right place – I hope it hasn't got too many bad associations for you?) and the date's ours if we want it! We're thinking of The Grange for the reception – what do you think? So, it's all systems go when you get back! Love Holly xxx

I'm so excited for Holly and write her a quick text: *Just got your email – SO excited! Of course I don't mind about Stowchester, it's the obvious place. Really looking forward to coming back now and helping you plan. Will try to sort the Jake thing. MUM x*

I dread telling Laura but agree with Holly, it's the only answer. I resolve to sort it when Adam's gone.

"WHATEVER HAPPENS WITH Jake, I'm going to come back at the beginning of July, Mum. I've got loads to sort out before uni and maybe, if I stay with you in Bath, I could get a job for the summer – it'll be a lot easier than when we lived in Stowchester. Could you look around for me?"

Adam, Jane and I are walking towards departures, my heart feels leaden with the thought of having to say goodbye to him, but it lifts when I hear this.

"Of course ... what type of thing would you want to do, ideally?"

"Oh, I don't know, I'm easy. I'd prefer not cleaning ... I'll definitely have had enough of it by then. Waiting ... labouring ... anything, really."

"I wonder if Ben would employ you for a few weeks? He might ... I'll ask."

"Cool ... have you told Dad, Mum ... about me?" He looks worried and I can see the little boy he used to be.

"No, I haven't yet ... are you sure you want me to? Wouldn't it be better coming from you? He'll be fine with it."

"Yea, maybe you're right. I've got to man up – ha ha! Yea ... I'll write to him when I get back to Byron. God, three more months of cleaning and Jake ... maybe I'll come back earlier."

"It'll fly by ... of course, come back earlier if you want to ... but I should stick with your plans. I'll work out what to do about Jake. Holly says I must tell Laura ..."

"I'll try and make him see sense, but I don't hold out much luck."

Jane hugs Adam and says she'll see him at Holly's wedding – she said they'd come over for it and stay for Christmas, the moment she heard the news. She walks away and looks at some magazines, leaving me to say my goodbyes to Adam, alone.

"Well, it's been a fantastic few days, Mum. I'm so glad I came. Thank you for being so understanding ... about everything." He puts his arms around me and I can't help it, but tears well up. As we pull away from each other, he sees my eyes and says, "Don't be upset, Mum ... I'll be home in three months and then you'll have me hanging around the flat, leaving things around for you to trip over and eating you out of house and home!"

"I know ... it's not long, but I hate goodbyes ... they're so ... final."

We hug again, and he walks slowly away, turning once to wave. And he's gone.

Jane grabs my arm and we walk in silence back to the car. "I'm going to miss that boy ..." says Jane. "He's turned into a really great person, Anna."

"I know, I'm so proud of him."

NOW THAT ADAM'S GONE, I have to do something about Jake – I've promised I would and I must follow it through. Adam's given me permission to ring Jake's uncle Brad, as long as I make it clear that he must never be implicated. He thinks if Brad has words with Jake, as his employer, from the point of view that he's not doing his job properly, that might go some way to sorting him out.

So, I take the plunge and ring his number. I explain who I am and how Adam is so concerned for his friend. Brad sounds like a lovely bloke and is really complimentary about Adam, but says he's noticed the change in Jake and was worried about him himself. He promises not to say anything about the phone call to Jake, but promises he'll give him a 'right kick up the backside and set him straight'. I ask him what I should do about Laura and he says he'll ring her if I write and let her know the situation. Hopefully, we've caught it in time, he says, but doesn't sound too convinced.

I sit down to write Laura the email. It's one of the most difficult things I've ever had to write. I know if I received an email like this, I'd be devastated. This is part of what I wrote ...

Adam's been here for a few days and I thought I really ought to write to you, as he told me something about Jake that you should know. I'd want to know, but I hate to be the bearer of bad news. He's been taking drugs – and Adam's worried about him. I think they both smoked weed at school, but this is a bit more than that. He assures me it's not heroin or anything, but other things. We talked for ages about what to do and Adam was keen for me to speak to Brad, although he didn't want Jake to ever know he'd told me. You know what kids are like, they don't want to be seen as a 'grass' and I can understand that. So, Laura, I rang Brad and he was great ... he says he'll give him a hefty kick up the backside and ring you in a few days.

I hope you'll forgive me for interfering, but we all love Jake and don't want him to ruin his life. I'm sure he'll be fine in the end – let's hope Brad scares him witless!

I feel I've done my bit – it's out of my hands now.

I KNOW I'VE NEGLECTED Ben with all these things going on, so I sit down and write him a long email, putting him in the picture – about everything. As I write it down, I see that Jane and Marcus, Adam ... and Jake are all striving to find their way into their futures and that hopefully, I may have helped in some small way. I never thought, when I came out here, that I would help solve other people's problems. I thought I was solving my own. But, helping others, being there for them, has helped *me* too. Behind all the grinning selfies, the happy status updates and smiley emoticons are just people, with everyday struggles. Facebook is fun, but it doesn't half mask the truth from us all.

Ben wrote: *You've certainly been through a lot since you've been out there, but what lovely news you've had about Holly. I know how happy that will make you; I can remember you saying you were convinced he was the 'one'.*

Now Adam is facing up to who he is, I'm sure he'll be fine.

I popped into your flat yesterday just to check everything – all's fine. Can't wait for you to be back here – Bath seems empty without you. Daisy was asking about you when I saw her last. By the way, I met 'him' the other day and have to admit I quite like him, so that's a relief. Daisy, who is the most important person in all this, seems comfortable with him and he's good with her. Grace is still the control freak she's ever been – I have to feel sorry for the bloke, being bossed around all the time! Good luck to him! Rather him than me.

Daisy's coming down next weekend – they're having a long weekend in Devon and I've got her for three whole days. I can't wait to spoil her rotten.

I expect your holiday is going way too fast now but, for me, I'm glad that it's under two weeks till I see you. And by the way, tell Adam I'm sure I could give him some hours – I've been inundated recently – I handed out some flyers and they seem to have done the trick. I hope he's good at wielding a paintbrush. All my love, Ben. xx

I WORRY AS I DON'T hear back from Laura. I imagine she's been in touch with her brother and maybe even Jake. I hope she hasn't spilt the beans about Adam and me. Then, about three days later, I hear from her. I open the email with trepidation, thinking that perhaps she's writing to end our friendship, but to my relief, it's not that at all. She's thankful I told her; she's been in touch with Brad and Jake's had his bollocking. We all have to wait and see if it works. She writes:

I'm just grateful you told me, Anna. That's what a true friend would do, so don't beat yourself up about it. I've been honest with Jake – I told him I'd been in touch with Brad – I never mentioned yours and Adam's involvement – and I told him how Brad is feeling about him. We didn't of course talk about the main problem, as I'm not supposed to know, but I made it clear to him, that he's got to pull himself together. Brad's going to watch him from now on.

The next week or so is a continuation of previous days – I go to the outdoor olympic size pool and swim up and down its long lengths in the sunshine, unburdened by dawdlers or overtakers. There are so few people in whenever I go, I wonder where everyone is ... but there are so many pools around, I don't think they ever get crowded. So, I can perfect my technique alone in my lane, breathing slowly under my left arm. In, out, in, out ... letting my thoughts float off into the azure waters.

I catch a glimpse of myself one day, walking towards the ladies changing rooms, reflected in the tall plate-glass windows. I see this woman, not skinny, but slim for her age – she's not wearing a hat or goggles and she's striding along, confidently. What a change from that woman, all those months ago. I can remember how I felt then, but it's as if it's someone else. The hurt's gone, the bitterness has gone and in its place is ... hope.

Chapter Twenty-eight

"Have you got plenty to read on the flight?" asks Jane. "Shall I go and buy you some trashy magazines to keep you occupied for a while?"

"Don't worry. I've got my Kindle, the Australian ... and I've already got a Hello magazine. I'm hoping I won't need to read too much on this leg – as it's night-time, I intend to take a sleeping pill again. Once they've fed us, I'll watch a film and then nod off – that's the theory, anyway."

My case has disappeared into the black hole and we're walking towards the place where we must separate. Marcus had a meeting tonight, so it's just me and Jane. My stomach is churning with the anticipation of saying goodbye to my sister. We've become so close during these weeks and have re-found that kinship we had as children – I hate the fact that we live so far apart.

Our arms are linked and our footsteps are in unison, as we walk across the concourse. "So, you'll keep me up to date with all your house news, won't you?" I say.

"Of course. These things always take ages, but at least we've had some interest already. And you've got to tell me all about the wedding ... and the handsome Ben ..." she prods me in the ribs, grinning.

"He's meeting me at the airport ... I wonder how I'll feel when I see him again? It's odd, I feel I've known him for years, but ..."

"You'll be fine. I like the sound of him ... can't wait to meet him."

"How long will you stay, when you come over?"

"I suppose it'll depend on how things are going but ... at least a month, I think. We can't go all that way for less. Don't worry, I know you've only got a small flat, we won't be with you all the time."

"No – don't be silly ..."

"No, seriously, Marcus wants to go up to Northumberland, where he lived when he was a boy ... why don't you come too?"

"Maybe ... let's just see what happens ... we don't need to worry now," I say. "Thank you so much, Jane ... I've had the time of my life!" I hug her to me and we don't let go for a long time.

"It's been so lovely having you and you've really helped. I don't know what would have happened to Marcus and me if you hadn't come. I mean it. I feel as if we were heading for disaster and now ... well, it's looking good again. And I'm so proud of you – you've handled everything so brilliantly." She kisses my cheek. "It's onwards and upwards for both of us now."

I fling my arms around her, one last time.

"Right ... enough of this ... I must go. Give Marcus my love. And see you at Christmas. I'm going to hold you to that. No excuses. No – "It's too far and I don't like flying"! You're coming, whether you like it or not!"

"Okay, big Sis, I get the picture." We stand opposite each other, all four hands linked, tears in our eyes; we kiss and I turn to go.

"Bye ... I'll email when I get home," and with that, I walk towards Passport Control.

WHEN I EVENTUALLY EMERGE at the other end of the journey, I feel as if I haven't slept for a year, never mind twenty-four hours. Needless to say, the sleeping pills only worked half-heartedly and I ended up watching about six films.

Having collected my luggage, I go into the ladies loos to try to bring some sort of order to my bedraggled hair and worn-out face. I let the cold water run and run, cupping it and splashing my face repeatedly. I hope that by smacking my face with water, I'll bring some colour back into my ashen skin; the tan I've acquired can't hide the tiredness lurking beneath. I want to look vaguely desirable for Ben – as much as I've restored faith in myself, I still have this secret fear of looking like his 'older' woman. So, despite my utter fatigue, I carefully apply eyeliner and mascara, vigorously rub moisturiser into my skin, put on a bright red lipstick and squirt expensive perfume all round my neck.

This actually makes me feel a whole lot better and I walk through the Nothing To Declare channel with a spring in my step. I scan the crowds of people at the barrier – and can't see Ben. All around me, there are people hugging and kissing, people holding placards aloft with names on and families with trolleys full of cases, making their way through the melée.

I go and stand to one side, so that I'm not in everyone's way. I look at my watch and realise I've got through quickly. Maybe Ben's having problems parking; maybe he's held up on the motorway? I turn my phone back on – no message from him. I look around – still no sign.

To pass the time, I quickly text Holly: *Hey, I'm back! Just waiting for Ben. Will ring when I've slept. Knackered! Love you, Mum.*

A reply quickly pings in: *Hi Mum – Welcome back!! Rushed off my feet today at work but all's good. Can't wait to tell you all our wedding plans! Speak tomorrow. Holly xxx*

I click on Facebook and scroll down my timeline, hoping to see Adam. There's one photo of both him and Jake with the words, *Off to surf ... Yay!* and a smiley face with *Feeling excited* by it. They've got their arms round each other – I scrutinise Jake's face to see if I can see anything different about him. He looks thinner – his cheekbones are more prominent – but apart from that, he looks okay. Still the cheeky grin and handsome face. Maybe this is good news; Adam had said he wasn't surfing – maybe he's trying to change?

That's the trouble with Facebook, you can read so much into one photo – who knows what it really means?

I'm so engrossed in my phone, that I don't notice Ben approach. He gently taps me on the shoulder and whispers in my ear, laughing, "You're always on your bloody phone!"

He makes me jump and perhaps it's the combination of feeling exhausted and thinking about the boys, I don't know, but I stare at him for a second, hardly able to speak.

"Ben! Sorry, I was ..."

He stops me in mid-sentence, by putting his lips on mine. We kiss for a long time, his arms are tightly round me and I relax into him. When we stop, he says, "God, I've missed you. I didn't realise quite how much, until then." Putting his hands on my shoulders, he kisses my forehead. "It feels like months since I saw you. It's probably different for you – do you feel as if you've only just left?"

I think about it for a while. "Yes ... and no. So much has happened, I feel like a different person, somehow."

"Does this new person still want to be with a boring painter and decorator from Bath?" he says, as he lifts my case off the trolley and begins to wheel it to the exit. He looks at me out of the side of his eyes, a grin dancing on his lips. "You didn't meet some Aussie macho man?"

"No, I didn't ... well, I *did*, but that's another story. I don't know any boring men ... I do know this attractive, younger bloke who picked me up in a pub ..." I say.

He reaches across with his spare hand and takes mine ... and it feels the most natural thing in the world.

AS WE DRIVE BACK DOWN the M4, I try to stay awake. Ben is chatting away, telling me all his news, but my mind is thick with sleep and eventually I fall unconscious, lulled by the windscreen wipers' gentle rhythm and the quiet background music, coming from the radio.

I dream I'm in the car with David, not Ben. We're driving to Cornwall, I don't know how I know this, but we are; the kids are in the back seat, arguing about something. David is glancing at me, smiling his lovely smile and he reaches for my hand. He often steers one-handed, his spare hand either resting on my knee or holding my hand, occasionally squeezing it. I can feel the warmth of his skin next to mine and I squeeze his hand back.

We are staring at each other ... and then, like a freeze-frame, I'm aware of him not looking where he's going.

"David!" I shout, but nothing comes out. I open my lips again, but there's no noise. I try again, "David," I scream. I can hear screeching brakes, feel the thud of metal on metal, the heat of tyres, leaving rubber on the road.

I wake myself up, whimpering. Little sounds are rising up from deep within me, bringing me back from my deep sleep. "Anna, darling ... are you okay? You were having a bad dream, my love." I feel his hand holding mine, squeezing it.

"That was ... that was horrible. I dreamt we were in a car crash, David and me and the children. It was so real ..."

"You're just exhausted ... you'll be fine, once you've had a good night's sleep."

"Why did I dream that? The children were little ..."

"You're okay, Anna. You're with me now. The children are fine. Try to go back to sleep, we've got at least another hour to go."

I close my eyes. The immediacy of the dream jumps into my head again. I open my eyes, not wanting to see and feel the crash again. I squeeze Ben's hand and taking his eyes off the road for a second, we smile at each other through the darkness.

HE PULLS UP OUTSIDE the flat. "Home at last," he says and jumps out to get my case from the boot.

I'm so weary I can hardly be bothered to get out of the car, but I haul myself up and stand staring at what is now my home. The thousands of miles I've travelled suddenly disappear and I'm back where I should be.

Ben goes ahead of me and unlocks the door; he goes in and stands aside as I come through. I go into the flat, put my bag down, take my jacket off and stare around me. I see the picture I bought in Cornwall – 'The Dawning of a New Day' – and vaguely realise its significance.

I go into the kitchen where, rather like a zombie, I fill the kettle and turn it on.

"Let me do that. You go and have a shower and get into bed. I'll bring you a cup of tea. Do you want anything to eat? I could whip up some scrambled eggs or something ..."

"No ... just tea. I'll go and shower." I shamble through to the bathroom, undress and stand impassively below the rushing water. Even that doesn't rouse me from my stupor and I emerge from it, to dry myself half-heartedly. Still slightly wet, I put on the only pyjamas I can find and throw back the duvet. I flop onto the bed and momentarily I'm aware of the familiar sounds of Bath around me.

I'm home, I say to myself, before I fall immediately asleep.

"GOOD MORNING, LOVELY," says Ben. "The tea's gone cold, I'm afraid. I'll go and get you another one. You were completely unconscious when I came in with it, last night."

"Sorry Ben. That was rude of me to fall asleep like that."

"Don't worry, I didn't take it personally," and with that, he's out of bed and off to the kitchen.

He's soon back with two mugs of tea. He's wearing nothing but boxer shorts and even through my sleepy haze, I can admire his physique. "What service," I say, as he hands me a mug.

"I've taken the morning off, so I can be with you," he says, as he gets back into bed. "Put your tea down, come here and give me a cuddle. I've missed you."

I take a quick sip of tea and put it back on the bedside table. Turning to him, I shuffle my body closer to his; we feel like two jig-saw pieces, inter-locking and fitting together.

"How are you now? Less tired?"

"So much better. I couldn't function last night at all. I'm so sorry."

"Don't worry. I wasn't expecting you to be full of beans. I've never flown that far, but it must be exhausting. I think it's worse coming back this way, than going out, isn't it?"

"Well, it certainly felt like it. I was tired when I got there, but at least I could *speak*," I grin.

"But ... it was worth it, wasn't it? Was it everything you'd hoped for?" He puts his lips on mine and we kiss for a long time before I answer.

"It was amazing. There was one big downside, though ..."

"Really?" he says.

"Yes ... I missed you, Ben. I kept wishing you were with me. I've missed this ..."

"I love you, Anna," he says. "I realised that, when you were away. I'm sorry I haven't said it before, but love is such an over-used word and I wanted to be sure. I couldn't believe after my disastrous relationship with Grace that I'd found someone else ... someone who felt so right."

"I love you, too Ben. I *never* thought I'd find someone else, either. David leaving me was the worst thing that has ever happened to me and it made me feel sad, inadequate and old, all rolled into one ... I don't know why I decided to go into the pub that night, it was completely out of character, but if Gaz and I hadn't gone in ... well, I hate to think what would've happened. But dear old Gaz introduced me to you ... we have *him* to thank."

Both of his arms are tight around me now and we kiss as if our life depends on it. The dream I had in the car flashes into my mind – I see David's smile and feel his hand holding mine, but I block it out. My marriage is gone. Perhaps it had gone a long time before I realised it. The dreamlike car crash was waiting to happen. I loved David but now it's time to move on and love the man in my arms.

My phone beeps and vibrates on the bedside table, but this time, I ignore it. Whoever it is will ring again – or text or Facebook message me – if it's important.

Everyone can wait ... it's time for me and Ben, now.

A FEW DAYS LATER, I'M in M and S, trying to find something nice to wear on our long weekend in Devon we've planned, but failing miserably. My phone vibrates and pings.

Message from Ben: *Hey, I've got an hour between jobs today. Can you meet me in the park for a picnic? You bring the sandwiches, I'll get a bottle of wine. Ben x*

This strikes me as odd as, usually, Ben doesn't take time off for lunch and he certainly doesn't drink wine when he's working. I wonder what's going on, but I text back:

That'll be lovely. Need a distraction – can't find ANYTHING I like! Will make some tuna sandwiches. May even treat you to a bar of chocolate. Love you, Anna xx

It's so lovely to write *Love You*. I do love him. I know for sure now.

I walk quickly home, pleased to get away from shopping dilemmas. I make the sandwiches and wrap them in foil, find a couple of chocolate bars and two apples and put them all in a bag. It's a bit early to leave, but I set off, with camera in hand. When I get to the park, I take some arty shots of flowers and trees for a while and then sit on a bench, waiting for Ben.

I text him: *I'm here! On bench, by the pond. See you soon, I hope! xx*

He doesn't respond straightaway and I while away the time, reading articles from the BBC and Huffington Post on my phone. Then, it pings.

Message from Ben: *If you raise your head from that f***ing phone, you'll see me!*

I look up and for a minute, I can't see him. *He* can obviously see me, so he must be near. Then, I see him – only he's not alone.

Bouncing by his side, eating its lead and generally being naughty, is a black labrador puppy.

Ben waves to me and as he tries to walk towards me (he keeps having to lean down and sort out the lead) I can see a broad grin on his face.

I slowly stand up, leaving everything on the bench and walk towards them. My heart is beating faster than normal and I can't stop smiling. "Oh my God, Ben ... who's this?" I bend down to stroke the puppy's head – it immediately puts its front paws on my legs and tries to bite my fingers. "What are you? A boy or a girl?" I bend to inspect and say, "Ah, a boy. You're gorgeous, aren't you? Is he yours, Ben?"

"No, he's not."

"How come you've got him, then?"

"Well ... he's yours ... a present from me to you ... if you want him, that is?"

He picks him up and the puppy starts to lick his face. Ben wrestles with him and laughs, saying, "Go and do that to your Mum ..." and hands him over to me. He licks me too, but then settles into my arms and quietens down.

"There, you see, you have the magic touch. Well ... what do you think? Do you want him? I can always take him back ..."

"NO ... don't do that! I love him already." I hold him up to my face again and breathe in the soft, puppy smell of him. I kiss the round top of his head, between his ears. "That's just so ... so ... thoughtful of you, Ben. I've wanted another dog so badly, but somehow ... felt guilty. I didn't want to 'replace' Gaz. But you've taken the initiative – how can I possibly resist now?" I laugh. I go up to him and kiss him, the puppy squeezed between us.

"So ... you don't want me to take him back, then?"

"No, I definitely don't. Where did you find him, anyway?"

"Well, when you were away, I went to a client's house and there, in the kitchen, was a basketful of black lab pups. I saw it as a sign. I said to the owner that I wanted a boy and there was one left who hadn't been sold ... this little fella. I didn't say anything to you, as I wanted to do this surprise. I've been so excited ... I've been dying to tell you, ever since. He's eight weeks old and he's had all the jabs he needs. He's yours, my darling Anna, for keeps."

We go back and sit on the bench. The puppy has settled into the crook of my arm and we sit together, me gently stroking the puppy's back, Ben with his arm round my shoulders, the sandwiches forgotten, at my side.

"What shall I call him?"

"I don't know ... your choice. I'm guessing you don't want to call him Gaz?"

"No, no ... there will only ever be one Gaz. But maybe something along the same lines ... with a football connotation?"

"Wayne?" laughs Ben.

"Definitely not ... I don't think I could call out 'Wayne' in the park and keep a straight face. Rooney would be quite cool, though."

"Alan?" says Ben, smirking. "After Alan Shearer, of course. I've always wanted to call a dog Alan ... or Keith ... or Brian?"

"Hold on ... what about Becks? Are you a Becks?" I whisper in the puppy's ear. "Maybe one day, we could get you a Posh ..."

"Yea, I like Becks. It suits him."

"Okay ... Becks, it is. I think he's fallen asleep completely now. He's passed out, like I did after the flight. It's all this excitement ..."

I extricate my arm and Becks sleeps contentedly on my lap, while we eat my rather uninteresting sandwiches and drink wine from plastic cups.

"Here's to Becks," I say to Ben, as we touch cups. "And here's to us. You realise he's going to become our surrogate child, don't you?"

"Yea ... I'd thought that. Two old idiots, spoiling a dog ... but who cares? We're happy, that's the main thing!"

As we sit there, talking and laughing, it strikes me that this time, a bench has led to something wonderful. The fateful bench in the rec is best forgotten – the place where this whole saga began. Now, though, here I am, sitting next to the man I love, with a snoring puppy on my lap.

Benches can be happy places, after all.

The Epilogue

The morning started at 6 am and has been a succession of dresses, hair and make-up, champagne, emotions, nerves and laughter, ever since.

Ben and I are staying at the hotel, along with lots of other guests, including, Laura, John, Rocco and Jake. Ben has spent the morning with Marcus, Adam and Daisy, while I've been on bride-support duty, with Jane alongside me and Holly's best friend and only bridesmaid, Fiona.

I've been with Holly every step of the way since I came back from Australia – we've had our fair share of emotional ups and downs, as you do with any wedding, but on the whole, it's gone smoothly. She didn't want all the fuss that brides go in for these days – both she and Jed were completely in agreement about the kind of wedding they wanted: A Christmas wedding in church, followed by a nice meal, and that's all.

She was adamant there was no need for canapés ('too expensive'); no need for little favours for the table ('it's not a kids' party') or themed tables and co-ordinating colours ('it's not Hello magazine'). No wedding present lists ('that just seems presumptuous'); no swanky gimmicks like photo booths, horses and carriages ('Dad can take me in his car, can't he?'). No expensive wedding photographer ('just throwaway cameras for everyone – far nicer to have everyone's snaps'). No wedding band, just music played from a computer playlist ('all our favourite songs'.) And certainly no pre-practised first dance ('if Jed and I did a Dirty Dancing type thing, I would run and jump at him, miss and we'd both fall over in fits of laughter'). They wanted a kind of 'stripped down' wedding, where they didn't get lost in all the detail.

When she finally emerges in all her glory, I'm the proudest mother of the bride ... ever. I know I'm biased, but she looks like an angel, in floaty chiffon. Her bouquet is small and perfect – lily of the valleys – her hair, natural, flowing down her back. Her eyes are shining, her skin radiant.

"Dad will be here in a minute. Are you ready?" I say, standing in the hotel bedroom, staring at her, with a silly grin on my face.

"As ready as I'll ever be," she laughs. I look at the heart-shaped gold locket she's wearing – the 'something borrowed' I've lent her – it looks perfect. David gave it to me on our wedding day – a day I remember so well and one that I can file in that folder, 'Happiness' now.

"Can you just help me on with this blue garter thing?" She hands it to me and sits down carefully, holding out one leg to me. I push it over her shoe and together we manage to get it above her knee. "God, the things we do for tradition ..." she says.

"Well, it'll bring you luck ..." says Fiona, as Holly stands up and shakes down her dress.

"Do you know what? I don't think I need luck, with Jed. He's the most perfect man ..."

"You two are sickening, you really are," laughs Fiona. "Have you absolutely *no* qualms?"

"Nope ... none," says Holly. "He's the one for me. End of. Where's my champagne?" she laughs.

We all chink glasses and toast Holly's happiness.

There's a knock on the door and I go to answer it ...and there's David.

It still comes as a shock when I see him. The man I spent so long with; the man who's so familiar, but yet who feels separate from me now.

He smiles at me, a shy smile, and putting his hands on my shoulders, kisses me on both cheeks. I haven't seen him at all since I got back. We've emailed each other about the wedding arrangements and I sent them a card when Noah was born, but apart from that, nothing.

The touch of his lips on my cheek, the smell of him, awakens the past for a few seconds. I remember, for some reason, Holly's christening, when we were such proud parents. We held her in her beautiful christening gown, like a piece of cut-glass that could shatter at any minute. We stood together, promising to protect her.

And now, here we are, standing together again ... Holly, in a white bridal gown, moving away from us, down the road into her own future, under the protection of Jed, not us.

Still proud parents, but with a gaping hole between us. "Suzie and the children have gone ahead to the church," he says. "They're so excited. Gemma's holding a bag of confetti – she can't wait to throw it."

David walks into the room and seeing his daughter, a look of wonder lights up his face.

"Holly, you look so ... beautiful ... so ... grown up." He goes slowly towards her and kisses her cheek. "I'm such a proud Dad," he says.

She takes his hands.

He turns back to me, smiling, his eyes shining with love, and suddenly, the chasm between us shrinks.

I see the man I loved ... still love.

"Doesn't she look ... amazing, Anna?" he says. "Our daughter. Our wonderful daughter."

I go over to him and put my arm through his. "We were clever, weren't we David, making her?"

"We certainly were ... we certainly were," he says and he takes my hand, squeezing it, as he always used to do.

THE END

About the Author

Sarah Catherine Knights is a British novelist and lives in the beautiful town of Malmesbury and has done since 1985. She came to Wiltshire, like so many others, because her husband was in the Royal Air Force. The family have now settled there and so she spends hours walking through the surrounding fields with her black labrador, Mabel and as she walks, she thinks about her next writing project.

Sarah studied English Literature at Birmingham University and went on to do a Creative Writing MA at Bath Spa University where she started to write her debut novel, "Aphrodite's Child" which was published at the beginning of 2014.

"Aphrodite's Child" grew out of the family's posting to Cyprus with the RAF in the early nineties. While there, Sarah realised it would make a great setting for a novel. With its microcosm of English life, the camp was a strange place to live. At that time, there was little or no communication with the UK and being somewhat cut off from the island too, life inside the camp became intensified and sometimes like a prolonged Mediterranean holiday. It was easy to dream up a dramatic storyline.

Having been an English teacher of both secondary level children and foreign business people, Sarah retired to concentrate of photography and writing.

Her three children have now all flown the nest but often come home for chaotic weekends of dog walks, laughter and noisy meals around the large kitchen table. The whole family, including Peter her husband, have been very supportive and patient with Sarah's late career change as a novelist, always willing to help with the plot or read a draft.

Read more at www.sarahcatherineknights.com.

Printed in Great Britain
by Amazon